DEADLY TERROR

Rachel McLean writes thrillers that make your pulse race and your brain tick. Originally a self-publishing sensation, she has sold millions of copies digitally, with massive success in the UK, and a growing reach internationally. She is the author of the Dorset Crime novels and the spin-off McBride & Tanner series and Cumbria Crime series. In 2021, she won the Kindle Storyteller Award with *The Corfe Castle Murders* and her last five books have all hit No1 in the Bookstat ebook chart on launch.

ALSO BY RACHEL MCLEAN

Detective Zoe Finch series

Deadly Wishes
Deadly Choices
Deadly Desires
Deadly Terror
Deadly Reprisal
Deadly Fallout
Deadly Christmas

RACHEL McLEAN
DETECTIVE ZOE FINCH BOOK 4
DEADLY TERROR

Copyright © 2020, 2024 by Rachel McLean

All rights reserved.

No part of this book may be reproduced in any form or by any electronic or mechanical means, including information storage and retrieval systems, without written permission from the author, except for the use of brief quotations in a book review.

This is a work of fiction. Names, characters, businesses, places, events and incidents are either the products of the author's imagination or used in a fictitious manner. Any resemblance to actual persons, living or dead, or actual events is purely coincidental.

Ackroyd Publishing

ackroydpublishing.com

Printed and bound in the UK by CPI Group (Uk) Ltd, Croydon CR0 4YY

CHAPTER ONE

SAMEENA KHAN HATED SHOPPING.

Even more, she hated shopping for shoes with her fifteen-year-old daughter Jamila.

For what seemed like the hundredth time in the last hour, Jamila picked up a pair of unsuitable shoes and shoved them in her mum's direction, eyebrows raised.

Sameena shook her head. "You know the answer."

"But Sarah's got these."

Sameena eyed the shoes. Black patent – at least the colour was sensible – with a tiny pink bow on the back – *not* in the uniform guidance – and a two-inch heel. Where would she start?

She sighed. "You know the rules. Flat, plain, black. Surely it can't be that hard to find a pair you're prepared to wear?"

"All the ones you like are disgusting."

"Disgusting? They're just plain black shoes." Sameena poked a slender foot out in front of her, turning it this way and that. "Like mine."

Jamila wrinkled her nose as if Sameena had let off a stink bomb. "Exactly."

Sameena checked her watch: gone three. She needed to be home by four thirty, to take Khaled to his football practice and then cook dinner. "Come on. I'm taking you to Clarks." She grabbed her daughter's sleeve and moved towards the shop exit.

"Mum!" Jamila tugged her arm from her mother's grasp, so violently that Sameena thought she might topple over. A tall white woman beside them looked round and pushed her glasses up her nose. Sameena wanted to tell her to mind her own business.

"There is no way I'm getting shoes from Clarks." Jamila folded her arms across her chest. The white woman chuckled and moved away. Sameena felt heat rise up her neck.

"You're making a scene."

"I'm making a scene? You're the one manhandling me in Hobbs."

"Let's just get out of here, alright? We can get a coffee or something. Work out where to go next."

"Only if you buy me a muffin."

Sameena gritted her teeth. "A small one."

A smile spread across her daughter's face. "You know what's even better than a muffin? Let's have churros."

"We don't have time."

"It's just over there." Jamila pointed over her mum's shoulder. "Come on, they're dope."

Sameena let her daughter guide her out of the shop and through the crush of Saturday afternoon shoppers. Unlike the rest of Birmingham this afternoon, Grand Central, the shopping centre over New Street Station, was at least dry. Which explained why it was so busy today.

They passed the escalators just as a young woman wearing a green headscarf tumbled off and towards them. Sameena glanced at her, wondering if she'd been pushed. The woman gave her a wary stare and picked up pace, brushing past the two of them as she hurried away.

"Oi," muttered Jamila.

"Shush," Sameena said.

"She hit me."

"She touched your arm with hers. That's hardly hitting."

Jamila rounded on her mum. "Are you saying I'm lying?"

Sameena took a deep breath. After the churros, she would take the girl home. She could wear her old shoes for another week. Gaping sole or no gaping sole.

"Come on," she said. "Let's get those churros."

"Bitch." Jamila rubbed her arm.

Sameena grabbed her hand. "I beg your pardon?"

"Not you. *Her.*" Jamila jerked her head towards the woman, who'd stopped at the barrier overlooking the station concourse and was leaning over. Sameena felt her heart stutter. She wasn't going to jump, was she?

Sameena flicked her gaze down to the crowded concourse below and back to the woman in the headscarf. The woman had straightened. She scanned the roof as if expecting to see something specific up there.

"I don't like you talking like that," Sameena said, dragging her focus back to Jamila. There was something about the woman that made her uneasy.

"It's not a swear word."

"Would you say it to a teacher?"

"Course not."

"Well, then. Don't say it to anyone."

"But she hit me."

They were approaching the woman. Sameena made for the opposite side of the walkway, steering away from her. But Jamila was insistent on approaching her.

"Jamila!" she hissed. "Get over here. D'you want those churros, or not?"

Jamila gave her a dismissive wave and stopped a couple of paces behind the woman. The woman was oblivious to her, staring across the void over the station concourse. Sameena followed her gaze and saw a man, standing in the midst of a throng of moving people like a boulder in a fast-flowing river. He stared back at the woman, his eyes hard.

"You hit me," Jamila said. She reached her hand towards the woman but didn't touch her.

The woman's eyes were locked on the man. He was heavily-built, wearing a hoody pulled up over a baseball cap. The steel in his eyes made Sameena shiver.

She grabbed Jamila's shoulder. "Stop it, Jamila. Leave her alone."

The woman shifted her weight, aware of Sameena and Jamila but not turning to them. She straightened, her eyes still on the man. For a split second she dipped her body, as if about to fall or throw herself over the railing. Sameena felt her breath catch in her chest.

"Are you OK?" she asked.

The woman had something in her hand. She gripped it.

A weapon?

Jamila was right. The woman was dangerous. But she looked scared, more than anything.

Sameena's training kicked in. As a social worker she was used to dealing with volatile and uncooperative people.

"Jamila, I need you to get away from here right now. Walk over there, to the churros stall. Wait for me."

Jamila turned. She must have seen the fear in her mother's eyes, because for the first time today she did as she was told.

When Jamila was safely out of the way, Sameena took a step forward. Her heart raced and her lips were dry.

"Are you alright? Do you need help? You're not going to jump, are you?"

The woman turned to face Sameena. On the other side of the void, the man unfolded his arms and scratched his neck. Sameena caught a glimpse of a tattoo before he disappeared into the crowd.

"Leave me alone," the woman said. She had an accent.

"I can help you."

The woman shook her head. She was sweating.

"Go. Now."

Sameena took another step forward. "It's OK, I'm not going to hurt you. I just don't want you to hurt yourself."

The woman flicked her wrists, her eyes on Sameena's face. Her coat – a cheap one made of blue polyester – fell open. Sameena looked down at her chest. She sucked in a breath.

She wore a kind of rucksack strapped to her chest. Wires trailed from it. It was dark, faintly reflective.

The object in her hand, Sameena realised, wasn't a weapon.

It was a detonator.

The woman's face tightened. Sweat beaded on her brow. Her nostrils flared as she blinked at Sameena. She was young, not more than twenty-five, and she looked as if she hadn't had a good meal for a while.

Sameena stared back at her, the words gone from her head.

The woman's breathing slowed. She stared back at Sameena, her eyes full of terror.

"Run," she said.

CHAPTER TWO

"Fancy a brew?" asked DCI Lesley Clarke.

"Yes please, ma'am." DI Zoe Finch sat at the tiny table in the dingy Force CID kitchen, making the most of the fact her boss was doing the honours. To be fair to Lesley, if she was making a cup for herself, she tended to make Zoe one too.

Lesley filled the kettle, her back to Zoe, her expression invisible. "How're things with your team?"

"They're fine," Zoe replied.

Lesley flicked the switch and turned to Zoe. "You sure about that? I've seen the way Connie looks at Ian."

"It's not a problem, ma'am."

"Does she know why he's here?"

"No."

"Should she?"

"With respect, I think that would make things even worse."

Lesley poured water into two mugs and snorted. "You don't need to do all that crap with me, Zoe."

"What crap's that?"

Lesley laughed. *"With respect.* Respect is earned. You know that, I know that. I hope you and I have both earned each other's respect, or regard at least."

"Yes, ma'am."

"Good." Lesley put Zoe's mug on the table. Black, no sugar. Zoe would have preferred something other than instant, but this would have to do. "Glad we got that sorted. But your DC should at least pretend to have a bit of respect for her DS, in my opinion."

"Connie's a good copper, ma'am. She's not letting her feelings towards DS Osman get in the way of her job."

"She hates him that much, huh?" Lesley sipped her coffee and pulled a face. "I should have got you to make this."

Zoe set down her mug, glad she didn't have to pretend to enjoy it. "He said some stuff that wound her up, when we were working the Lovetree case."

"The Digbeth Ripper."

Zoe cringed. Her last big case had led them to a man who was attacking gay men and leaving them behind or inside pubs in Digbeth's gay village. Alive or dead. "I thought we weren't calling him that."

"Everyone else is, might as well join in. Come with me."

Zoe stood up. The office was quiet today, only a few people in besides herself and Lesley. Her friend DS Mo Uddin was out investigating an organised prostitution racket but otherwise, things were low-key.

As they left the kitchen, a uniformed constable ran along the corridor.

"Ma'am."

"Calm down, Constable. The place isn't on fire, you know," Lesley replied.

"There's been a bomb threat at New Street Station."

CHAPTER TWO

Zoe felt herself tilt, like she might lose her balance. Lesley's face slackened. "When?"

"We got the call at three fourteen pm."

"Shit." Lesley turned to shove her coffee mug into Zoe's hand. "I'm designated Silver Command this weekend. Our chat'll have to wait."

"Anything I can do?"

"Wait here. If we need you, we'll call you. Uniform and anti-terror will be there."

"Ma'am."

Lesley dashed into her office and ran out, dragging a stab vest over her silk blouse and suit jacket. She paused as if to say something to Zoe, then nodded.

"Good luck, ma'am." Zoe watched her boss run towards the exit, her heart racing.

CHAPTER THREE

A SQUAD CAR was waiting for Lesley. She threw herself into it and stared out at the dimming January afternoon as they sped towards the city centre. She checked her suit pockets for her ID and a few essentials – phone, notebook, pen. Everything would be laid on for her when she got there. She wondered if they'd established a base yet, and who would be there. Superintendent Gavin Sanders was designated Gold Command. She'd never worked with him before but had heard he was calm under pressure.

Would she be? She was in a speeding car, heading towards a scene everyone else would be fleeing. She didn't even know if *bomb attack* meant detonated bomb. Yet.

The car came to an abrupt halt in Severn Street, quarter of a mile from the station. A cordon was being established on Navigation Street, Uniform hurrying to move the public away from the station.

No sign of an explosion. Lesley felt her breathing level out.

CHAPTER THREE

A female sergeant held the door open. "A base has been established in the Mailbox, ma'am. Please follow me."

"Where's Sanders?" Lesley climbed out of the car and raised her hand to shield her eyes from the low sun.

"He'll be here soon."

"I asked where he is, not when he'd get here."

"He's outside the station, ma'am. On the ramp above Stephenson Street." A pause. "Briefing the negotiators."

The 'ramp' was a pedestrian walkway leading up to the Grand Central shopping centre, immediately over the station. Being at the scene, briefing the negotiators – that was Silver Command work, not Gold.

"Then that's where I need to be." Lesley stuck her head back in the car. "Can you drive me to Stephenson Street?"

"Yes, ma'am," the driver said.

The sergeant outside the car came closer. "Ma'am, I've been told that we need at least one of you safely away from the scene."

Lesley turned to look up at the woman. "What's your name?"

"PS Wareham, ma'am."

"Well, PS Wareham, tell your senior officers that you passed the message on but that it didn't get through."

"But—"

"No buts, Sergeant. I'm going to the ramp, now. Maybe I'll see you later. Maybe not."

Lesley slammed the car door as it sped towards the cordon. She grasped the passenger door handle as they sped through it and round the bulk of the station complex.

At Stephenson Street she jumped from the car and sprinted up the ramp. Superintendent Sanders stood near the top, talking to a woman and a man. Between them and the doors to the centre was the inner cordon, which right now comprised three armed officers facing the doors.

"Lesley."

"Sir."

"You're not supposed to be here."

"Neither are you, I believe."

"Touché. Right, I'm nearly done with these guys then I'll brief you."

"Is there a suspect in there?"

The swing doors to the shopping centre opened and two armed constables emerged with a group of shoppers. They stared at the officers as they were hurried down the ramp towards safety, their faces wide with fear.

"A woman," said Sanders. "Mid-twenties, wearing a green headscarf. She's got an explosive device strapped to her chest."

"But she hasn't detonated it."

"Not yet."

"That's good."

"I don't think anything about this situation is good, Silver Command."

"She's got doubts," Lesley said. "She's reconsidering. At the very least, she could be waiting until we've evacuated the place."

"It's one of the UK's busiest railway stations. There are still trains on the platforms, people being brought off them. It's far from empty."

"Which could be why she's still waiting."

"Silver, you need to get to the ops base. I need you co-ordinating the armed response units."

"Are they already in there?"

"They are."

"Can she see them? The bomber?"

"There's CCTV being set up at the base. You'll be able to find out there."

"They'll scare her."

"She's standing in the middle of a shopping centre with an explosive device on her chest. I think she's already scared, don't you?"

Lesley chewed her bottom lip. The doors opened again and a gaggle of people stumbled out, this time unaccompanied by police.

"How many still in there?" she asked.

The woman that Sanders had been talking to nodded at Lesley. "Could be over a hundred, ma'am."

"Shit. And you are?"

"Inspector Jameson, ma'am. Lead negotiator."

"Good. Why haven't you gone in yet?"

"With respect, ma'am, we were about to when you arrived."

"Go then," Lesley said. "Don't wait for me."

Jameson eyed Sanders, who gave her a nod. She conferred with her colleague and the two of them passed the armed officers and pushed through the swing doors, their hands raised. Both wore stab vests: no protection against a bomb.

"What's their angle?" Lesley asked Sanders.

"They don't have one yet. We have no idea who this woman is, what her motive is. No group has claimed involvement. They're going to have to talk to her, find out what they can."

"We got any witnesses? Any muggles who spoke to her?"

"Muggles?" He wrinkled his nose.

"You know what I mean. If any members of the public saw her, spoke to her even, it'll help us."

"I've no idea. We'll be putting out an appeal, but in the meantime..."

"Of course." Lesley peered towards the glass doors. The shopping centre beyond them was still. "Do those two have recording devices?"

"Too risky," Sanders said. "They wanted to go in clean."

"OK." Lesley sucked in a breath. "CCTV it is." She turned for the car, then reconsidered. "I'm going in there."

"No. You're not."

"Somebody in charge needs eyeballs on the scene. It can't be you. I won't get involved. I won't go far. But I want to see for myself what's going on."

Sanders put a hand on her arm. "That's folly."

Lesley yanked her arm away and shook her head. It felt like someone had pumped it full of liquid fire. By the time she got to the ops base, and accessed the CCTV, it could be too late.

A radio crackled behind her: Sergeant Wareham had arrived. She gave Lesley a wary look and turned to the Super.

"Sir," she said. "We've got a feed in the ops base. I can relay an account of what's happening."

"Can't you patch it through to a phone?" Lesley said.

"Sorry, ma'am. They're working on it, but not yet."

They all turned as the junior negotiator came through the doors. He'd been running.

"She's got a girl," he panted.

"The bomber has?" Sanders said.

"A hostage."

"Why?" asked Lesley. "She's got a bloody bomb strapped to her chest. Why does she need a fucking hostage?"

CHAPTER THREE

Sanders raised an eyebrow. "If you don't mind, Silver."

"Oh, don't mind me. She wants something. She's not going to blow the place up. Not now she's got another bargaining chip."

"We can't make any assumptions," Sanders said.

"Sir," said Wareham. "Ma'am. You really need to come with me. At least let's retreat to the cordon."

A clump of vans sat at the bottom of the ramp, more of them no doubt snaking their way up New Street. The city centre was emptying out. Good.

"Very well," Sanders said. "What's the latest from the feed?"

"The bomber seems to be talking to Inspector Jameson," Sergeant Wareham said. "She's got the girl in a tight hold at her side, leaving her other arm free for the detonator."

"That's how she was when I left," said the junior negotiator.

"She's still holding the detonator?" Sanders said.

Wareham lifted the radio to her ear. "Yes, sir."

"Have we got snipers on her?"

"Six, sir. Three inside the centre and three on the roof. They have a visual but we don't know if a bullet will go through the ETF plastic."

"The what?" Lesley asked.

"The clear plastic they built the roof from," Sergeant Wareham replied.

The shopping centre's roof was made of a double-layer polycarbonate, light over the vast span it had to cover but insulated against the elements.

"No one can tell us?" Sanders asked.

"We're trying to get hold of the company that manufactured it, sir."

"If it's in doubt, and let's face it, it will be regardless of what the manufacturers say, then the armed officers on the roof can't possibly take that shot. They could hit the girl, or the negotiator."

"Sir."

"What about the other three? Have they got a line of sight?"

"This is my job," said Lesley.

"I beg your pardon?" Sanders turned to her.

"Sir. You're Gold Command. Your job is strategic oversight. Coordination with other services, allocation of resources. Mine's operational. Leave this to me."

"If I leave you in charge, you'll go running in there."

She said nothing.

He sighed. "Wareham will stay with you, brief you on what we're getting from the feeds."

"Thank you, sir."

"Hmm."

Lesley knew she'd pay for her insubordination. But Sanders was micromanaging. He needed to do his job, so she could do hers.

"Right," she said to Sergeant Wareham as Sanders reached the bottom of the ramp. "I want to see. I'm not going inside, but I'm going as far as those doors. OK?"

"Ma'am."

"Tell me if you get anything important from that feed."

"Ma'am."

Lesley made for the glass doors. She hated not being able to see what was happening. She knew her place was far away from the scene, where she could safely co-ordinate the operation. But first she had to see what the situation was.

She put a hand on the door and leaned forward to look

through the glass. Ahead of her was a broad corridor flanked by shops. At the far end was a group of restaurants, and off to the right, unseen, more shops.

"Where's the bomber now?" she asked Wareham. She put a hand up against the glass to block reflections.

"She's next to Caffé Concerto."

"Where's that?"

"It's overlooking the station concourse. Up ahead, and to the right. Not far away."

"Has she been there all along?"

"We think so, ma'am."

Lesley put pressure on the door. She wanted to push it open, to go in there. She saw movement to one side and tensed.

"Someone's on the move," she said.

Wareham paused. "It's Jameson. She's on her way back. She's got the hostage."

"Well done that woman." Lesley let out a long breath.

"Ma'am."

Lesley watched as the negotiator walked towards the doors. She was moving briskly but not running. She had a girl of about sixteen with her, who walked ahead of the inspector with jerky movements. Lesley watched both of them, willing them to hurry. Jameson would be aware of the bomber's eyes on her back, she would have been told not to run.

Inspector Jameson was five metres from the door. The hostage was in front of her, two metres away. Lesley shifted to one side to look past them. As she did, Jameson surged forward and pushed the girl through the doors. Lesley caught her as she stumbled out and the doors swung back.

There was a flash of light from the right. Through the glass of the door Lesley could see Jameson turn towards it. A moment later her head snapped back like someone had yanked at it. She spun in midair and hurtled towards Lesley, her arms flailing. In the same instant, the flash of light grew and engulfed her.

"Back!" Lesley yelled. She threw herself in front of the girl. Behind her, Sergeant Wareham shouted to her colleagues on the cordon.

Lesley wanted to run to the negotiator, to rescue her. But it was too late. Her body slammed into the reinforced glass. A wave of sound followed behind her.

The glass doors shattered. Lesley shrieked and raised her hands, just as her feet left the ground. A pulse of air knocked her backwards and sent her slamming back into the ground, glass shattering over her.

CHAPTER FOUR

Zoe sat in the team office, BBC News on Connie's computer monitor. Her own laptop had too small a screen and her eyes were aching.

She rubbed them as the door opened: DS Mo Uddin.

"What's going on?" He grabbed Rhodri's chair and positioned it next to Zoe's then sat down.

"There's been a bomb threat at New Street. Lesley's Silver Command."

"I know about that. What's the latest?" His voice was strained.

She sighed. "I don't know. The cordon's too wide, the cameras can't see a thing."

"Can't you find out direct?"

"There's no way I'm disturbing Lesley. And relaying updates back to the office isn't exactly priority number one right now."

"Fair point." He stood up. "Can I get you a coffee?"

"That would be perfect. Strong, please. Stick an extra spoonful in."

Mo screwed up his face and ignored the look Zoe gave him. She leaned back in her chair, eyes fixed on the screen. She knew she should be focusing on her caseload but she couldn't tear her eyes away. She'd been out this morning interviewing a shopkeeper who'd been the latest victim of a spate of armed robberies in Chelmsley Wood. Grunt work, but she'd been the only person available. CCTV had captured two men – faces covered, no surprise. There was paperwork to do, of course.

That could wait.

Onscreen, there was movement. Uniformed officers led a group of shoppers past the cordon. The officers looked grim, eyes down and mouths tight. The members of the public were pale and agitated. A small girl in a bright pink coat was being carried by her mum, both of them crying.

Zoe tapped her foot against the desk leg. Her breathing was ragged and her chest tight. She hated being stuck here like this, but she knew she had no part to play in what was unfolding in the city centre.

Her phone rang: DI Carl Whaley, her boyfriend.

"Hi," she said, leaning back in her chair. "Are you watching?"

"BBC. D'you know what's happening?"

"Lesley's there, but that's all I know."

"That's good news. She knows what she's doing."

"Yeah." Lesley was experienced and competent, good at coping with pressure. Zoe hoped her boss would be safe.

"This mean we're off for tonight?" Carl said.

"I don't know. Sorry." Zoe watched the journalist onscreen speak to a woman with a bright blue hat and a faraway look in her eyes. "We keep doing this, don't we?" she said.

"Comes with the territory. At least it's both of us."

"Yeah. Look, I'll try and call you—"

The door opened behind her. Zoe swivelled her chair round, her hand over the phone. "I hope it's good and strong."

"You hope what is?" Detective Superintendent David Randle stood with his back to the door.

"Sir." Zoe stiffened. What was he doing here on a Saturday? He should be at home, enjoying the perks of seniority. "Anything I can help you with?"

"You've got the news on. Good."

She shivered, uncomfortable at being caught skiving. But she needed to know what was happening to her boss.

"Carl, I'll speak to you later." She hung up, wondering if Carl had heard Randle's voice.

"Take a seat," she said, hoping he'd decline.

He sat in the chair Mo had vacated and made himself comfortable. The door opened again and Mo entered holding two mugs. Zoe gave him a perplexed shrug.

"Sir," Mo said.

"DS Uddin. You're working the weekend too?"

"Working on the Sparrow case, sir."

The muscle under Randle's eye twitched. He eyed the mugs. "Wouldn't mind one myself, if that's OK."

Mo pursed his lips but nodded. "No problem, sir."

Randle gave him a patronising smile and turned back to Zoe. She took the two mugs off Mo and placed them on her desk. He'd made hers eye-wateringly strong. The fact that it could blow the top off her head distracted from the taste.

She grimaced, aware of the inappropriateness of the thought.

Onscreen, the reporter spoke to camera, relaying the lack of information. He stood in the centre of New Street, out of sight of the station and towards the Bullring shopping centre. Behind him was quiet, the only people uniformed officers.

"So," said Randle. "How are things here at Force CID?"

Randle had worked in these offices in Harborne until three months earlier, when he'd been promoted to Detective Superintendent. He'd been a DCI, Lesley's colleague. He was head of Force CID now, but based out of HQ at Lloyd House.

"Busy, sir. As always."

"Glad to hear it. Wouldn't want to be over-resourced, not with the budget pressure we're under."

Zoe nodded. David Randle hadn't come in here to talk to her about budget cuts.

"You have a new DS in your team," he said.

He knew that. He'd come across DS Ian Osman before.

"We do, sir."

"I imagine you're missing Mo."

"That's not relevant, sir," she said. "DS Osman's an experienced detective. I'm glad to have him on the team."

Randle's shoulders shifted in a suppressed chuckle. He knew as well as she did that Ian wasn't a welcome member of the team. He was argumentative and borderline lazy, and he rubbed the constables up the wrong way.

"Glad to hear it," Randle said. "Look after him, will you? I wouldn't want to see him getting a raw deal compared to his predecessor. I know you're not one for favouritism."

"I treat all my team the same, sir."

"Glad to hear it." Randle stood up.

"You're not waiting for that coffee, sir?"

"I need to head off."

She nodded. So he'd wanted Mo out of the room.

Randle patted down his hair. He wasn't wearing his

habitual dark suit, but was as well turned out as ever, an ironed blue shirt and a pair of chinos that made Zoe think of politicians on their days off.

"Your coffee, sir." Mo was back.

"Thank you, DS Uddin, but I won't be needing it. I'm sure DI Finch will drink it."

"I'm sure she will, sir." Mo gave a hesitant smile.

"Thank you." Randle put his hand on the back of Zoe's chair, close enough for her to feel a breeze brush her neck but not quite making contact. She held herself very still, determined not to shudder. After a few moments, he patted the chair and walked out.

"What was all that about?" Mo asked.

"Beats me," said Zoe. "He wanted to know how Ian's getting on."

"Ian?"

Zoe had her own ideas about why Randle was interested in her sergeant. She turned back to the screen, where people were running past the reporter.

"What's happened?" she sat up in her chair.

She turned up the volume to hear a low rumble in the background. Her stomach clenched.

Mo's mouth hung open. "That doesn't sound good."

"No," she said.

The reporter put his hand to his ear. He blinked into the screen a few times, then spoke fast, barely intelligible. "There's been an explosion inside New Street Station."

Zoe and Mo looked at each other. She'd watched them evacuating people, knew that Uniform would be doing all they could to clear the place. But on a Saturday afternoon in the January sales, the place would be packed.

She leaned in, almost toppling the two cups of coffee.

The scene onscreen was chaotic, people running. Either the picture had dulled, or there was smoke.

The door crashed open again. Randle.

"DI Finch," he said. "Come with me."

CHAPTER FIVE

SOFIA PICHLER HUGGED herself as she stared out at the aeroplanes unloading their cargo.

Behind her, one of her boyfriend's employees, Adam, barked into a mobile phone. He paced back and forth as he spoke but never moved more than six feet away from her. He'd driven Sofia here in her boyfriend's second Mercedes.

He, and his colleagues, drove her lots of places.

The aeroplanes were vast and beautiful, gliding towards their positions alongside the gates. The one she longed to get a glimpse of would arrive unseen at the far end of the arrivals hall. But for now, just gazing out from the viewing lounge was enough to fill her with anticipation.

She checked her watch: 3:50. Andreea's plane would arrive in twenty minutes. Then there would be passport control, and the luggage carousel. Within the next hour Sofia would be reunited with her sister.

Only two months ago, she'd been on the other side of that glass. She'd taken the journey Andreea was taking today, from Bucharest to Birmingham, and been delivered to her devoted new boyfriend. Titi, she called him. She still couldn't quite believe her luck meeting him the way she had.

"Move." The man had put his phone away and was standing in front of her. "Time to go now."

"Go where?"

"To fetch your sister."

She allowed herself a smile, ignoring his look of disdain. She wondered what the men said about her behind her back. That she was a gold digger perhaps. That she'd only come from Romania because of his money.

Sure, she wasn't complaining about the money. Her boyfriend's modern house in the countryside south of the city was the sort of thing only a politician would own in Romania, and the jewellery he gave her made her squeal with joy. But he was more to her than a meal ticket. He was the man who'd opened her eyes to the real world. The world outside her backward, old-fashioned country with its hangups about the past and its fear of the future. The man who'd given her the confidence to make a new life here in the UK.

And now Andreea was getting her chance to do the same.

"She won't be coming through for at least half an hour," Sofia told the man. "Longer, if she's got luggage."

Andreea wouldn't have much luggage, she knew. A few torn t-shirts, some of her trademark fishnet tights. A gallon of hair gel. But Andreea didn't own much apart from her clothes.

"Boss says we go now. Come wi' me." Adam had a thick Birmingham accent and Sofia couldn't always understand him, but his body language was clear enough.

"Can I talk to him?"

He shook his head. "Sorry, love. He's busy."

CHAPTER FIVE

He was always busy. When they'd met in Bucharest he'd had all the time in the world for her. He'd taken her for meals she could never afford on her meagre salary. They'd strolled through city streets that had looked so different at his side. He'd been relaxed and attentive.

When she'd first arrived here, things had been similar. But since Christmas he'd become more and more preoccupied with business. Now she was lucky if she saw him for an hour at dinner in their echoing dining room.

She picked up her handbag – Gucci, a gift – and followed her minder. He took her not towards the arrivals gate as expected, but back to the exit.

"You're going wrong way."

He shook his head. "*The* wrong way. You need to talk properly."

"*The* wrong way. You're going *the* wrong way."

"Uh-uh. This way."

They had time to spare. Maybe he was taking her to meet Titi. Maybe they would welcome Andreea together. He hadn't met her sister, and Sofia wasn't sure what he'd make of her, with her grungy look and her bad manners. She steeled herself.

"We'll need to be back here soon," she said.

"Don't worry." Adam stepped out of the airport building. She followed, wishing she'd brought a coat. It was usually warmer here than at home, but today was an exception.

A van pulled up. Not the Mercedes. Adam yanked open the side door and eyed her.

"Get in."

"Where do we go?"

He rolled his eyes. "Where *are we going*, is what you mean to say."

"Where *are we going?*"

"You'll see."

"Where is boss?"

He clenched a fist. "I told you. Just get in, will you?" He placed a hand on her back and steered her into the van.

Inside were three rows of seats. All empty. She sat in the closest one and shuffled to make herself comfortable. Titi did this sometimes. He had her taken places to meet him, without telling her where. Not that she knew her way around the city anyway. She liked the air of mystery. And it always turned out for the best.

Sofia smiled, determined to show a brave face to Adam and the driver, who she didn't recognise. The two men spoke together in low tones so she couldn't listen in.

They sped away from the airport building. Sofia looked behind her at the people streaming in and out of the doors. Andreea was back there somewhere. What if Sofia missed her? Andreea would be lost in an alien country.

She took a deep breath and muttered a prayer in Romanian, crossing herself. Adam turned to fix her with his thin blue stare. She met his gaze, her handbag clutched in her lap.

They raced away from the roadways in front of the building and swung around bends, leaving the airport behind. Sofia turned to look through the back window, her heart racing. What would Andreea do if she emerged from those gates to find Sofia missing? Would she wait?

Andreea was short-tempered and unpredictable. She might do anything.

They turned another bend and the van slowed. They were on a narrow road now, not much more than a country lane. Trees arched overhead and there was a gate in front.

The van shuddered to a halt and the driver slung his arm

across the passenger seat, turning to look out of the back as he reversed. Sofia blinked, not wanting to stare at him. There was a scar under his right eye and his face had been pockmarked by acne. Adam had his phone to his ear.

"He's definitely on the plane?" he grunted. He scratched his neck as he waited for a response. Sofia watched, her heart racing.

"Good," he continued. "Teach those bastards what happens if you step into our business." He hung up and sat back in his seat, shuffling his shoulders.

They stopped at right angles to the gate, the van filling the road.

"What is happening?" Sofia asked. "Why do we stop here?"

Adam raised a finger to his lips: *shush*. He chewed his bottom lip.

She leaned across to see out of the window. Beyond the gate, which was made of mesh, was a neat grassy mound. It was long and straight, running parallel to the van. A plane taxied along, above their heads. The runway?

There was no sign of the Wizz Air plane. It would be here soon. The plane Sofia could see had a green and black flag on its tail. She wondered where it had come from, whether it was full of wealthy holidaymakers or people seeking a new life like Andreea.

The plane slowed as it passed. Steam rose from its surface into the cold January air. Sofia watched it slow and prepare to take another bend.

Without warning, the plane was engulfed by a ball of flame. An ear-splitting bang followed the sight, pushing Sofia down in her seat. The tail collapsed and crashed to the ground. Black smoke billowed from beneath the plane, while flames spread towards the cockpit.

Sofia stared, terrified. Her feet were rooted to the floor of the van. The two men in the front threw their doors open and jumped out.

Sofia couldn't tear her eyes away from the burning plane. Her chest felt full and empty at the same time, and tears pricked her eyes. She leaned forwards into the front seat to see better, whimpering. Nausea rose from the base of her stomach.

The side door to the van slid open.

"Out," said Adam.

Sofia stared at his face then back at the plane. How was he so calm?

"We have to help. We have to tell someone," she croaked.

"They know. It's not your concern." He leaned in and grabbed her arm. His fingers dug into her flesh through her thin jacket. Another gift, wildly impractical.

"Now," he said. His voice was low and full of threat.

She stumbled from the van. Heat from the fire washed over the side of her face. She turned to look, her mind racing.

Those poor people. The plane was fully ablaze now. No sign of anyone escaping. Sofia's knees buckled.

"Move!" Adam grabbed her hand and dragged her away from the van.

"Stop! You made me drop bag!"

He yanked at her arm. "Get it when we come back. Move!"

It was getting dark, the growing dusk accentuated by the brightness of the fire. She let herself be pulled along as he crossed the road and made for the fence. She could smell the smoke, sharp and bitter.

Andreea. What did they do if a plane was about to land and something like this happened?

Her question was answered by the sight of another plane standing further along the mound. Wizz Air. It had landed.

The driver huddled against the gate. He held wire cutters. Adam pointed to the Wizz Air plane. "We're getting them out. You have to help."

Sofia stared back at him.

"Don't you understand?"

The driver jumped back as a hole appeared in the gate. An alarm sounded.

"Yes," Sofia said.

"Good," Adam replied.

Sofia ran with him.

CHAPTER SIX

"I'm fine. Just let me do my job."

"There's glass embedded in your neck and you're in shock."

"I'm fine." Lesley explored the skin of her neck with her fingertips.

"Please don't do that," the paramedic told her. "You'll make it worse." She muttered something unintelligible under her breath.

Lesley dropped her hand. "I'm Silver Command on this operation. My job is to tell you and your bosses what to do, as well as a whole bunch of my own lads and lasses. Now just let me go so I can get on with my job."

The paramedic sucked her teeth. She was pale with curly dark hair, slightly overweight. Lesley had learned how strong she was when the woman had manhandled her away from the top of the ramp and down to the waiting ambulance, arguing with her all the way.

"OK," she said. "I'll patch you up. I'm putting a neck

brace on you, so you can't get at your injuries. As soon as you're done here, you get a police car to take you to A&E."

"That's the right decision."

"A thank you would be nice. And a promise that you'll do as I say."

This paramedic was a feisty one. Lesley liked her. She saluted. "Aye, aye."

The paramedic's face softened. "Good." She slid the brace around Lesley's neck. Lesley immediately felt like a dog coming back from the vet with a cone. She slid her fingers into the edge of the brace, screwing her face up.

"Don't mess with it."

"Fair enough." Lesley hauled herself upright and tried to ignore the dizziness that hit her. She had no idea where Sanders was.

A uniformed sergeant was nearby, briefing two of his constables.

"I need your radio," Lesley told him.

"I'm sorry?"

"My name's DCI Lesley Clarke. I'm Silver Command on this thing. Now are you going to give me your radio, or aren't you?"

"Ma'am."

She snatched it off him. "What channel's the ops base on."

"Nine, ma'am."

She flicked the radio to that channel, wondering if she should give him a bollocking for not demanding her ID.

"Jackdaw operation base, please keep this channel to urgent comms only."

"This is Silver Command. Detective Superintendent Lesley Clarke, call sign FD582. Where's Gold?"

"One moment please."

Lesley waited for Sanders to come on the line. The sergeant whose radio she'd nicked watched her. He looked uneasy. She did that to people.

"DCI Clarke, I heard you'd been injured."

"Just a few surface wounds, sir."

"That's not what I've been told."

"I'm fine. I'll go to A&E to get stitched up when this is all over. Not before."

"As long as you're sure."

"I wouldn't be using this radio if I wasn't. What do we know?"

"Thirty-seven people were inside the building when the bomb detonated. It was a nail bomb, which is a blessing of sorts. Two dead, eight critical, seventeen walking wounded."

"What about the negotiator?" Lesley couldn't remember her name.

"One of the deceased, I'm sorry to say. Inspector Jameson. The bomber is dead too."

Lesley blew out a thin breath. Her mouth tasted of soot and metal. She closed her eyes, wishing there was a wall or something she could hold onto.

"There was a girl, a hostage," she said.

"She's fine. They're checking her up, at City Hospital. But she's just got some bruises. You saved her life."

"Inspector Jameson did, you mean."

"DCI Clarke, we'll need you here. There's a search operation underway in case there are any victims we haven't yet found, and Forensics need to know when it's safe for them to go in too. You're liaison."

Lesley opened her eyes. The giddiness washed over her. She swallowed and put her hand over her mouth.

CHAPTER SIX

"Surely it would be better to do it from here."

"Silver, just get in here, will you? Coordination is from the base. I don't want you putting yourself at risk any more than you already have."

"I'll be right there. Sir."

Lesley passed the radio back to the sergeant who hurried away. A barrier stood next to her, one of those things they'd put in to protect the Christmas market a few years back. They hadn't considered nail bombers.

She felt bile rise in her throat. She scanned the street and leaned down behind the barrier to vomit. Her mouth was dry and only phlegm came out. Her stomach felt like someone had pulled it out and stuffed it back inside out.

She pushed herself up and let the barrier take her weight as she took a step. She couldn't have people see her like this. She pushed out her chest and let go of the barrier, focusing on her balance, on moving. Parked in front of her, on a road normally reserved for trams, was a squad car.

She opened the passenger door. The driver turned to her, startled.

Lesley held up her badge. "Take me to the Mailbox. Ops base."

"Yes, ma'am." The constable radioed in her destination and revved the engine. Lesley leaned back in the passenger seat, pushing away the image of the negotiator's body flying at her on the other side of those glass doors.

CHAPTER SEVEN

Zoe sat in Randle's Audi, remembering the times she and Mo had observed this car with suspicion while they were investigating the murder of the Assistant Chief Constable.

At the Five Ways roundabout, Randle took the ring road east.

"This isn't the way to New Street," Zoe said.

"We're going to the airport," Randle replied. They stopped at the Bristol Road lights, the blinking indicator the only sound.

"I don't understand, sir."

"There's been an explosion."

"What?" Zoe sat upright. "When?"

"I got a call after we left your office. An aeroplane. On the runway."

Zoe's skin bristled. "Oh my God."

"It could be a coordinated attack. Sanders and Lesley are at New Street, so you and I will need to be on this one."

"But we haven't been briefed." *And I only completed the*

CHAPTER SEVEN

Bronze Command training a week ago, she thought. She wasn't ready for this.

"I'm Gold, DCI Donnelly's Silver. You're one of three Bronze Commands."

DCI Chris Donnelly was from Erdington, Zoe's old station. She'd worked with him as a rookie detective.

"Your role will be to ensure the responders preserve forensic evidence, as far as possible," Randle said.

Zoe worked through the training in her head. She didn't remember anything about forensics, but it made sense. "Are Uniform already there?"

"Airport security are running through their standard evacuation procedure. Uniform are en route."

"They're evacuating people from the plane?"

He shook his head as they pulled away from the lights. "Looks like there are no survivors."

She slumped in her seat. "None?"

His upper lip twitched.

"How much do we know about the evacuation procedure?" she said. "What's the priority?"

"Other planes, I expect. The airport buildings will be chaos. Forensics will be... I don't know where forensics will be."

"On the exploded plane," she said. "No issue about the evacuation affecting that. The airline will want access."

"Search and rescue will be going through it, when it's safe. Firefighters, God knows what."

Zoe stared at the brake lights ahead of them.

"Hold on," Randle said. He flicked a switch on the dashboard. Blue lights and the wail of the siren were enough to startle the cars in front into moving aside.

"That's better," he muttered. They pushed through the

traffic, picking up speed as other drivers became more aware of their presence. Zoe gripped her seatbelt, thoughts racing. Were the two explosions related? Was this second one even an attack?

"The plane might have malfunctioned," she said. "Fuel leak, something like that." She knew nothing about planes.

"On any other day, you'd think that. But within an hour of a bomb going off at New Street?"

"True." Zoe's mouth was dry. They were on the Coventry Road now, speeding towards the airport. The signs on the gantries were changing, warning people of diversions and blockages ahead. She and Randle would be ploughing through them all, heading straight to the scene. She wondered what they'd find when they arrived.

CHAPTER EIGHT

The two men ran up the grassy mound. Sofia followed, her eyes darting between the two planes: the one that was in flames, and the one that held her sister.

At the top of the mound, the airport opened up before them. Planes had halted on the tarmac. Lights and sirens blared.

No one had emerged from the plane that had exploded. Smoke filled the air, leaving a bitter taste in Sofia's mouth. What would it be like to be in there, trapped with fire raging and smoke choking your lungs? On her flight here the plane had been full. She'd had a window seat, the seat next to her taken by an overweight man who ate chocolate bars all the way over. How would you get past someone like that?

She glanced at Adam. He watched the blaze, his mouth twitching at the corners, hands in his pockets. She felt panic wash over her.

She snapped her focus back to Andreea's plane. The side doors had opened and people were visible in the openings.

Someone hurled an object to the ground: the inflatable slide. It hit the tarmac and filled with air.

She needed to get closer. She needed to find her sister.

She was about to run for the plane when Adam grabbed her. He spun her round to face him and shouted into her face.

"The boss has got instructions for you."

She nodded. "Where is he?"

"He's not here. But you have to do as he says."

"OK." She glanced towards the plane, tugging at his arm.

He leaned in, his breath stinking of the roll-ups he smoked. "You have to listen to me."

"OK. Just tell me."

He shoved his free hand into his pocket and brought out a sheet of paper. "There are kids on that plane," he said. "They've come from a school, in Romania."

She nodded as he crumpled the paper into her hand.

"On there are names. Seat numbers."

She frowned. Nobody would still be in their seat.

"Find those kids. Get them off the plane and bring them here. If you can't find them, just pick eight kids."

"Why eight?"

"Just do as you're told, will you?"

"What about Andreea?"

"I'll worry about her."

A second van stopped beyond the gate, behind the one Adam had brought her in. Sofia stared at it. Had Titi come for her?

Adam shook her arm. "We'll take care of your sister. You have to get those kids off. You got that?"

"I do."

CHAPTER EIGHT

She could find the kids and look for Andreea. If she had time.

The second van's doors opened and three men tumbled out. One of them carried a gun. They ran to the gate and shoved their way through it.

Sofia felt ice run through her veins, remembering the men who'd come to their village with guns when she was a child.

"What's happening?" she asked Adam. "Where's Titi?"

"Boss is fine. He's somewhere safe."

What about me? she thought. *Why aren't I somewhere safe?*

Adam dug his fingernails into her wrist. "Eight kiddies. You speak their language. You find them, you get them off the plane, you bring them back here. Got it?"

"Got it." Sofia wanted to spit in his face, but the man with the gun made her scared to breathe.

Adam let go of her arm. "Good. Now run."

CHAPTER NINE

Randle stopped in front of the main entrance to the airport. Zoe jumped out, scanning the scene.

People were being herded away from the building, onto patches of open land. She knew there had to be a system, but she couldn't see it.

"Remember," said Randle. "The forensics."

Zoe nodded. They ran into the building, pushing past the crowds coming the other way. Suitcases and bags were strewn across the luggage drop-off hall, abandoned in the panic. They had to swerve and jump to get through the chaos, but eventually they reached the doors to the security offices at the far end.

"Ops base will be in here," Randle said. Zoe blew hair out of her eyes.

"How d'you know all this?" she asked.

"The May Day preparation exercise. June last year. Don't you remember?"

She'd been a detective sergeant at the time, unconcerned with emergency operations like this. She didn't reply.

CHAPTER NINE

"Right," he said, after a moment's silence. "You'll need to speak to Donnelly."

Zoe tensed. The last time she'd spoken to Chris Donnelly had been the day she transferred to Force CID. It had not been a friendly conversation.

But more important things were at stake.

They ran along corridors until they came to a set of double doors with security signage. Randle pressed an intercom buzzer.

"Detective Superintendent Randle. I'm Gold Command. Let me in."

The door opened. Beyond, the room was being set up. Staff dragged long tables into place and set up computer monitors. A notice board was being erected. People rushed this way and that, all busy, all focused. The room was hushed, patches of conversation interrupting the quiet.

Donnelly was leaning over a woman at a computer two tables along. He wore cords and a brown sweater. So, he hadn't been on duty.

Randle approached him. Zoe hurried to keep up, not wanting to trail behind. Randle stretched out a hand.

"DCI Donnelly," he said.

Donnelly looked from Randle to Zoe. He raised his eyebrows at his former DC then returned his attention to Randle. "Sir."

"What's the situation?"

"Come with me."

Donnelly led them to a bank of monitors. Three techs flitted between them, threading wiring between the screens and plugging in more.

"Eleven aircraft are in a holding pattern above the airport," he said. "Air traffic control are looking after that but they need to get them down before they run out of fuel. The runway's unsafe, apparently the heat has affected the tarmac within a three hundred metre radius of the explosion."

"What about survivors?" Zoe asked.

Donnelly glanced at her and then back at Randle. "There are six planes out there right now, either just landed when it happened or preparing to take off. Nothing is allowed to land or take off until they've secured the airport and sorted the tarmac."

A woman in a dark blue suit approached, her hand out towards Randle. "Barbara Rolands, Head of Airport Security."

"Ms Rolands."

"I'm second Silver Command along with DCI Donnelly here. You're Gold?"

"I am. This is DI Finch. She's going to be working with Forensics to ensure—"

"I don't think so."

Randle leaned back. "I beg your pardon?"

"The airline is going to want first dibs on investigating what happened."

"We have a potential terror attack here," Randle said. His blue-grey eyes bore into hers. The woman stared back, refusing to be cowed. "The priority is to identify potential perpetrators so we can stop them striking again," he said.

Rolands opened her mouth to speak. Randle turned away from her to confer with Donnelly.

"Do we have video of the incident?" he asked.

"From three angles," Donnelly replied.

"Good. We need everything we can get, and fast. You do know about the New Street attack?"

"Yes, sir."

CHAPTER NINE

"We have no reason to believe the two are connected," said Rolands. "The likelihood is failure in the aircraft."

Randle gave her a condescending look. "With respect, Ms Rolands, I think the chances of two major incidents in the Birmingham area within an hour of each other are slim to say the least. We are treating this and the New Street incident as a coordinated terror attack."

Zoe felt the breath leave her. Hearing Randle say it out loud highlighted the scale of what was happening.

"I'm going to check what's happening with the plane," she said. "Find whoever's in charge of search and rescue."

Randle nodded. Donnelly gave her a smile that didn't touch his eyes. She returned the same.

Zoe passed the next bank of monitors. Security personnel and police officers mingled, some staring into screens and others darting between them, carrying printouts and talking into phones. To one side was a group of men. Two of them wore heavy jackets with West Midlands Fire Service logos on the back. She made for them, identifying the grey-haired man at their centre as the most senior.

She was almost on them when a door to her right opened and a man came out. He was short with dark hair and a nondescript face.

Zoe stopped walking. "Ian?"

DS Ian Osman stared back at her, his face losing what little colour it had. "Boss."

"What the hell are you doing here?"

"Helping with the investigation, boss."

"What investigation? There is no investigation yet."

His gaze flicked over her shoulder. She turned to see Randle watching the two of them.

"Did he call you?" she said as she returned to her sergeant.

"Got a call from the office, boss. I've done major incident training. You're Bronze, I hear."

"It was your day off." She narrowed her eyes. "Why did they call you out?"

"To help you, boss."

"If I needed your help, I'd have asked for it."

He shrugged. "I'm here now. Might as well make the most of it, eh?"

CHAPTER TEN

The squad car pulled into the underground car park beneath the Mailbox and sped towards its rear, tyres squealing as it turned corners. The car park was deserted, access denied to all but residents and those involved in the operation.

At the rearmost lifts, the car stopped with a jolt. Lesley opened the passenger door. Her vision was hazy and she didn't entirely trust her legs to take her weight when she got out.

But she couldn't let the driver see that.

She heaved herself up, using the door frame as support, then pushed away from the car, focusing all her energy on staying upright.

"You alright, ma'am?"

She waved in dismissal, not turning for fear of losing her balance. "I'm fine. Leave me."

The car drove off. Lesley took a few long breaths and made for the lift doors. She pressed the button for the top floor. There was an events suite, normally rented out for parties and conferences, that the police used for incidents in the city centre. They hadn't needed it before, but today it would afford a good view and a large space they could fill with the equipment they needed.

The lift door opened and Lesley shuffled inside, glad to be able to lean on the back wall as she travelled upward.

Her neck hurt. She reached her fingers inside the goddamn brace and touched her skin, feeling for where she'd been cut. The paramedic had been attempting to remove the shards of glass but Lesley hadn't let her check she'd got them all.

It hurt less when Lesley put pressure on her neck, inside the brace. So she did.

The doors slid open. Ahead of her was a blank wall, a corridor leading to the room she was heading for. She was familiar with this, had rehearsed it in the May Day practice event that had brought together police, fire service and ambulance crews to prepare for incidents like these.

She turned right and then right again, reaching a flight of stairs which she took two at a time. Halfway up she felt dizzy, and slowed her pace.

At the top of the stairs she took another left turn and came to a door. A buzzer and camera were mounted on the wall beside it. She leaned towards the camera and checked her image in the screen. She was pale.

She pressed the buzzer.

"DCI Clarke, Silver Command. Let me in."

"Ma'am." There was a click and a buzz and the door opened. Lesley pushed her fingertips against it and it gave under the pressure.

Overcome by disorientation, she tried to stop herself toppling forward, the pressure of her hand against the wood

CHAPTER TEN

threatening to pull her over. She shifted her feet, regaining her balance just in time.

Sanders was twenty paces away, talking to a senior fire officer. He turned towards her. His expression fell.

"DCI Clarke. You shouldn't be here."

"Get me a glass of water," Lesley muttered. She put a hand out to the wall to steady herself, and raised the other to her neck. The skin below her blouse collar throbbed. Her hand felt wet. When she brought it in front of her face, it was covered in blood.

"I'm, I'm not..." she said. She leaned on the wall, grateful for its solidity. She closed her eyes.

Gravity sucked at her. She let the ground pull her down, slumping against the wall as she slid to the carpet and the world went black.

CHAPTER ELEVEN

THE PLANE WAS dark and still in the low light of evening. People threw themselves down the inflatable slide. At the top, a woman argued with a stewardess about her shoes. The stewardess yanked the shoes off and gave the woman a shove. She slid down, shrieking all the way.

Towards the rear of the plane, steps had been lowered. The men were making for them, Adam at the front. Sofia followed, hoping she wouldn't miss Andreea.

They ran up the steps. There was no one at the top to challenge them, no one to tell them they shouldn't be here. Sofia covered her face with her sleeve as she waded into the plane. It stank in here: urine, sweat and shit. The smell of people scared for their lives.

Adam turned to her, jabbing his finger at her hand. The list. She had to find those children.

She sniffed and scanned the plane. How would she find eight children in all this?

People were climbing over the backs of seats, standing on one another in their desperation to escape. A woman in a purple headscarf huddled in the seat next to Sofia, her head in her hands. She sobbed, making no attempt to get out.

Sofia dipped down to check the woman's face. She knew it wasn't Andreea, her sister wouldn't be seen dead in a headscarf. But she had to be sure.

"You need to get out of here," she told the woman in Romanian. The woman's face softened at the sound of her own language.

Sofia felt a hand on her shoulder. A tall, blue-uniformed woman wearing heavy makeup stared into her face. She frowned.

Sofia looked away, terrified this woman would identify her as an intruder. Instead the woman gave her a smile.

"Make your way calmly to the doors behind aisle 37," she said in English. "Remove any heels and leave your belongings behind."

Sofia nodded. The woman smiled. Her makeup was sliding down her face, her forehead beaded with sweat. A man came up behind her, wearing a similar uniform. He shouted into the woman's ear and she shrugged wildly.

"Sofia, over there!" Adam was up ahead, gesticulating at her. The eerie illumination provided by the emergency LEDs along the floor only added to the sense of strangeness. When Adam was sure he'd got her attention, he pointed at a group of children further forward in the plane. There were twenty of them at least. Not eight.

She had to get through. Andreea would have been near a door, she was the cautious type. She'd be out by now. Sofia could only hope she'd wait somewhere for Sofia to find her. Maybe the women and men in the tight blue uniforms would take her somewhere.

Sofia muttered an apology to the head-scarfed woman

and placed her hands on the back of her seat and the one opposite. She braced herself and shoved through the crowd, apologising as she went.

A man turned to glare into her face. "You wait," he barked. Behind him, Adam approached. The man grunted and slumped to the floor.

Sofia clambered over the man. She tried not to look at his face. He was solidly built and tanned. She hoped he'd get out.

Adam and the other men had disappeared into the crowd. The children were close now and Sofia reached them easily once she'd struggled past the man.

There was no sign of an adult with them. Maybe their teacher was up ahead, working out how to get them out. Maybe there was no teacher.

Sofia squinted at the list. She angled it down to the floor lights for a better view, stooping to read.

"Alexandru Balan!" she shouted. "Is Alexandru here?" The first name on the list.

The kids looked at her as if she was insane.

"Alexandru Balan!" she repeated.

"That's him!" came a shout. A hand went up, hooking over to point at a blond boy who looked twelve or thirteen years old. He turned as hands landed on his shoulders and shook him. They all pointed back at Sofia who threw the boy a smile.

"Wait there!" she called. She looked behind her. The route to the steps was clear, if you ignored the stewardess pushing people towards the slides.

"No, come here!" she called. Alexandru let himself be shoved towards her by his friends.

She repeated the exercise as he approached, calling out

names and summoning children to her. Five of the names on the list were accounted for and she soon had a gaggle of children surrounding her.

"Are you their mother?" the stewardess asked. "We need to get them off first."

Sofia nodded at the woman, pretending not to understand. She called out the last three names but no one answered.

Just get eight kids, Adam had told her. He was gone, along with the other men. They were up at the front of the plane somewhere. Doing what?

She scanned the plane for signs of her sister. Andreea would have heard her calling the kids' names, would have recognised her voice. No, that was impossible. She wouldn't have heard her in the chaos.

Sofia took a huge, gasping breath and shouted as loud as she could. "Andreea Pichler!"

No response.

The stewardess shoved Sofia forward, pushing the kids along with her.

Three more kids. All the kids on her list were twelve or thirteen. She singled out three more the same age and grabbed each of them in turn. The stewardess put a hand on her arm, shouting in her face.

"What are you doing?"

Sofia shrugged. *I don't understand*. She threw her arms out wide to encompass the kids. The slide was closer now, the panicked crowd shuffling jerkily forwards. If she went that way, she'd lose them.

"Kids! Come with me!" she called in Romanian. The kids looked at her and then between themselves.

"Trust me!" she cried. Alexandru, the boy she'd picked first, nodded at his friends.

Sofia turned to push the stewardess out of the way. The woman was skinny and it wasn't difficult to overcome her. She yelped as Sofia shoved her down onto a row of seats.

Sofia pushed the children past the stewardess. She pointed to the open door. "Out! That way!"

The children did as they were told. *Romanian children*, she thought. *So much better behaved than English brats.*

The stewardess hauled herself up and lunged at Sofia. "What are you doing?"

"Sorry!" Sofia gave her another hard shove and ran to the door. She sped down the steps after the children.

At the bottom, they had stopped to wait for her. They looked scared and confused, years younger now.

"Come with me," she said. Sofia ran towards the gate she'd come through.

"Hey!" A voice came from behind. "Where are you going?"

A bus stood on the tarmac a hundred metres from the bottom of the slide. People crashed onto it, shoving their way in. Other children piled on with them. One of them called out to Sofia's group. A name: Elena.

The girl she'd grabbed last, one of the ones not on the list, called back. She broke away from Sofia's group and ran towards the bus. She leaped onto it just as the doors closed. She stared back through the glass, her eyes on Sofia.

Sofia had seven children now. She hoped that would be enough for Titi. He wanted to give them a new life too, like he had her. That poor girl had missed her chance.

"Come with me," she said. She ran for the gate. Up ahead, Adam held the wire aside as the other men led a group

CHAPTER ELEVEN

of women through. Sofia's heart lurched to see her sister in the middle of them.

"Andreea!" Sofia picked up pace. They were rescuing her sister, too. Bringing them together.

Energised by joy and relief, Sofia ran as fast as she could. At the gate, she stopped to let the kids through. Adam was already through, which made her the last.

As she turned sideways to squeeze through the gap, her trouser leg snagged on the wire. She tugged. The children were in the van she'd arrived in, and the engine was running. The other van had gone, Andreea on it. She couldn't be left behind.

She grabbed her trouser leg and tore at the fabric. Her leg came through.

Sofia let out a cry and ran to the van, sliding into a seat just as it sped along the narrow road it had come in by.

CHAPTER TWELVE

Zoe sat in the back of a fire service car, being driven out onto the runway. It was fully dark now, the January night closing in. Behind her, the lights of the airport building blazed. Up ahead, planes were dotted across the tarmac, abandoned like she was driving across some kind of aeroplane graveyard.

The fire had been extinguished and smoke rose up, lighter than the night sky behind it.

"I still don't get why you were called out," she said to Ian. "And how you got here so quickly."

He shrugged. "M6 brings me straight here from Castle Vale. I was shopping at the Fort with Alison and the kids."

"So you've abandoned them there?"

"Of course not. I got them an Uber."

"How *are* your kids?"

"Getting better. Slowly. I'd rather not talk about it."

Ian's kids – Maddy, aged twelve, and Ollie, aged four – had been abducted the previous October. Ian had been brought onto her team after they'd been found. Brought wasn't really the right word. Parachuted in was closer. Professional Standards wanted him in Force CID, gathering evidence against David Randle. They suspected Ian was bent himself, which made him the perfect poacher turned gamekeeper.

"OK," she said. "The brief I've been given by the Super is to do everything we can to preserve forensics. If this is a terror attack, then FSI will need everything they can get to find out how it happened and who's responsible."

"Surely someone'll claim it."

"You know it doesn't work like that anymore."

"Or it could be a lone nutter. Take explosives onto a plane, kill yourself in the process, get your seventy-two virgins in the afterlife."

"First off, we don't know it's Islamist terrorists. Secondly, getting explosives onto a plane as a passenger isn't exactly easy."

"If it's made of plastic, won't trigger the detectors."

"It won't get past the dogs."

"Yeah." Ian screwed up his nose. Zoe eyed the man driving the car. He was in plain clothes, not a firefighter. But not senior. Clive Junger, who she'd correctly identified as the man in charge back at the ops room, had summoned him and told him to escort her.

"You're right," she told Ian.

"I am?"

"Whatever evidence might have been on that plane will have been destroyed. We need to focus on the airport."

"But the plane just landed. It hadn't come into contact with anyone here as far as we know."

She sighed. "That means it's the airport at the other end. Where did that plane come from?"

"Karachi, ma'am," said the driver.

"That doesn't help." The plane would have taken off hours ago. If someone had got explosives onto the plane there, maybe by infiltrating the baggage handlers, they'd be long gone.

"We're never going to get anything," she said. "It's useless."

"This is bigger than you and me," Ian pointed out. "It's an international incident."

"Still. We're here and we've been given a job to do."

The car stopped a good distance from the plane.

"Don't go too close, ma'am," said the driver. "Authorised fire service personnel only."

So he was more than just the driver. He'd been sent here to stop her interfering. "I understand."

She opened the door and swung her legs out, not ready for the sharp smell of burning aeroplane. She was overcome by the feeling that Randle had sent her out here to get her out of the way.

CHAPTER THIRTEEN

The van was full of women and smelled of sweat and perfume. Andreea looked out into the night, hoping she was being taken to Sofia. She had no idea who these other women were. She'd seen them on the plane sitting near her, none of them talking to each other. It was unusual to see so many single women travelling like that. But she'd been lost in anxiety and guilt.

Her sister had a boyfriend. He was a big deal, according to Sofia. Someone who could make things happen. He had a job lined up for Andreea, Sofia had told her. What kind of job, she hadn't said. But something that paid well.

Andreea wondered why the boyfriend hadn't found a job for Sofia. At home, she'd worked in a coffee shop in Bucharest, the kind of place only tourists and businessmen could afford to drink at. He'd taken her away from that, promising a new life and riches she could only dream of.

Andreea wasn't so sure. If something's too good to be true, then it's probably a lie, was her motto. But anything had to be better than life at home. Stuck in that rundown farmhouse with her ageing mum and sick dad, she'd had enough of fetching and carrying, of being at her parents' command.

She'd told them this was a holiday, a chance to see Sofia. They knew as well as she did that she had no plans to come home, but no one was saying it.

The van slowed. It was surrounded by cars, headlights bright. The road was wide, with occasional groups of shops. Most of the shops were open, even after dusk. Some of them looked luxurious. The shops were interspersed with restaurants, mainly Indian, some selling pizza or Chinese food. Andreea wondered if English people ever ate English food.

They turned onto a narrower street that was choked with traffic. The men in the front of the van were talking between themselves. One of them, the one who'd pulled her off the plane, looked pissed off. He'd looked pissed off from the moment she'd first seen him. She wondered if any of the men were Sofia's boyfriend.

A woman in the row in front turned to her. "Do you know where we're going?" she asked in Romanian. Her accent was heavy, rural. Andreea shrugged.

"They're taking us to a hotel," another woman, skinny with lank hair, said.

The first woman rubbed her hands together. "It's cold here."

"Should have brought a coat," the skinny woman told her.

"Shut up back there!" The angry-looking man turned to them. "We're trying to concentrate."

Andreea's English wasn't good but she knew enough to tell that this man wasn't happy to be here. She wanted to ask where Sofia was. But she wouldn't get a sensible answer out of any of them, she knew. And she wasn't about to let them humiliate her.

Streetlights reflected off puddles in the road. The cars coming the other way moved slowly past them, drivers intent on the road ahead. Bucharest's roads would be busy at this time on a Saturday night, but not as busy as this.

The man driving the van muttered something to the angry man, who slapped him around the ear. Andreea shook her head. She'd seen plenty of that kind of thing: the way her dad treated her mum, for starters. Until he'd become too ill to keep up with her.

The driver stopped the van. He shunted it back and forth until it was on the other side of the road, facing back the way they'd come. They started to move.

"Where do we go?" Andreea asked.

"You'll find out," the angry man said. He turned back to the third man. They spoke to each other, shaking their heads. The driver looked nervous.

Why were they going back to the airport?

She squeezed past the gap between the seats and jabbed a finger into the angry man's back. He turned to her.

"Get back in your seat, for fuck's sake. You'll get us all arrested."

"Where do you take us? Where is Sofia? My sister?"

"You what?"

"My sister. Where is she?"

A snort. "Don't worry about that, darling. You'll see your sister soon enough." He gave her a shove in the chest. "Now sit the fuck back down."

Andreea curled her lip at him. Men like him didn't scare her. She retreated into the back of the van, her eyes not leaving his as she took her seat and fastened her seatbelt.

CHAPTER FOURTEEN

"This is useless," Zoe said. She stared across the tarmac at the smouldering plane, Ian beside her. "I have no idea why we're here."

"Preserve evidence," Ian said.

She turned to him. "I know that. But we can't bloody well do anything with the firefighters not letting us on the plane."

He shrugged. "Maybe we just wait."

"Wait."

Zoe didn't like waiting. She grabbed her phone, tempted to call Randle and confront him.

Firefighters had started entering the plane now, searching for survivors or, more likely, bodies. No one had come out alive yet. The fuselage had a jagged hole where the explosion had hit, like something had taken a bite out of it. The tail had sheared off and was two hundred metres behind the rest of the plane along the taxiway. The plane was stained with scorch marks and soot, the airline's logo obscured.

The firefighters emerged with a stretcher. They took it to a patch of ground that had been cordoned off in front of the plane and laid what looked like a body on the ground.

"Come on," Zoe said. "If we can't get onto the plane, the only forensics we've got is going to be those bodies."

Ian shivered and followed her.

A woman was crouched over the body.

"Thank God for that," said Zoe. She picked up pace. "Dr Adebayo."

The woman stood up, her hands in the small of her back. She was tall and willowy, with piercing eyes. She grimaced as she stretched then smiled at Zoe. "DI Finch. I didn't know you were here."

Adana Adebayo was Zoe's favourite pathologist. Direct and abrasive, but damn good at her job.

"I'm working on preservation of forensic evidence," Zoe said. "You're the lead pathologist?"

"For now. There are going to be so many victims that I imagine this'll be taken out of my hands."

"Do you have an ID for this body?"

They looked down at the body. It was a woman, her face covered in blood. A deep gash ran round the side of her head and her arm had been all but torn off.

"Give me a minute, Inspector," the pathologist said. "I'm not Superwoman."

Ian made a guttural sound. Zoe gave him a warning look.

Two more men approached with a second body: a man this time. They laid him next to the first, with a gap of half a metre. Adana looked at the man, her mouth tight. "Nothing prepares you for a job like this."

"No." Zoe stepped forward. "Do we have a suspect? A bomber?"

"How should I know?"

"Surely they're logging where on the plane people are being found?"

"That's what I hope they're doing. Maybe you should check."

Zoe turned to Ian. "You stay here. Flag me down if there's anything interesting."

"OK."

Zoe ran to the metal steps that had been wheeled into position next to the plane.

"Who's in charge of bringing victims off the plane?"

"I am," said a tall man in protective gear. "Who are you?"

Zoe raised her ID. "DI Finch, Bronze Command. I need you to chart where each survivor or victim is being found. It would be better if you'd let me and my colleagues on board."

"No chance," he said. "It's not safe for anyone other than the fire crews."

"We need to send a forensics team in there," she said. "If the explosion started inside the plane..."

"It didn't."

"No?"

"It was near the wheel housing. Rear right hand side. You won't find a suicide bomber on this plane, if that's what you're thinking."

"So how did it happen?"

"The airline investigator will be working on that."

"We don't believe this is a malfunction. We believe it's a deliberate attack."

"On what grounds?"

"This was the second explosion in the city in less than an hour."

"Who's to say they're linked?"

She sighed. "West Midlands Police do. That good enough for you?"

He grunted. "You'll have to speak to Clive Junger. He's in charge of the fire service response. I can't authorise any police ingress on that plane."

"I've already spoken to him. As Bronze Command I outrank him."

"You aren't my boss. Sorry."

She dug her fingernail into her palm. "What's your name?"

He straightened. Behind him, another body was being brought off the plane. "Sam Hetherton. Incident Response Manager for West Midlands Fire Service."

"Well, Sam Hetherton, have you received major incident training?"

"Of course I have."

"Well in that case you know that Bronze Command outranks your bosses, no matter how loyal to them you might be."

"You're a mardy bitch, aren't you?"

"I..." Zoe stopped herself. Letting this man rile her would get her nowhere. "Look, just let us take a look."

"They're still looking for survivors. No chance you're getting in the way."

"Wait."

Zoe walked back to Ian, her body fired up with anger. The bodies were accumulating on the tarmac, a dozen of them now. Adana moved between them, making notes on an iPad. Ian was crouched over one of the bodies.

"What's up?" Zoe asked him. "Seen something?"

He stood up quickly, rubbing his hands together. "No. It's... it's tragic, is what it is."

She nodded. "I don't imagine any of these bodies will provide us with evidence. It'll be on the plane. But right now, they're not letting us near it."

Ian opened his mouth to speak but she put a hand up to shush him and took out her phone.

"Gold Command."

"Sir, it's DI Finch."

"You're supposed to use the radio. Find a grunt who'll give you access."

"I need your authorisation to go onto the plane."

"They aren't letting you?"

"Some jobsworth from the fire service is saying that he won't let me and Ian on until Clive Junger gives the all-clear."

"Ian's with you?"

"He is."

She glanced at Ian, who raised his eyebrows in acknowledgment.

"Sir?" Zoe said.

Ian had his phone out. "Forensics are onsite," he said, moving his thumb across the screen. Zoe nodded.

"Wait a moment," Randle said. "Junger's right here. He wants to know who you've been talking to."

"Sam Hetherton. Says he's Incident Response Manager."

A pause. "Junger's been in contact with him. Looks like they're bringing off survivors. You know we can't obstruct that."

"Sir, you told me to preserve the scene."

"Their work takes priority. You don't need me to tell you that, do you?"

"No, sir."
"Right. Get back here, you can brief the forensics guys."
"Sir."
She turned to Ian. "Looks like we've wasted our time."
He shrugged and looked back down at the bodies. He turned towards the airport building and she followed.

CHAPTER FIFTEEN

Sofia sat amongst the children, ignoring the way they kept looking at her as if she knew what was happening. She had no idea who they were, why their names had been added to that list. Except for two of them, who hadn't been on the list. Should she have taken them? What about the one who'd run to the bus?

Maybe their parents were back on that plane or at the airport, looking for them? She couldn't imagine what that would be like.

She pictured Andreea, being led away from the plane. She'd gone through the same gate as Sofia, been led into the first van. Sofia could only hope the two vans were heading to the same place.

A girl sitting behind Sofia began to cry. Sofia turned to her.

"Hey, it's OK. You're safe now. We're going to take you somewhere nice where you can get some food. Maybe there'll be chocolate."

The girl stared back at her. She continued crying.

"Did you have anyone with you on the plane?" Sofia asked.

The girl ignored the question. Sofia turned to the two boys sitting next to her. They were huddled together, shivering. They didn't have coats, just the jeans and t-shirts they'd been wearing on the plane. She wondered where their luggage was.

"What about you two? You look like you're good friends."

One of the boys nodded. "I'm Marius. He's Florin. Where are we going?"

"There was an explosion, on another plane. We got you away, safe."

"Where are we going?"

Sofia looked at Adam, sitting in the front. He stared out of the windscreen, his feet up on the dashboard and ankles crossed. She swallowed.

"We'll find out soon," she said.

They were heading for the city centre. Titi had had a flat not far away, when she'd first come here. They'd moved out within days of her arrival, to the echoing, sparkly house in the countryside. She hadn't met any of the neighbours, had never even glimpsed them. Adam and the other men took her shopping or to the hairdresser's. And Titi, of course. He took her to all sorts of places, when he was around. Restaurants with dishes that would have cost her a month's salary. One time, a hotel suite. It was a luxurious lifestyle, but she longed for friends.

It would be easier now Andreea was here. They could go places together, Sofia could show her the city. They'd escape her minders and find some freedom.

The boy gave her a look as if it was all her fault. She couldn't blame him. She'd grabbed him and his friends from the plane, bundled them onto this van and driven them away into the night. She was amazed they weren't all crying.

"Shit," Adam said. Sofia perked up. She leaned forward.

He slammed his phone into the dashboard and turned to the driver. "Bad news. Looks like it wasn't as clean as we'd hoped."

"What, you mean he might have walked out of that?" the driver asked.

Adam shrugged. "Who knows? Turns out even the so-called experts can't get a fucking bomb right. But the problem now is us and where we're going. They've cleared the place out. Too close to New Street."

"They've what?"

"It's not safe, apparently."

"So where are we going then?"

Adam slapped a palm to his forehead. "Beats me."

The boy next to Sofia put a hand on her knee. "What's happening?"

"We're just finding the best route," she told him in Romanian. "Won't be long now." She tried to smile.

"We're lost," the other boy, Florin, said.

"No," she reassured him. "See out there? That's a mosque. Biggest one in the city. I know this area. I've eaten in a restaurant not far from here."

She hoped she wasn't mistaken. Titi had driven her this way a week after her arrival, taken her to a fancy French restaurant. But she couldn't remember where it was.

She leaned forward.

"Where do we take the children?"

"Just keep them quiet, alright? We'll worry about that."

"They're tired. They're scared. They need food."

"They'll be fine."

"Did you say you cannot take them where you were planning?"

"You listen too much."

She clenched her fists. "You don't know where you're going."

He jerked around in his seat, his eyes blazing. "Shut up, woman. Just cos the boss is shagging you doesn't mean you're immune."

She glared back at him, ignoring the trembling in her limbs. "They need to go somewhere safe. Where are parents?"

"No parents. School exchange programme."

She looked back at the children, her body cold. These children had no one to stand up for them.

"Where is the teacher?"

"Buggered if I know."

Sofia slumped back. She hadn't had time to ask questions when they'd arrived at the runway. She'd never asked why they were taking the kids, who they all were.

"We take them home," she said.

"Don't be daft."

"Not their home. My home."

Adam exchanged a look with the driver.

"It is a big house. They will be safe there. Titi will look after them."

Adam laughed. "Oh, he'll look after them alright, lady."

She wanted to hit him. The impulse made her think of Andreea, and her quick temper.

"Take me home. I explain to him."

"You *will* explain, is what you mean."

She waved her hand, irritated with his correction of her English. She'd like to see him try to speak Romanian.

"I'll have to call the boss," Adam said.

Sofia squared her shoulders. Her boyfriend was a good man. He'd brought her here, and he was doing the same for her sister. So the kids couldn't go to their intended hotel, so what? There was plenty of space in her house. Six bedrooms, two living rooms.

"Call him," she said.

Adam gave her a thin smile as he raised his phone to his ear. He stared at her as he waited.

"Fuck." He put down the phone.

"What is it?" Sofia asked.

"No answer."

"Then I decide. We take the kids home. Now."

CHAPTER SIXTEEN

"DI Finch, DS Osman. You're back."

The ops base had filled up since Zoe had left it. Almost all the monitors were turned on and airport and police staff lined the desks. There was an air of hurried calm.

"Sir. I'm not happy about the—"

Randle raised a hand. "You got your answer, DI Finch. Just shut up and do as you're told, eh?"

It felt like he'd slapped her, and with Ian right next to her too.

"Where's Adi?" she asked.

Randle jerked a thumb behind him. "Getting computers set up with the other techs. Waiting for you."

"Good." She walked past Randle and made for the Forensics team. No way was she letting him see he'd rattled her.

"Zoe," said Adi. For once he didn't smile. She'd known Adi Hanson for years, and he never failed to flirt with her when they came face to face at a crime scene. This one, it seemed, was the exception.

"Adi." Zoe turned to his colleague, Yala Cook. She was bent over a computer, setting up software. "Yala."

"DI Finch." Yala turned and gave her a tight smile, then returned to her work. Another tech, a young man Zoe hadn't met, worked with her.

"So, what are we working with?" Adi asked.

Zoe plunged herself into a chair. The techs had been allocated a row of desks in a corner of the room. They were setting up their own computers, not getting any help from the incident IT team. "Not much, right now," she said. "The explosion was beneath the passenger compartment, in the hold, I imagine. We'll need to get schematics of the aircraft."

"Leave that with me," Adi said. "I've already spoken to the manufacturers. They'll be sending their own investigative team. I'm just hoping they'll work with us."

"Me too." Zoe wasn't holding out much hope, the way this day was going so far. "They're still bringing people off. Bodies, mainly, but they seem to have found survivors."

"That's something."

"Yeah." Zoe wanted to speak to Ian. He was still with Randle.

"Ian?" she called. "Get over here, will you?"

He looked up from his conversation with the Super. "Sorry." He nodded at Randle then hurried to join her.

"What was all that about?" she asked.

"He wanted more information about the crime scene," he replied.

"There are a range of possibilities," Adi said. "If someone detonated that bomb from inside the plane, then whatever they used was probably destroyed. And I can't see them getting it past security anyway. We'll need to go through the hold contents, or what's left of them."

"The plane came from Pakistan," said Zoe. "We'll need to find out what security checks would have taken place."

"If there was a detonator, there might be traces of it on the plane," added Ian. "Even if it's just fragments."

"You got an idea what kind of thing you might be looking for?" Zoe asked Adi.

"Some. Not much. Most of the people on that thing will have been carrying electronic devices. Phones, laptops. They could have used a phone."

Zoe slumped in her chair. She checked her watch: 9:42pm. Almost six hours since it had happened.

"OK," she said. "Seeing as we can't get access to the plane right now, what else can we be looking at?"

"In terms of forensics?" asked Adi.

"Course."

"The bodies," he said. "If we can get access to them, we can check for devices, phones and the like. Take them in, look for any unusual apps. And we'll need to take devices from survivors, too."

"That'll be my job," said Yala. "It could be a lot of phones to go through. Or it could be none. Depends what state they're in."

"We always have to consider the possibility it was just a fault in the plane," said Adi. "The airline investigator doesn't like that idea."

"I bet not. What type of plane was it?" Zoe asked.

"Airbus A320."

"What's their safety record like?"

"Very good," said Yala. "One crash per ten million flights." She shrugged, catching Adi's expression. "I did some googling on the way here."

"So that makes it more likely that this was human activity," Zoe said.

"I know," said Adi. "We'll be ready, when we can. We'll secure the plane, make sure there's nothing that's going to degrade. I want to work fast, though. I'm worried that when the airline investigators turn up tomorrow, they'll bring things to a halt."

Zoe sighed. "Ian? You've been very quiet."

He frowned. "There's always pathology," he said. "We might find evidence on the bodies."

"Luckily we have Adana working on that."

"She's got access already?" asked Adi.

"She's out there now." Zoe jerked her head in the vague direction of the runway. This room didn't have windows and for all she knew, she was gesturing in the opposite direction.

"Nice one, Adana," said Adi. He shook his head. "Wish I could be as persuasive as her."

"You'll get your chance," said Zoe. "Meanwhile, what can you tell me about New Street?"

The bomb in the city centre had been playing on her mind. She'd had to push it away since she'd arrived at the airport and focused all her attention on the incident here. But she'd heard nothing since seeing the explosion on TV.

"You haven't heard?" said Adi.

Zoe tensed. "What?"

"DCI Clarke. She collapsed in the ops room."

"She did what? Why?" Lesley was made of steel.

"She was right by the doors when the bomb went off," said Adi. "That's all I know, but it sounds like she was injured."

"Where is she now?"

"City Hospital."

"Shit." Zoe felt an urge to drive straight to the hospital, to find out how her boss was doing. To be there in the same way Lesley had been there for her over the years.

"Who's at Force CID?"

Ian shrugged. "I haven't been in, remember?"

Zoe gave him an irritated look and grabbed her phone.

"Zo."

"Mo, I just heard about Lesley. Is she OK?"

"She's in surgery."

"Surgery?"

Adi and Yala exchanged glances.

"She got shards of glass lodged in her brain stem," Mo said. "Made her black out."

Zoe gripped her chair's armrest. "Where are you?"

"I'm at New Street. Working with Uniform, trying to compile a list of witnesses. It's not easy."

"I can imagine."

"There were hundreds of people here at the time. Thousands. But no one says they saw anything. We've got CCTV of a woman talking to the bomber but no one knows who she is."

Zoe put her hand over the receiver. "Yala, do you know about this woman who spoke to the New Street bomber?"

Yala shook her head.

"I'm putting you onto Mo. Maybe you can work on that while you're waiting for access to the plane."

"Let's get out there," said Adi.

"No point yet," Zoe said.

"Like I say, I want as much time as I can before the airline guys arrive. If I'm on the runway, I'm ready. You coming, or not?"

"I'll join you when I can." Zoe turned to Ian. "You go with Adi. Keep me informed."

"No problem, boss."

CHAPTER SEVENTEEN

The van turned into a driveway on a street lined with large, shabby houses. Andreea shivered and wrapped her arms around herself.

Sofia had told her she was living in a large house in the countryside. This must be it. Andreea let herself relax for the first time since they'd led her off the plane.

The side door to the van opened.

"Out," said the man.

Andreea jumped down along with the other women. She had no idea why these women were coming with her. Maybe they were friends of Sofia's boyfriend.

She grabbed the woman closest to her by the wrist. "Why have they brought us all here?"

The woman pulled her arm away. "They told me I'd have a job waiting for me, a place to stay. Maybe this is it."

"Shut up, you two." The man with the scarred cheek pushed them apart. Andreea stared back at him. She didn't know who he was but he wasn't pushing her around like that.

"Let go of me," she said. "Take me to Sofia."

"Will you shut up about your fucking sister." The man turned to his friend and laughed. Their eyes were hard. She'd known men like that, back at home. She'd learned to avoid them. Was this the kind of man Sofia was befriending now she was in the UK? Or were they all like this?

"You don't push me around."

"Don't I?" The man flashed his eyes at her. He gave her a shove in the chest. "I think I do."

She lunged at him, her fists clenched. He smirked.

"You're priceless, you are. They're gonna love you."

"Stop it, Cal," the man who'd been angry with her said. Andreea could see his face now. He was older than the others, old enough to be her father. "Just let's get them inside before someone hears us."

The younger man backed away, his eyes not leaving Andreea's face. She glared at him, her chest heaving.

The men shepherded the women along a pockmarked gravel driveway that reminded her of her parents' farmhouse.

"Here we are," grinned the older man. "Home."

The building wasn't the mansion Sofia had described. It was big enough, sure. But that was where the similarity ended.

"There has been mistake," Andreea said. "You leave others here, take me to Sofia."

"*There has been mistake*," the older man repeated. "Are you all like this?" He grabbed her arm and shoved her towards the building. She tried to free herself, but his fingers dug in.

The building had been grand once. It was broad and imposing, with tall windows and a roof that disappeared up into the night sky. But almost half of the windows were boarded up and weeds grew around the steps leading up to the front door. The place looked like it would fall down if Andreea gave it a sharp kick.

The man banged on the door with his fist. Flakes of paint fell to the ground. Andreea coughed.

The door opened and a thin woman wearing a black fleece and torn blue jeans confronted them.

"You're late."

"We had to take a detour. Too many pigs."

The woman spat. "Get them in 'ere then." She had dyed red hair and her roots were showing.

The man pushed Andreea forward. The woman stood back to let her pass. Her eyes were sharp, like a crow's. She peered into Andreea's face, sizing her up. In return, Andreea shot her a look of disdain.

"You're going to be trouble," the woman said. "We'll tame you."

Andreea felt her skin bristle as she passed the woman and entered a broad hallway. Wide stairs with carved wooden railings rose to one side and the walls were partly covered in wood panelling. Patches of it were missing, crumbling plaster showing through from underneath.

"This is not Sofia's boyfriend's house," she said.

"Hah! That's a good one," the woman said. "No, you can certainly say this is not his house. Although he did pay for it."

"You have brought me to wrong place."

"No idea what you're talkin' about, hen." Her accent was different from the men, sharper.

Andreea stared back at the woman. For the first time, fear threatened. "Take me to Sofia," she said, struggling to keep her cool.

"We'll find you a nice comfy bed," the woman said. "And

give you some food. If you're good." She prodded Andreea's stomach. "You could do with fattening up."

Andreea swiped at the woman's hand but she was too fast. The woman leaned in, her breath stinking of cigarettes.

"You'll learn to behave yourself, lass. If you know what's good for you."

Andreea blinked back at her. Behaving herself wasn't something she did.

The other women had gathered behind her. Andreea turned to see them huddling together. Who were these mice? There were twelve of them, three men, and this scrawny woman. They could overpower them, no problem. But none of them looked like they had the guts to do so.

She blew out a breath. She'd have to get away under her own steam. Find Sofia. Wait for her boyfriend to arrive: this was his house, after all.

She'd watch, and she'd wait. And then she'd act.

CHAPTER EIGHTEEN

At last Zoe had been given the all-clear to enter the plane. Adi was already there, directing his team as they pushed a set of steps up to the hold doors.

"How helpful will the hold be now they've cleared it out?" she asked him. Luggage, mostly burnt, lay jumbled on the tarmac not far from where they stood. Apparently it was standard procedure to clear out the hold in case anyone was hiding inside.

"Not very," he said. "Got to cover all bases though."

"I'm going to check the passenger compartment. Shout if you find anything."

Adi brushed her arm with his hand. "Be careful, yeah?"

"I won't disturb anything, if that's what you mean."

"You know what I mean."

Ian was near Adana, surveying the bodies. Ambulances lined up behind them, collecting the wounded. Sam Hetherton was still at the bottom of the steps, coordinating firefighters. Zoe approached him.

"How many survivors?" she asked.

"Just forty-one." His eyes were bloodshot and his skin sagged. He looked like he'd aged five years in the two hours since she'd seen him. "At least six of them won't make it."

Her shoulders slumped. "We didn't get in your way, did we?"

"Not too much."

Her chest tightened. "Sorry."

"Yeah. I'm used to it, from your lot."

She clenched her fists. "We've been given the all-clear to go in there."

He twisted his lips together. "So I hear."

She started up the steps to the passenger compartment. The bodies had been removed from the plane now, along with the survivors. It had taken almost three hours.

"Ian?" she called. Ian left the pathologist and hurried to meet Zoe at the steps.

"We allowed in?" he asked.

"We are. Go carefully, yes?"

"You really think I'm incompetent, don't you?"

"I'd say the same to Mo, or anyone. Just park the paranoia, please."

He wrinkled his nose and pulled up the hood of his protective suit. Zoe sighed.

"Wait," Hetherton called from the bottom of the steps. "You'll need these." He held out breathing apparatus.

"Still that bad?" she asked.

"Precautionary."

Ian took the two masks and handed one to Zoe. They were both already wearing forensic suits, not that it would make much difference now the firefighters had stomped all over the inside of the plane.

"Right," she told Ian. "The explosion was towards the

rear of the plane. We can't go too close until Adi has marked out the scene, but we can take a look."

"Stay by the doors. I get it."

"Good." *Preserve the scene. Protect the evidence.* That was her job, and she was damn well doing it.

Zoe hurried up the steps, ignoring the fact that they swayed as she moved. Ian was right behind her, his breathing heavy as he pulled on the breathing apparatus. At the top, she fastened hers around her head and plunged inside. Her vision was obscured by the steaming visor, and the sound of her breath assaulted her ears. How was she supposed to spot anything in these conditions?

The passenger compartment was wrecked. Seats had buckled and molten plastic formed into stalactites that hung down from the overhead lockers. People in dark firefighters' uniforms moved slowly through the space, gesturing at each other.

Zoe looked to the left, towards the front of the plane. The curtain separating them from the toilets had partially disintegrated and the door to the cockpit hung open. A leather holdall, undamaged, sat against the back of one of the pilots' chairs.

Zoe turned back to the main compartment. Ahead of her, propped on a window seat, was a doll, its face black with soot. Zoe felt her legs weaken.

She glanced back at Ian, sharing a grim but silent reaction. This was like nothing either of them had seen before.

Zoe took a tentative step forward and felt something soft under her foot. She flinched, squeezing her eyes shut. She took a heavy breath though the mask and looked down. A foot. A single, small foot wearing a pink sock.

She felt her stomach convulse. *Keep it down*, she told herself.

"Finding forensics in the middle of all this is going to be a nightmare," she said. She looked up, away from the foot.

Ian pointed towards the back of the plane. "There's definitely more damage back there."

Seats had been torn from their anchor points and were piled up at the back of the plane, a twisted tangle of metal and fabric. Overhead lockers hung open and the floor was strewn with bags and suitcases, many of them charred. Their contents spilled out: clothes, books, toys.

Zoe went to plunge her fist into her mouth but was stopped by the mask.

"We need floodlights," she said. Ian grunted agreement.

"Come on," she told him. "There's nothing we can do here. Not now."

She descended the steps, all but pushing Ian down in front of her. A woman had joined Sam Hetherton. She wore a thick black fleece over a grey suit.

"Who are you?" she asked as Zoe and Ian reached the tarmac.

Zoe pulled off the mask, glad to breathe in the cold night air. "Detective Inspector Zoe Finch. I'm co-ordinating preservation of the scene."

"I'm Sue Turbin. Fire scene investigator, West Midlands Fire Service."

Zoe put out a hand and the woman shook it.

"Our FSI guys are in the hold," Zoe said. "They'll want to coordinate with you."

"Yes."

Hetherton gave the fire investigator a look. Zoe smiled to herself.

CHAPTER EIGHTEEN

"Have you worked on explosions like this before?" she asked the woman.

"Plenty of explosions. Mainly gas, one bomb when I worked in London. Nothing involving planes though."

"What can you say from what you've seen?"

"I'm not about to jump to conclusions, Inspector."

"Do you think it was a bomb, or a malfunction?"

Sue folded her arms. "You aren't going to persuade me to speculate. Not till I've taken a proper look."

"Fine." Zoe felt fatigue drag on her limbs. This woman might have been a plodder, but she could trust her to work with them.

"Sue," Adi approached, smiling. "How's my favourite fire investigator?"

Zoe stared at him. How well did this pair know each other?

"Adi." Sue leaned in and kissed him on the cheek. Zoe exchanged raised eyebrows with Ian.

"Sue's one of the good ones, Zoe," Adi said. "If this is suspicious, you can bet that between us, we'll get to the bottom of it."

CHAPTER NINETEEN

SOFIA SAT on the vast leather sofa, her legs curled beneath her. Her senses tingled, alert for sounds of the children. She'd allocated them rooms, none of them alone. She figured a bunch of kids who'd been through what they had would want company.

Adam and the other men had left an hour earlier. Adam had argued with her, but she'd put her foot down and got her way. She had precedence over him, as the woman Titi loved.

Good.

She heard a noise from the hallway. A girl stood at the bottom of the carpeted stairs.

"I'm thirsty."

Sofia flicked the TV off; she hadn't been able to concentrate on it anyway. She walked into the hallway and gave the girl a look designed to convey concern and kindness. She was careful not to touch her.

"That's OK," she said. "Come to the kitchen, I'll get you a glass of milk."

A smile flashed across the girl's face and quickly disappeared. These children had no idea who she was. They would be unsure whether to trust her. She hoped to show by her actions that they could.

In the kitchen, she opened the massive American-style fridge and brought out a carton of milk. She poured a generous glass and placed it on the marble worktop in front of the girl. The girl stroked the worktop then grabbed the glass and downed the milk in one lengthy gulp. Sofia stepped in to refill it. The girl took a step back.

Sofia stood back. "Sorry," she said. "You must be scared."

The girl said nothing. Sofia refilled the glass and placed it down, then retreated.

"What's your name?" Sofia asked.

"Gabriella."

"I've got a friend called Gabriella. Or at least I did."

Gabriella had worked with her in the coffee shop where she'd met Titi. She'd been Sofia's supervisor, barking orders at her morning till night. They'd gone for a drink after work a few times, when she'd loosened up and been less officious.

"You must be wondering why you're here."

The girl finished the second glass, her brown eyes not leaving Sofia's face. She shrugged.

"Truth is, I'm not sure myself. But I do know there was an explosion, at the airport. We got you out safe."

The girl's eyes narrowed.

"Were your family on the plane with you?"

There'd been no adults in sight, and she'd been told it was an exchange programme. But Adam might have been lying to her.

Gabriella shook her head. "School trip."

Sofia relaxed. "That's nice. Visiting England." She

wondered what there was in Birmingham to entice a group of Romanian children on a school trip.

"We'll find your teacher," she said. "We'll make sure you're back with your other friends. My boyfriend, Titi. He's a good man, he'll—"

"What's that about me?"

Sofia turned to see him standing in the doorway. His tie was loose and his face red.

She hurried to him. "Titi. This is Gabriella. We rescued her and her friends from the airport today. Like Adam told me you wanted. She was on the same plane as Andreea."

He gave Sofia a peck on the cheek and walked past her. The girl shrank back, rounding the kitchen island.

"What's she doing here?" he asked.

"We could not take them to hotel. Some problem, a bomb. At the station. I brought them here. Just one night."

The girl stared at him, her shoulders rising and falling. He turned to Sofia, his movements measured. "You did what?"

"Adam tried to call you. I tried to call you. We could not get you. Titi. I did not want to le—"

He put a hand up to silence her. *"Don't call me that. This is my home."* He eyed her. *"Our home."*

"Sorry. It is very big. Plenty of space, huh? And just one night."

He narrowed his eyes, looking at her as if she were stupid. Had she been stupid? Would someone be looking for these children? Would they think she'd kidnapped them?

"I am sorry. Maybe it was not such a good thing to do. But I wanted them to be safe."

He looked back at the girl. She'd grabbed the glass of milk and held it up, staring across the rim at the two of them. Titi smiled at her, his eyes cold. She didn't smile back.

"They shouldn't be here," he said. "Adam shouldn't have let you."

"Was not his fault." Sofia approached him and lifted a hand to his cheek. "I am sorry, honeybun. I forced him."

He raised an eyebrow. She stroked his cheek. His flesh was hot. Her heart pounded against her ribs. "Do not be cross with your munchkin, please?"

His body loosened. He grabbed her hand and put it to his lips, then kissed it gently. "It's been a rough day, but I could never be cross with you."

She bit her lip. She was right. Titi was a good man. She looked at Gabriella as if to say *I told you so*. The girl stared back, her face pale.

Titi turned to the girl. "Leave us."

Sofia nodded at her, gesturing for her to leave. The girl placed the glass on the counter and ran around the island. Sofia heard footsteps recede up the stairs.

Titi clutched her hand. His eyes flashed at her. He liked rough sex, it was a weakness of his. It had taken her by surprise when he'd invited her to his hotel room in Bucharest, but she was getting used to it. Enjoying it.

He spun her round. She stumbled into the kitchen island, her hip hitting the marble.

"Take off your top."

She pulled her t-shirt over her head, her eyes on his. Warmth radiated through her body. She glanced at the door. "We should close it."

He shook his head. "This is my house. Our house. We leave it open."

He gestured for her to remove her bra. She unfastened it

and let it fall to the floor. She wore only her jogging bottoms now and her pink panties, the lace ones he'd bought her.

Two paces brought him up against her. He had an erection. He placed his hands on her waist and lifted her up onto the counter. He grabbed the waistband of her trousers and pushed them to the floor. She lifted her butt off the counter to help. His eyes held her in place. He had a look of calm, of power. It turned her on.

He leaned in to kiss her. He plunged his tongue deep into her mouth and she let him possess her, her body filling with fire.

CHAPTER TWENTY

Zoe leaned against the front door. It was past midnight and every muscle in her body ached.

The cat lay stretched out on the stairs in front of her. The second step up seemed to have become her favourite spot lately.

"Hey, Yoda." Zoe slung her coat on the hook and picked the cat up. She nuzzled its warm fur. "You must have been wondering where I was."

She went into the living room. The coffee table was empty, no sign of the mugs she'd left there this morning. The floor had been cleared too, no discarded books or clothes awaiting the journey upstairs to the washing basket.

Nicholas had been tidying.

Zoe laid her fingertips on the surface of the coffee table. He'd been dusting, too. And hoovering, by the tracks in the carpet.

Her son cleaned when he was anxious. She hadn't rung him all night.

She glanced back towards the stairs. Should she knock on his door, let him know she was home?

She didn't want to wake him. And she was too tired for an argument. In the morning, she'd have the energy to explain herself.

The kitchen door opened. "Mum."

Her body slumped. "I'm sorry. You've been worried."

"I've been fine." His voice was thin.

"You've been cleaning."

He shrugged. "The place was a tip. I needed to fill the time."

"Come here." She placed the cat on the sofa and reached her arms out. Nicholas approached and let her hug him. He patted her back.

She pushed him away and held him at arm's length. He was just an inch taller than she was.

"I should have called you, let you know I was safe."

"They said a detective had been injured."

"Oh, my God. I'm sorry, I didn't think. That wasn't me. It was Lesley."

"Your boss Lesley?" His eyes widened.

She nodded. "She was hit by glass, at New Street. I... I don't know much else."

What time had she spoken to Mo? Hours ago. She'd been preoccupied with cordoning off the plane, establishing a potential crime scene. Randle had still been there when she left, managing the ops room. Ian had left hours earlier. She'd sent him home, thinking of Alison and the kids.

"I need to call the hospital," she said.

"You think they'll talk to you?"

"You're right. Her husband. I don't even know his name."

She frowned. She knew Lesley had one daughter, but wasn't sure about a husband.

"It can wait till morning, surely," Nicholas said. "I'm just glad it wasn't you."

She smiled. "Thanks, love. I appreciate you saying that."

He shrugged. "We need to talk." He turned for the kitchen.

"OK." She followed him. The clock above the hob said 12:35am. "What's up? Is it Zaf?"

"No."

"He not here tonight?"

"He had revision to do. So did I, not that I got any done." He switched the kettle on.

"Sorry," she said. "Again."

He leaned on the kitchen counter. Their kitchen was tiny, barely enough space for two people. Zoe shuffled against the fridge, ignoring the handle digging into her back. "Whatever it is, you can tell me."

"Hmm."

"Please. You've got me worried now."

He met her gaze. "It's Gran."

She craned her neck to stare up at the ceiling. "And there was me thinking it was something important."

"Gran *is* important."

"Yes, love. But she's predictable. If there's a problem with your gran, then it's nothing new for me to worry about."

"She's in the spare room."

"She's *what?*" Zoe's eyes shot upwards. "Why?"

"She was at New Street. When it happened."

"Doing what?" Annette wasn't the shopping type.

"I dunno. But she called me, from a phone box on Corporation Street."

"They still have phone boxes?"

"She was scared, Mum. Confused."

"Drunk, you mean."

"A bit."

A bit drunk, for Annette Finch, meant half a bottle of gin. On a good day.

"So she came here," Zoe said.

"I went to get her. I took a taxi. There was some cash in your room." His voice dropped. "I hope you don't mind."

She'd left fifteen quid on her bedside table that morning. Money for the window cleaner. "Of course I don't mind. Why didn't you call me?"

"The network was down."

Of course. The first thing to happen after a major incident was that everybody in the vicinity hammered their phones.

She grabbed his hand. "Well done, love. You did the right thing."

He puffed out a breath. A lock of hair blew upwards; he'd been letting it grow. "I thought you were going to give me a bollocking."

"Tomorrow." She winked.

He laughed, a tired laugh that spoke volumes about the day he'd had. "Yeah. I'm off to bed."

"Good. See you in the morning, sweetie."

"Don't call me that."

As he left the room, she looked up at the ceiling again. Her mum was above her head, in the small room at the back of the house that she worked from when she needed to but that also housed a single bed. Asleep, or awake? Listening in?

Right now, she didn't have the energy to care. She'd deal

with it tomorrow. She trudged up the stairs, avoiding the cat and ignoring the clenching of her stomach as she passed the spare room door.

CHAPTER TWENTY-ONE

Zoe lay in bed, scrolling through her phone. She knew she should go downstairs, but that meant facing her mum.

There was a voicemail from Carl, checking up on her. She wasn't used to accounting for herself. It was nice having people who worried about her, but it could be a chore.

She dialled his number. "Sorry, Carl. I hope you got my text last night."

"I got it. Did you get my message?"

"Sorry, only just picked it up. You know what the networks are like when this kind of thing happens."

"Were you at New Street?"

"I went to the airport. With Detective Superintendent Randle and DS Osman."

Carl whistled. "My two favourite people."

"Yeah. Ian was supposed to be on his day off. He told me he'd had a call from the office, made his way straight there from a shopping trip. I'm not so sure."

"You think it's suspicious?" Carl asked.

DI Carl Whaley was Zoe's boyfriend, but he was also

an officer in the Professional Standards division. He'd planted Ian in Zoe's team to have him watch Randle. Ian had struck a deal with him, and now Zoe was stuck with the man.

"It's just odd, that's all," she said. "He doesn't have a role in the incident command structure, and he was there before me. And *I* got a lift with Randle in his Audi."

"Maybe Randle told him."

"I was with Randle the whole way there. And besides, the two of them aren't exactly mates."

"We don't know that," Carl said.

"You haven't found any evidence that they've worked together. Surely that's why you're happy for Ian to spy on Randle."

"We have to be open to all options, Zoe. Let me know if anything else happens. Anything odd."

"Will do. Has Ian been reporting to you?"

"Nothing of interest yet. My Super is starting to put the pressure on."

"Surely Ian knows that if he doesn't give you anything soon, he'll lose his deal?"

"I never explicitly said that. But yeah. I'm not sure what happens to Ian if he doesn't keep up his side of the bargain, but it won't be good. He knows that."

"Poor Alison."

"A bent copper is a bent copper, no matter what his family situation."

"She's been through a lot."

"Zoe, let's not discuss the ins and outs of my job, huh? I just wanted to check you're OK."

"I'm fine." Carl was bristly this morning. Had she pissed him off by not returning his call?

"So you'll be on the investigation team for New Street, then?" he asked.

"And the airport. We need to establish if the two were linked. Adi Hanson's working on it, with some woman from the fire service he seems to be sweet on."

Carl laughed. "I thought he was sweet on you."

"He's just a mate."

There was a knock at her door. "Gotta go, Carl. I'll come round to yours tonight, after I finish."

"Looking forward to it."

"It could be late."

"I know. Wake me if it is."

She smiled. "I will."

Another knock.

"Wait a minute!" she snapped.

"Sorry. I'll go," said Carl.

"It's just Nicholas. He got a scare last night, thought it was me who'd got injured."

"How is Lesley?"

"That'll be my next call."

The door opened and Zoe hung up. Nicholas rarely disturbed her in the morning, especially on Sundays.

"Zoe."

She slumped back against the pillows. "Mum."

"Did I disturb you?"

"It's fine. I need to get to work."

"It's Sunday."

"I don't exactly have a nine-to-five job, Mum."

Annette gave her a sheepish smile. "I know, love."

Zoe grimaced. She hated it when her mum tried to be affectionate. She'd spent most of Zoe's childhood ignoring her, too engrossed in the bottom of a bottle. Now when she wanted attention herself, Zoe wasn't inclined to give it.

She threw the duvet aside. "Nicholas told me you were in town when it happened."

Annette's eyes widened. "It was terrifying."

"Were you in the station?"

"No. I was... I was further along New Street."

Zoe tried to remember the pubs along there. Annette would have been in the Briar Rose, one of her usual haunts.

"You rang him, and he came to pick you up."

"He came in a cab. You've raised a fine boy there, Zoe."

Zoe threw a shirt over the t-shirt she'd been wearing in bed. *No thanks to your example*, she thought.

"How long are you staying?" she asked as she fastened the buttons.

Annette clung to the doorframe. "A couple of days."

"Surely you need to be at home."

"I'm scared, Zo."

Zoe gave her a look. Only Mo got to call her that.

"Zoe. Sweetheart."

Zoe ground her teeth.

"Two terror attacks in one day," Annette continued. "When you get to my age, your nerves..."

Zoe snorted. Annette's nerves were nothing to do with her age.

"OK," she conceded. "You can stay till Tuesday."

Annette's face broke into a smile. "Thank you." She reached her arms out. Zoe frowned and shook her head. Annette let her arms drop to her side.

"Just don't eat all the food." Zoe pulled on her jeans. "And don't bring any booze into the house, alright? I don't want you giving it to Nicholas."

"He's eighteen, love. It's perfectly legal."

"Drinking with his alcoholic grandmother isn't how I want my son spending his time when he's got A levels to prepare for."

"Oh, go easy on him, love. He'll be at university soon, able to do his own thing."

Zoe took a step towards her mum. "I said you can stay here. But leave Nicholas alone, alright? He doesn't need you messing things up for him."

"I won't mess things up for—"

Zoe yanked the door open. "I've got work. Just keep out of trouble and I'll see you later."

She slumped. She couldn't go to Carl's for the night now. And there was no way she was bringing him here with her mum staying over. "I'll get a takeaway."

"A curry would be lovely."

"Hmm."

Zoe hurried down the stairs and into the kitchen. Nicholas was buttering toast.

"Mum."

She gave him a peck on the cheek. He winced and rubbed the spot where she'd kissed him. She opened the fridge: four cans of lager. "I'm getting rid of these, alright?"

"They're mine, Mum."

"I don't want your gran drinking them."

Annette was in the doorway. Her dressing gown hung off her and she was pale. Her cheekbones were sharp and her limbs stick-thin. Zoe gave her a look of disgust.

"I'm taking them," she said, as much for Annette's benefit as for Nicholas's.

"Fair enough," Nicholas said. "I'll go to the pub with Zaf."

"You've got school tomorrow."

"I won't stay out late. You said you were going to stop doing this."

She clenched her fists. He was right. She'd been overprotective of him when she'd been working her last big case, a killer targeting gay men. She'd agreed to cut him some slack. But having Annette here threw her off balance.

"Sorry, love. You go to the pub if you want."

He grinned. "Cool. I'm going back to bed."

Zoe checked the clock: seven thirty. She'd be late for the eight o'clock briefing.

She brushed past Annette and made for the front door. Yoda stirred from her spot on the stairs and miaowed at her.

"Can you feed Yoda?" she called as she opened the front door.

"I'll do it." Annette was in the doorway to the living room. She picked the cat up. Zoe shuddered. *It's alright*, she told herself. *You can trust her with a cat.*

She gave her mum a final look and yanked the door open, hoping she could calm herself down on the drive into work.

CHAPTER TWENTY-TWO

RHODRI AND IAN were in the team room when Zoe arrived. She slung her coat on the back of her chair in the inner office and re-emerged with a notebook.

"I'm late for the briefing," she said. "Why aren't you in it already?"

"We were waiting for you, boss," Rhodri said. "How's the DCI?"

She stopped in her tracks. "Not good. She got glass lodged in her brain stem. Five hours in surgery. But she's recovering now. We'll know more later."

Rhodri gave her a nervous smile.

"Come on then," said Ian. "Don't want Randle picking us out for public ridicule."

Zoe gave him a look. "Hmmm."

She pushed the door open and they sped along the corridors. "Is Connie already there?" she asked.

"No sign of her yet," said Ian.

Zoe skidded to a halt. "She's not in?"

Ian shook his head. "Not unless she went straight there."

CHAPTER TWENTY-TWO

Connie wouldn't have even known there was a briefing until she spoke to Ian. But she would have seen the news, would know to be in early.

"Knowing Con, she's already in there," said Rhodri. "Keen as mustard, like."

"Let's hope so." Zoe paused then opened the door to the briefing room.

It was already full. A dozen heads turned to her and she smiled, trying to hide the awkwardness. *Damn*.

"Morning," she said, trying to make it sound as if she *should* be late, not that she'd been dealing with her alcoholic mother and had to rush into work.

"DI Finch, glad you could grace us with your presence." Randle was at the front, sitting with a man she didn't recognise.

"Sir."

Zoe scanned the room: no sign of Connie. She turned to Rhodri who shrugged then took a chair. She shuffled past him, wishing he'd thought to sit further along, and sat next to DI Dawson. He gave her a wry smile which she chose to ignore.

Randle was fiddling with a laptop, barking at a woman in a pale blue dress to get the damn projector working. So they hadn't missed much. Randle liked his Powerpoint presentations. Zoe preferred a board, as did Lesley.

The room felt empty without the DCI. She'd be sitting at the front, eating one of her yoghurts and not taking any bullshit from Randle.

She'd be back soon. Hopefully.

At last the projector decided to behave and Randle's carefully formulated slides appeared on the screen behind him. Zoe wondered how late his secretary had stayed up preparing them.

"Right," he said. "Before we start, introductions." He gestured towards the man next to him. "Detective Superintendent Silton is head of the anti-terror division. His team will be analysing existing intelligence and identifying what fits with this incident. I expect Force CID teams to work closely with his officers, to share information."

Zoe raised a hand.

"We haven't got to questions yet, DI Finch," Randle said.

"You're referring to one incident, sir," she replied. "Not two."

"We believe this is one co-ordinated attack. The same people responsible in both cases."

"Do we have intelligence that confirms that?"

Randle narrowed his eyes at her. "Not yet, Zoe. But we will do. Don't you worry about it."

She wasn't worried, not in the way he thought. She eyed Ian, who was focused on the Super, his face steady.

"So," Randle said, "if I can be permitted to continue?" He stared at Zoe, his lips twisted in irritation.

"Sir," she said. Beside her, Dawson suppressed a smile. She dug her fingernail into her palm.

"OK." Randle pointed at the screen, which had moved on to photographs of New Street Station and the airport. The slides advanced, more and more images of destruction flashing up in front of them. The interior of the shopping centre above the station was devastated. The wide walkway over the concourse gaped open, wiring and pipework hanging out and spilling to the floor below. Shop fronts had blown out and their contents littered the ground: charred scraps of clothing, smashed crockery. The row of shops next to the spot where the bomber had stood looked like something from a war zone. Their interiors were blackened and ruined, signs torn down from their positions, each store a gaping void of darkness.

At the airport, the carnage was confined to one plane, but the human cost had been higher. The room plunged into silence as Randle flicked through photos of bodies laid out on the tarmac and in a hangar, where they had been transferred. The jagged hole in the bottom of the plane seemed larger in daylight than it had in the dark. Zoe felt her stomach hollow out as she gazed at the images.

So much destruction. So much death.

"No one has claimed it yet," said Detective Superintendent Silton. "And if they haven't yet, they're unlikely to. Which means one of two things: it's a new group, or it's an individual or small group of individuals who want to remain anonymous."

"The groups you're aware of, would they all have gone public?" DI Dawson asked.

Silton nodded. "There are three groups we've been watching in the city and surrounding areas. All of them are associated with other groups abroad who behave in fairly predictable ways. If any of them were responsible, we would expect them to tell the world."

"We're still keeping a close eye on social media and Islamic news outlets," said a woman Zoe didn't recognise in the next row forward. "And YouTube. They like YouTube."

Randle advanced the slides, and the photos were replaced by a structure chart.

"This is how we'll be organising the investigation," he said. "Anti-terror will be collating existing intelligence, following up sources, linking it to any evidence we're able to collect. Force CID will be working with the FSIs and pathology team to glean what we can about the attacks. This is no different from a normal investigation, people. We examine the scene, we follow up leads. It may be bigger, and the eyes of the world may be on us, but we do our jobs."

"Sounds good to me," said Dawson. Randle gave him a tight nod.

"How will Force CID teams be allocated?" Zoe asked. She was determined not to let Dawson eclipse her on this one. He'd been a DI five years longer than she had, and he'd been her boss. But she was his equal now.

"Good question, Zoe." Randle flicked to the next slide, a CCTV still from the station. It showed two women facing each other, standing a couple of metres apart. One, her back to the camera, wore a green headscarf. The other carried shopping bags and was staring into the first woman's face.

Randle pointed at the woman carrying the bags. "Sameena Khan, out shopping with her daughter. She tried to engage the bomber, but got away before the bomb went off, fortunately. Uniform spoke to her briefly, but she was in too much of a state. We'll need to go back to her."

He shifted his pointer to the woman in the headscarf. "This is our bomber. We find out who she is and who she associated with. She might have been forced into this, or she might have been a willing sacrifice. She might have masterminded the whole thing, or been a nobody. We need to know which."

Randle fixed his gaze on Zoe. "Your team's job is to find this woman. Identify her, if you can. Find out if she's got a record, if she's involved with any of the groups that Detective Superintendent Silton's lot are investigating."

Zoe looked at Silton. "Could she be one of your targets?"

CHAPTER TWENTY-TWO

"No one we've been following closely. They're all men. But she could be an associate of one of them. Or a girlfriend."

"Presumably the blast did her significant damage?"

"She's at City Hospital, in the morgue," said Randle. "Or at least, the parts of her we were able to recover are."

Zoe wrinkled her nose. Beside her Rhodri made a high-pitched sound. *It's alright*, she thought. *I won't be sending you there*. This was her responsibility.

"Sir," she said.

"Good." He flicked to the next slide. Zoe bit her lip.

"There was one other casualty," Randle said.

The image showed a woman in a blue suit and white shirt. She lay twisted on the floor of the shopping centre. Her body was covered in cuts, her suit shredded on one side. Blood pooled around her body.

Randle cleared his throat. "Inspector Ashanti Jameson, chief negotiator. Killed in the line of duty."

The room fell into silence. Zoe felt her throat constrict.

Randle sniffed. "It was a nail bomb. Comparatively speaking, it didn't cause as much damage as it might have done. But this officer..."

Rhodri pulled in a shaky breath, his fists clenched on his knees. The door at the back of the room opened and Zoe heard an exclamation.

She turned to see Connie standing against the wall, her hand clutched to her chest. *Where have you been?* she thought.

Randle glanced at Connie and then at Zoe. She met his gaze, willing him to move onto the next slide.

After a few excruciating moments in which Rhodri tried to mutter into Zoe's ear and she did her best to ignore him, Randle turned back to the screen. The next slide showed the airport hangar, bodies lined up in rows. "Frank, I want your team on the airport."

"Wait," said Zoe.

Randle raised an eyebrow. "What for?"

"I was there last night. With DS Osman. With the forensics team and the pathologist. I've got a head start. Wouldn't it make sense for my team to focus on the airport, and DI Dawson to take the station?"

Randle leaned back in his chair, tipping his head back to stare at the ceiling. When he righted himself, he was staring at Zoe. "Nothing changes with you, does it DI Finch?"

"Just trying to do the best job I can, sir."

"You were like this on Canary. On the Jackson case. Just do as you're told." He turned back to the room. "Now, Detective Superintendent Silton is going to brief you all on the kind of behaviour you're looking for from a terrorist group."

CHAPTER TWENTY-THREE

Sofia stretched, basking in the winter sunlight that slanted across the bed. This bed was broad and soft, as big as her entire bedroom back in Romania, and she loved waking in it.

She turned towards Titi's side: empty as usual. She was getting used to this. He liked to rise early. He said he preferred not to disturb her, that it was an act of kindness. No matter how many times she told him she'd rather see him before he left for work.

She swung her legs out of bed and slipped on her fluffy slippers. The floor was warm, underfloor heating toasting her toes. From downstairs she could smell toast and bacon. She hated bacon, but didn't have the heart to tell Titi.

She slid down the wide stairs and padded into the kitchen. Mrs Brooking, the housekeeper, was at the stove. Sofia didn't like having a housekeeper, especially one who cooked for them. She was perfectly capable of cooking. She wanted to make her boyfriend the meals she'd grown up with, as well as the ones she'd enjoyed after leaving home and discovering that Romanian cooking wasn't all meat and potatoes.

She missed the kind of food she was used to eating back in Romania. Mrs Brooking cooked decent food, good food, even, but sometimes Sofia just wasn't in the mood for it. She was losing weight. Titi had complimented her on it, so at least there was an upside to sometimes feeling hungry.

"Good morning, Miss Pichler," Mrs Brooking said. "I've made your breakfast."

Sofia sniffed. "I will have muesli. If you do not mind."

A shadow crossed the housekeeper's face. "Of course, miss. Let me get it for you."

"I will do it." Sofia opened the door to the fridge and pulled out a carton of milk. She tried four cupboard doors before finding the muesli, then tipped it into a bowl. At first it had reminded her of rabbit food, but she was getting used to it. It beat the greasy bacon and eggs Mrs Brooking liked to make.

"Are the children awake?" she asked as she sat in one of the high stools at the kitchen island.

"Children?"

"Romanian children. Seven. We brought them last night. They were in plane crash." That wasn't strictly true, she thought. Today she would call the airline, find out who these children were and where they were supposed to be.

"I'm sorry, miss, but I don't know anything about any children."

Sofia pushed her bowl away. "Must be sleeping." Not surprising: it had been almost midnight when they'd settled. And they'd been through enough to make any child sleep for a week.

She hurried upstairs and stopped outside the first

CHAPTER TWENTY-THREE

bedroom door. She'd put two of the boys in here, sharing a vast double bed.

She knocked. When there was no response, she knocked louder. Waking them might be difficult. When she'd been that age, the only way her mother could rouse her was to send their two dogs into her room. Danut and Bogdi, her best friends.

She pushed the door open a crack. It was dark inside, the curtains drawn as she'd left them last night.

"Marius? Florin?" She pushed the door a little more. "Time for breakfast." These boys would appreciate eggs and bacon. She'd ask Mrs Brooking to cook more.

No answer. No movement in the bed. Sofia pushed the door all the way, sending a shaft of light across the room from the hallway.

The bed was empty. It was neat and tidy, as if it had never been slept in.

She stepped into the room and looked around. The children hadn't carried any luggage, but they had brought a few belongings with them. She'd gathered up their clothes and draped them over a chair after they were in bed.

The chair was empty. The clothes were gone.

She ran to the room next door. She stopped herself, pausing to knock. "Hello? Time to get up."

"Are you alright, Miss Pichler?" The housekeeper was behind her. Sofia wanted to shake answers out of her, demand that she tell her what had happened to the children. But she'd said she didn't know about any children.

She opened the door. This room held three single beds. All empty. There were no discarded clothes, nothing to show that she'd left three girls in this room the previous night.

She ran to the other two rooms and did the same, flinging

the doors open and running inside to search. If the children had been scared in the night, she thought, they might have gathered together for comfort.

But the clothes. Where were their clothes?

She turned to Mrs Brooking. "Where are they?"

Mrs Brooking held her hands out, her eyes wide. "Miss Pichler, I think you should sit down. There's been nobody in these rooms. Not since you moved in."

Sofia spotted something sticking out from under the bed. She ran to it and held it up, triumphant.

"Then how you explain this?"

The housekeeper peered at the doll in Sofia's hand. Her brow furrowed. "Maybe it was left by the previous owners."

Sofia shook her head. "House was empty. Titi and I picked furniture. Nothing was left behind."

"I'm sure there's a sensible explanation. Why don't you come downstairs and I'll make you a nice cup of tea?"

Sofia shook the doll in the housekeeper's face. It was a representation of an adult woman, the kind of doll that girls liked to dress up. A cheap imitation of a Barbie.

"This is explanation," she said. "There were seven children in house last night. I know, because I brought them here. I gave them all bedrooms, put them to bed."

She turned back to the room. She flung a duvet aside, hoping to find evidence of the bed being slept in. The sheets were undisturbed.

Her shoulders slumped. She felt Mrs Brooking's hands on her shoulders, and tensed. Was she going mad?

"They were here," she whispered. "I know they were here."

CHAPTER TWENTY-FOUR

"Where were you?"

Zoe had waited until they'd got to the team room before putting Connie on the spot. The DC had followed her along the corridors, struggling to keep up with her boss's long strides. Zoe didn't have to look behind her to know that the two constables were sharing worried looks. Combined with puzzled looks, in Rhodri's case.

Connie placed her bag on her desk and remained standing, her hands clasped together.

"Well?" said Zoe as Ian closed the door behind them.

"I went to see the DCI, boss."

"You did *what*?"

"In hospital. I- I wanted to know how she was."

Rhodri breathed out. Ian snorted.

"She's the DCI, Connie," Zoe said. "You're a detective constable. Why would you decide to go visiting?"

"Sorry, boss."

Zoe tapped her foot on the floor. "So?"

"Sorry?" Connie stared back at her.

"So how is she?" Zoe perched on the edge of Rhodri's desk. "I imagine we all want to know."

Rhodri nodded, a stray hair bobbing. Ian cocked his head.

"She's stable," Connie replied.

"Did you get to see her?"

Connie lowered her eyes. "No."

"So you went gallivanting off to the hospital when you should have been here doing your job, and you didn't even get to see her?"

"I spoke to her husband."

"I didn't know she had a husband," said Ian.

"Probably cos it's none of your business," said Zoe. She turned back to Connie. "What did he say?"

"He was appreciative. Of me being there. Said it was above and beyond."

"I should say so," said Zoe. She reached up to the back of her neck and massaged the knots that had been forming. "Constable. It's laudable that you care how the DCI is. Even better that you've ingratiated yourself with her husband."

"I didn't mean to—"

"But next time, you come into work first, alright? If you want to go visiting fellow officers in hospital, you check with me. Or with DS Osman."

"Yes, boss."

Zoe leaned back. "What d'you expect the DCI would say about this? D'you think she'd prioritise the touchy-feely stuff, or buckling down and finding the bastard who did this to her?"

"Finding the bastard," Connie muttered.

"Exactly. Now." Zoe bit her upper lip. "Sit down and forget this happened, alright? We've got a job to do."

"Yes, boss."

CHAPTER TWENTY-FOUR

"OK." Zoe turned to the wipe board that filled the wall at the back of the team office. She grabbed a cloth and started cleaning it.

"Er, boss?" Connie said.

Zoe paused. "Yes, Connie?"

"There's important information on there."

"She's right, boss," said Rhodri.

"Shit." Zoe stood back and surveyed the board. "Did anyone take a photo of it, by any chance?"

"I take a snap on my phone every night before I leave," said Connie. "I took one on Friday. Unless..." She looked between her colleagues.

Ian shrugged. Rhodri shook his head.

"Anyone else put anything on this board over the weekend?" Zoe asked.

"Don't think so," replied Ian.

"Good. Connie, email me that photo. Upload it to the shared drive. Whatever, just make sure we've got it."

"It's the workings from the Chelmsley Wood robberies," said Ian.

"I know," Zoe replied. The case was still live. But no one had been hurt, just threatened. It would have to take a back seat to this one, for now.

"Right," she said. She continued to clean the board then wrote *New Street Station* and *Birmingham Airport* at the top. Below the first, she wrote *bomber?*

She turned to her team, the marker pen pointing to the last word. "We need to get any and all video footage of the bomber from before the attack. CCTV, social media. See if we can trace her movements, find out where she came from. Was she on a train, and if so, which? Or did she walk into the station? I want to know that woman's movements prior to the attack, right back to what she had for breakfast."

"I don't think we'll be able to find that out," said Rhodri.

"It was a figure of speech, Rhod."

"Oh. Sorry."

"I'm putting you on that. Talk to any businesses or individuals with cameras in the area. Search Facebook, Instagram, Twitter. Get footage from the hour before the bomb went off. And talk to New Street Station, get all camera angles."

"I'll talk to the station," said Connie. "And I can help Rhodri with the social media."

"OK. The two of you work together, that'll speed things up."

Connie and Rhodri sank behind their computer screens. Connie's stiffness had faded but she looked relieved to be getting on with work.

Zoe went into the inner office. Ian followed and closed the door.

"What's up? Don't say *you've* got plans to head off to the hospital with a bag of grapes," she said.

"She's turning into a liability, boss."

"Connie's a good copper. She acted from concern. Bloody stupid of her, but her heart was in the right place."

"We don't need her heart to be in the right place. We need her arse in that chair."

Zoe allowed herself a smirk. "I don't think she'll be pulling a stunt like that again."

"No? Not after what she did on the Digbeth Ripper case?"

"You kicked her out of the office when I expressly said

she should stay. Are you surprised she wanted to do her job regardless?"

"She accessed the suspect's social media accounts, illegally, using public wifi."

"She helped us track down a monster who'd have killed her brother next."

"She wasn't thinking straight."

Zoe folded her arms across her chest. "Ian, you made your feelings about Connie crystal clear at the time. I don't need you to do it again."

"Just saying it as I see it."

"I know."

The sergeant's job was to question her, she knew that. Mostly it was to work with her, obey orders when they were given. But she knew that having an experienced DS as a sounding board made her a better DI.

She just wished it wasn't Ian Osman.

"Anyway, Ian, you've got a job to do." Zoe grabbed her coat. She'd bought a new one after her sheepskin coat had been ruined by torrential rain on her last case.

"And you?"

"I'm going to the post-mortem, Sergeant Osman." She noticed his grimace. "Wish me luck."

CHAPTER TWENTY-FIVE

Dr Adana Adebayo had two post-mortems to do this morning. She'd already begun the first when Zoe arrived at the morgue.

Zoe hurried to put on the white wellies and apron, then steeled herself as she entered the mortuary.

"Zoe," said the pathologist. "Glad I've got you, and not one of your minions. There's no way that Welsh boy would keep his breakfast down today."

"Good to see you too, Adana." Zoe held out her hand. On spotting that the pathologist's glove was covered in substances she'd rather not identify, she withdrew it.

Adana gave her a curt nod. "So. This is your bomber, or what remains of her."

Zoe turned away from the table and took a breath before looking at the body. She'd attended plenty of post-mortems in her career in CID, but never one where most of the body was missing.

"So I think we can hazard a guess at what killed her," she said.

CHAPTER TWENTY-FIVE

"It's not as straightforward as that. I need to ascertain the precise cause of death."

"There are enough candidates."

Adana looked down at the body. Her face was mostly obscured by a surgical mask but her eyes looked sad. Zoe felt her sadness, but not for this woman, who had wrought such devastation.

"It was quick, that's for sure," the pathologist said.

Zoe dragged her eyes to the body. It wasn't a body in the conventional sense. Instead, laid out on the post-mortem table were fragments of something that had once been human. At the top, the remains of a head, the skull intact but the flesh missing on the right side and half the brain scooped out.

Zoe swallowed. She struggled to breathe.

The rest of the remains were in three parts. The torso, which stretched from the collarbone to the pelvis and, remarkably, was intact except for a gaping wound to the left side. The upper right arm was still attached, everything below the elbow gone. A segment of the left arm sat beside the torso: just the section around the elbow. The left leg was missing and of the right, there was only the section from just above the knee to the ankle bone. The skin was torn open and splintered bone protruded.

"She was hit by multiple objects, mostly sharp, at high velocity," Adana said.

"Nails."

"Not just nails." The pathologist pointed at the torso. "This gash here was caused by something jagged. See the edges?"

Zoe nodded.

"Parts of the unit that housed the bomb. There are fragments of fabric seared into the wounds, too."

"Have you found any of the bomb itself embedded in the body?"

"Yes." Adana took a jar down from a shelf. It held fragments of black plastic and sheared-off metal. "Give this to Adi Hanson."

"Adi's working the airport. They've brought in another team for the station forensics. From East Midlands."

"That much to do, eh? Poor Adi."

"What about the other body? The negotiator?"

"Inspector Ashanti Jameson. Good Ghanaian name. Come."

Adana led Zoe through a set of swing doors into a room where a second body lay on a table. This one was more easily recognisable as human. The body was whole, pitted with scorch marks and incisions.

"Most of the damage was caused by ignition of an explosive substance. It's all on her back, but easier to see on this body," the pathologist said.

"Can you tell me what kind of explosive substance?"

"Not a powder. We'd see a blast pattern if that was the case, kind of like magnified snowflakes. I think this was a plastic explosive."

"No traces of the explosive on either body?"

"We're running tissue tests. I'll be able to tell you later if they find anything.'

"Thanks."

Zoe gazed at the woman. Ashanti Jameson. Killed doing her job. The video footage would hopefully help them understand what had led up to that moment.

"What's happening with the bodies from the airport?" she asked.

"We've set up a special facility there," Adana told her. "There's no way they'd fit here." She sighed. "It never gets easier."

"No."

"First priority is to identify them all. They're using dental records to help, although about a quarter of the victims had passports on them, which makes it easier. We'll try DNA where necessary. But the chances of people being in the database are slim. Next priority is to look for evidence of one of them being responsible for the explosion. A detonator, explosives residue."

"I'm hoping Adi will be able to run DNA tests."

"What for?"

"The area around the explosion. You never know, there might be traces."

"Good luck with that."

"Yeah."

Identifying the perpetrators wasn't going to be easy. Zoe had to start with the woman whose body was laid out in pieces on Adana's table. Who was she, and why had she sacrificed her life to terrorise the city?

CHAPTER TWENTY-SIX

DI Dawson slammed the door to the office. Mo flinched, along with DC Fran Kowalczyk at his side.

"You heard the man," Dawson said. "We're on the airport. Fran, I want you to talk to the incident team. Get a full record of what happened yesterday, everything from start to finish. I'll head over there, talk to the forensics people and the pathologist."

"What d'you want me working on, boss?" asked Mo.

Dawson shook his head. "You've got to pick up the slack on our other cases."

"The Super made it clear this is the priority."

Dawson took a step towards Mo. "Look, DS Uddin. Half of West Midlands police is on this investigation. They ain't gonna miss one crummy DS. But if we drop the ball on our other cases, *that* will get noticed."

Mo pushed his shoulders back. "I can keep an eye on that at the same time as working this case. I just don't think Randle will be happy if we—"

"You let me be the judge of what keeps David Randle

happy, eh? You're an experienced copper, you can handle this case alone."

"I'll need more involvement from Sheila Griffin." Sheila was a DS in the Organised Crime division.

"She's already helping you, isn't she?"

"She's got a full caseload. It'll need to come from up the chain."

"I'll talk to her DI." Dawson pushed his specs up his nose. He'd only started wearing them a couple of weeks ago and they made his eyes seem tiny. "But make sure it stays our case. This is gonna be Force CID's collar, not Organised Crime's."

As far as Mo was concerned, it was irrelevant who took credit when they eventually did arrest the men behind the brothels that had been springing up around the city like a rash. The important thing was to make the arrest.

But he knew better than to tell DI Frank Dawson that.

"Sir."

He sat at his desk and opened up his computer. At that moment, more than anything, he wanted to walk out of the office and yell at a wall. He wanted to find Zoe and let off steam. But she'd been given the task of tracking down the bomber: she'd be busy.

Lucky Zoe, he thought, as he started trawling through case records.

CHAPTER TWENTY-SEVEN

Sameena Khan lived in a 1930s semi in Hall Green, in the south of the city. The house had probably started off cramped and dark, but a vast glass box at the back now filled it with light.

Zoe sat on a large leather sofa, a mug of coffee in her hand that Sameena had insisted her daughter make. Jamila. The girl had been a witness too. She'd looked distracted as she stirred instant coffee into hot water. She didn't notice her waist-length dark hair spilling into Zoe's mug as she stirred.

Sameena sat opposite Zoe on an identical sofa. She had her feet on the floor, her legs together and her hands folded in her lap. Her jeans looked like they'd been ironed.

"I'm sorry to have to make you relive it," Zoe said. "But we need to find out anything we can about the woman. You're the last person who spoke to her."

Sameena nodded. She glanced at her daughter, who sat on a high stool next to the kitchen island, twirling her hair and staring at her phone.

CHAPTER TWENTY-SEVEN

"Jamila love," she said. "Why don't you go to your room for a bit? You can watch YouTube."

"But it's only eleven."

"I'll relax the rule today."

Jamila perked up. "OK." She slid down from the stool, grabbed a pack of Chocolate Digestives and left the room.

"It's hard on her," Sameena said. "She thinks I should have done as the woman said. Not talked to her."

"Done as she said? What was that?"

"She said 'run'. When I approached her. She opened up her coat." The skin under Sameena's right eye twitched. "Then she looked at me and said 'run'."

"But you didn't?"

"No. I... I'm not sure what I was thinking. Foolish of me, with Jamila there. I told Jamila to get away, to go to the churros bar." She looked up. "We were heading there, you see."

"And did she?"

"Sorry, did she what?"

"Jamila, did she move away?"

"Not as far as I wanted her to. She stayed where she could see me. Where she could hear."

"And what did you do then?"

Sameena pursed her lips. She sipped her coffee and looked out of the window. The garden was small, bare at this time of year.

She looked back at Zoe. "I'm a social worker. I'm used to... difficult situations. People. I've been threatened plenty of times in my job, had people pull knives on me. I was punched once." She pulled her hair back to reveal a scar on her temple. "The man went down for two years. He shouldn't have, he wasn't a criminal. Well, not before that."

"Tell me what you said to the woman. With the bomb."

Sameena blinked. "Sorry. My mind. It wanders, since..." She put the coffee on a glass-topped coffee table and plunged her hands into her lap, together as if in prayer. Her fingernails had been bitten. "I tried to talk her down. To persuade her not to do anything. I assumed that someone would have spotted her, that maybe I could distract her until the police arrived."

"Did she talk back to you?"

Sameena shook her head. "She just stared at me. There was me, standing there, babbling on like some fool. The world disappeared. It was like she was at the end of a tunnel, shooting back and forward in front of my eyes. Everything else went blurry. I don't know if anyone else was nearby, if they'd called the police."

"What did she look like?"

"Medium height. She wore a green headscarf, I couldn't see her hair. She had... I'm not sure what colour her skin was. She wasn't Asian, I can tell you that. If you're thinking this was an Islamist group, then she wasn't from Pakistan or Afghanistan."

Where the bomber came from had little bearing on her motives, Zoe thought. "How do you know?"

"When she said run. She had an accent, but it wasn't one I recognised."

"Did she have any distinguishing features? A birthmark, scars, wounds?"

"There was a bruise on her cheek." Sameena raised her hand to her own cheek. "Right here. It was yellowing."

"What about her clothes? Were they clean?"

"Scruffy, but clean. She wasn't homeless, if that's what you're thinking."

CHAPTER TWENTY-SEVEN

Zoe wrote in her notepad. "So you were talking to her, and then what happened?" Sameena had got out of the building unscathed.

"After a while she started screaming. She told me to" — a glance at the door — "to *fuck off*. It snapped me out of it. My trance, or whatever you want to call it. The world came back, I saw Jamila shouting at me, crying. So I ran. I grabbed my daughter's hand and I pulled her out of that place as fast as I could."

"Where were you when the bomb detonated?"

"Halfway up New Street. Your vans were there by then, I saw police running towards the station. I read that she had a hostage, a girl." Sameena gasped. "When I think that could have been Jamila..."

Zoe gave her a reassuring smile. "You did the right thing. You protected your daughter. And the hostage survived."

Sameena grabbed a tissue from a box on the coffee table. "The right thing? Really? If I'd carried on talking to her, your lot might have got to her. She might not have killed that policewoman." She blinked. "I could have stopped it."

Zoe shifted forwards in her chair. She wanted to put a hand on this woman's knee, but felt uneasy. "You couldn't have stopped her. And it wasn't your job. That was our job."

Sameena's chin trembled. "We all failed." A tear dripped onto her jeans.

Zoe straightened her back. "You didn't, I promise you. You and your daughter got away uninjured. You did the right thing for her." She imagined what she would have done if she'd been caught with Nicholas in a similar situation. Would her maternal instinct kick in first, or her training?

"I do hope you're right, detective. Because right now I think I'm going to regret this for as long as I live."

CHAPTER TWENTY-EIGHT

Sofia phoned Titi for the fifth time. She didn't bother leaving a message; she'd left three already.

Mrs Brooking watched her, eyes narrowed, as she paced the kitchen. What was the woman thinking? Had she seen the children, but was lying about it? Had she been involved in getting them out of here?

"They must be somewhere," Sofia said. She would call Adam. He'd seen the kids, he'd been with her.

She didn't have his number. They all used unregistered phones that didn't leave a number when they called her. Titi said it was for security, that everyone did it here. He'd set her phone up the same way.

She hadn't been to his office. He'd told her it was in Solihull, a wealthy commuter town not far from the house. But she had no address and no knowledge of Solihull.

"Perhaps I can get you a cup of tea," said Mrs Brooking. "That might calm your nerves."

"I don't need nerves calm. I need to speak to Titi."

Sofia rubbed her forehead. The children were missing,

and more importantly, so was her sister. She'd been on that plane, she'd been led away by her boyfriend's men, but she hadn't been brought here.

"Do you know where Andreea is?" she asked the housekeeper.

"I'm sorry, I don't know who that is."

"You have heard us talk about her. She is my sister."

"I don't eavesdrop on your conversations, miss."

Sofia clenched her fist. This woman heard everything they said, she was sure of it.

She blew out a long breath. "I want to go shopping."

"Very well. You'll need a driver."

"I will call a taxi cab."

"I'm not sure if that's such a good idea, not when we have—"

Sofia held up a hand. "I go upstairs, get dressed."

She ran up the stairs and flung open her bedroom door. She wanted to run into the other bedrooms again, to check for the children. But she'd already done that enough times, Mrs Brooking following her from room to room like a shadow.

How were the beds so clean? What had happened to the children's clothes? Only one person tidied up around here, and that was the housekeeper.

She knew.

Sofia had to get away from her.

The doll was in her pocket. She dumped it on her bed and stared at it as she got dressed. It was the only evidence she had. It might lead her to the children.

And if she found the children, maybe she would find Andreea.

She straightened the jacket she'd picked out – designer,

bought for her by Titi the week after she'd arrived – and went into the cupboard where she kept her handbags. She had a white one that matched it.

She stopped.

There was a space where yesterday's bag should be. Her pale blue one, the Gucci one, the one she carried most often. She hadn't put it away.

She always put her bag away. Every night, she emptied it and put it in the cupboard. Handbags this expensive needed to be looked after, they were precious. And she didn't want Mrs Brooking going through them while she slept.

She ran downstairs, racing through the kitchen and checking the surfaces: worktops, chairs, bar stools. She went into the living room and searched the area around the sofa where she'd waited for Titi the night before.

"Mrs Brooking, have you seen my handbag? It is blue one, with flower embroidery."

The housekeeper was in the doorway, watching Sofia's panic. "Sorry, miss. You always put your bag away at night."

"You have not tidied it?"

"I haven't." A frown. "Have you lost it, miss?"

Sofia gave her a look of disdain. *Don't patronise me*, she thought.

Maybe she'd put it on one of the children's rooms, when she was tucking them in. But she'd searched those rooms when she'd been looking for the children. She'd found a doll under the bed, surely she would have found her favourite handbag.

Had she left it in the van? Her heart lurched: Titi wouldn't be happy if one of his men found it.

She leaned against a wall. Losing the bag was a setback, but it wasn't the most important thing. She had to focus.

CHAPTER TWENTY-EIGHT

She picked up the phone in the hallway. She'd never seen anyone use it, but she assumed it worked.

There was a dial tone. But how was she supposed to find the number for a taxi?

"Miss? Can I help you?" Mrs Brooking asked.

"I want taxi, so I can go shopping."

"Leave that with me," the housekeeper said. She pulled a mobile phone from her pocket. Sofia eyed it jealously.

"Kyle? Miss Pichler wants to go shopping. Can you send a car for her?"

Sofia felt her body hollow out. *Damn.* She'd never find Andreea or the children if she had yet another of Titi's men with her.

CHAPTER TWENTY-NINE

"How'd it go with the witnesses, boss?" Rhodri was at his desk, a cup of tea and a half empty packet of Hobnobs at his side.

Zoe took a Hobnob. She grimaced at the tea: so strong it was orange. "The woman who spoke to the bomber didn't get much more than that she had a bruise. Ian spoke to the hostage, but she was in too much of a state to remember anything useful."

"Post-mortem must have been rough."

Zoe ate the last of her biscuit and took another one. "The bomber is in pieces. At least Inspector Jameson wasn't in such a bad way."

"It's tragic," said Connie.

"All the more reason to find out who was behind it. Are you getting anywhere with the CCTV?"

"We've got the recordings from the station," said Connie. "And one from a building opposite the back entrance that we think shows the bomber going inside."

"Anything from social media?"

"Plenty," said Connie. "Half of Facebook was videoing Sameena Khan talking to the bomber."

"Any close ups?"

"They all stayed a sensible distance away."

"They should have got themselves out of the building, not filmed the bloody thing."

"Too right," said Rhodri. Connie shrugged.

"OK then. Show me the best images you've got." Zoe put her coat on the back of Ian's chair and dragged it up to Connie's desk. Ian would be back soon.

"Boss. The CCTV is on my computer." Rhodri gave her a sheepish grin from behind his monitor.

"Right." Zoe dragged her chair round to his side of the desk. Connie did the same.

Rhodri pressed some keys and an image of the back of New Street Station came up on his screen.

"Where's this taken from?" asked Zoe.

"Office building," said Rhodri. "Right opposite."

She nodded.

The steps leading up to the station entrance were busy. It was a Saturday afternoon and the city would have been full of shoppers. This side of the station, despite officially being the main entrance, was the quietest, since it didn't lead directly to the main shopping area.

"What am I looking for?" she asked.

Connie pointed at the right-hand edge of the screen. "She's going to appear here in a minute. Green headscarf, bulky black coat."

Zoe leaned in. After a few moments a woman came into shot, just as Connie had described.

"Do we know for sure that's her?"

"We've pieced together her movements inside the

station," said Rhodri. "We've got her right up to the moment the bomb goes off."

The woman walked up the stairs to the station. She moved steadily, not rushing and not dawdling. She was careful to avoid making contact with the people she passed, swerving to avoid a family and stopping to let a man in a hoody pass as she got to the top.

She disappeared into the darkness of the station and Zoe tapped her fingers on her knee, impatient.

"What's next?"

"This one," said Rhodri. The picture on his screen was replaced by a shot from inside the station. The camera was above the door the woman had just entered by and showed her walking from the bottom to the top of the screen, heading into the station.

"I assume you've watched these all the way through?" Zoe asked.

"We have," said Connie.

"I don't need to see it all if you have. Show me the highlights. Does she talk to anyone? Does she go into any shops, buy a train ticket?"

"Watch this," said Connie.

Rhodri flicked to a video of the top of the escalators leading up from the station concourse to the shopping centre above. He pointed to the closest escalator. "She's on that one."

The woman in the headscarf moved into shot as the escalator brought her to the top level. At the top, she stumbled off as if she'd tripped.

"Run that again," said Zoe. "Slower."

Rhodri rewound the video and the woman slid into shot

CHAPTER TWENTY-NINE

once again, moving upwards at a snail's pace. Once again, she stumbled as she reached the top, almost losing her balance.

"Why does she trip?" Zoe asked.

"She could have caught herself on the top of the escalator," Connie said. "Happens to me sometimes."

"She would have been distracted, like," said Rhodri.

"No," said Zoe. "She would have been careful. There's a bomb strapped to her chest. She doesn't want to go setting it off by accident."

The door opened and Ian walked in. "That was rough," he said.

Zoe gave him the best smile she could muster. "Ian. Grab a chair and help us with this video."

"You've got my chair."

"So find another one."

Ian went into Zoe's office and brought out her chair. He placed it behind her and sat down, his breathing loud in her ear. She wrinkled her nose.

"We've got video of the bomber entering via Station Street," she said. "Then we've got her at the top of the escalators, stumbling as she gets off. I reckon she might have been pushed."

"Pushed? Why?" asked Rhodri.

"Maybe someone wanted to make sure she went ahead with it. They were steering her into place."

"That would have been risky," said Ian. "If she had an accomplice, they wouldn't have wanted to be anywhere near the bomb."

"Let's watch it again."

They all fell silent as the woman slid into view once again. Behind her the escalator was crowded. Immediately behind her was a man in a grey hoody and a cap that obscured his face.

"Typical," said Connie.

"Sometimes I wish we could ban bloody baseball caps," said Zoe.

Onscreen, the woman stumbled. Momentum propelled her forward and she almost hit two women walking past.

"That's Sameena," said Zoe. "Pause it."

Rhodri clicked his mouse. Onscreen, Sameena was looking at the bomber. Behind her was her daughter Jamila, staring over her mum's shoulder. The man in the baseball cap was heading away from them, towards the nearest shops.

"If she was with him and he pushed her, she'd look at him," Ian said.

"She's distracted by Sameena and Jamila," Zoe said. "Looks like she might have crashed into them."

Sameena hadn't mentioned this. Maybe she hadn't remembered, or didn't think it was important.

"We'll have to go back to Sameena," Zoe said. "I want to know if she saw that man."

"He's just a random man," Ian said. "That escalator's slow, I get shoved on it all the time."

Zoe raised an eyebrow. "You an expert?"

"I live in Erdington, remember? When I go into town on my day off, I use the train."

She tapped her teeth with her pen. "I want you to find footage of the man in the cap after he leaves the escalator."

"Boss," said Rhodri. He clicked his mouse and the image on the screen changed again. Sameena's hand was on Jamila's shoulder, and Jamila was looking at the bomber. The bomber turned away and started walking towards the far side of the shopping centre, but Sameena and her daughter followed her.

Rhodri hit fast forward and the women started making jerky movements, hurrying away from the escalators.

"Stop," said Zoe. "What's she looking at?"

The bomber had stopped next to the café overlooking the station below. She looked out over the empty space, her eyes ahead. She wasn't looking down at the station, but across at the other side of the shopping mall.

"What's she looking at?" Zoe said.

"Maybe your mystery man," Ian replied.

She turned to him, her eyes sharp. *Don't mock me.*

The bomber turned to Sameena. The video was indistinct and Zoe couldn't tell if they were talking. Then the bomber opened her coat and Sameena grabbed Jamila's arm. She turned to her daughter, their faces close. After a few moments like this, Jamila walked away, turning back to stare at her mum until she was out of shot. The bomber had closed her coat again.

Sameena stood facing the bomber.

"They're talking," Zoe said. "She's trying to talk her down."

The bomber looked back at Sameena. From time to time she turned to look behind her.

"Something over the other side is certainly bothering her," said Connie.

"Yes. And we need to find out what, or who, it is," said Zoe.

CHAPTER THIRTY

Mo had been trawling through mugshots for two hours. He was trying to identify a man that Sheila Griffin's surveillance cameras had seen on two occasions with the prostitutes they'd been watching. The man hadn't invited any of the women into a car, which meant he was probably a pimp rather than a punter. Mo didn't recognise this man, not from previous cases or anywhere else. And Sheila was at a loss too.

The problem was that this man looked like a million other lowlifes. He had a shaved head and a squat, dumpy body that spoke of too much time on his backside. He wore the same generic grey hoody that Mo could swear was being given out to all the local criminals as a kind of uniform. He was white, with hair of indeterminate colour due to the shaving, and had no visible scars, tattoos or other distinguishing features.

To make things worse, the photo sitting next to Mo's computer had been taken at night and was illuminated by a dim streetlamp. Half of the man's face was cast in shadow and the other wasn't sharp enough to be helpful.

He was getting nowhere.

He sighed and picked up the phone.

"Mo." DS Sheila Griffin sounded as tired as he felt.

"Sheila. This photo you've given me. Haven't you got anything better?"

"Sorry, mate. He only stood under that light for a few seconds. Guy knows what he's doing."

Mo lifted the photo and peered at it. He considered tracking down a magnifying glass, but he knew that would get him nowhere. Sheila's techs had enlarged it to the point where if he zoomed in any further, the picture would disintegrate before his eyes.

"In that case, we're no further on," he said.

"I thought as much. Still, worth a shot. We had something odd happen last night though."

"Go on."

"Macauley Street's cleared out."

"How d'you mean, cleared out?" Mo put the photo down and leaned back in his chair. The office was empty, all the other members of the team at the airport.

"No girls. Women. It's like the place was never active, let alone one of their most lucrative spots."

"What about the punters?"

"A couple of cars drove up and down the street, according to the surveillance team. Slowly, like they were looking for the women. Then they buggered off. No cars after midnight. It's like they all got a memo or something."

"So there were no women working Macauley Street last night?"

"Not one."

"You think they knew you were watching them?"

"It's an option. But we've been watching them for weeks now. And we've been bloody careful. Why would they suddenly clear out?"

Mo considered. "Maybe they finally spotted the cameras."

"I think there's something more to it," Sheila said. "There was no activity at the house on Curton Road."

The house she was referring to was home to a shifting population of between eight and twelve women. Four of them seemed to be permanent residents, the others came and went. Most of them also worked Macauley Street. They'd had cameras on it for two weeks now, but had seen no sign of the women's pimps.

"Maybe they all stayed inside and kept off the streets. Sounds like they've rumbled us."

"Rumbled us, DS Uddin? What's this, Hawaii Five-Oh?"

He laughed. "You know what I mean."

"Yeah. Things have been hotting up. A couple of known pimps have turned up dead in the last two weeks. Three mid-level drug dealers."

"You think it's connected?"

"I'm not sure. I think there might be a new gang trying to stake some territory. The beginnings of a turf war."

"Any idea who?"

"Not yet. But we'll be keeping an eye on things. Anyway, we've applied for a warrant to go into the Curton Road house tonight. Official grounds is the usual, but between you and me I'm worried about those women."

"You haven't seen anyone else go in?" he asked.

"No. But..."

"Yeah?"

CHAPTER THIRTY

"I'd like you with us when we go in," Sheila said.

"What time?"

"Depends when we get this warrant, but it'll be late. Worried about getting home past your bedtime, Mo?"

"No." Past his daughters' bedtime, he thought. But that was the nature of the job. His wife Catriona would understand: her job was unpredictable too.

"I'll see you later, Sheila. We'll find out what's going on."

"Let's hope so."

CHAPTER THIRTY-ONE

"It's nothing," said Randle.

"She was pushed off the escalator by this man," Zoe replied. "And afterwards, she doesn't look round, doesn't even react. If a stranger shoved you off an escalator, you'd flinch at least."

"She's carrying a bag full of explosives on her chest. I think she's likely to avoid confrontation."

"With respect, sir," Zoe ignored Randle's raised eyebrow, "I think we should follow this up."

They were in the briefing room, Zoe standing opposite Randle with the rest of Force CID and half the anti-terror division looking on. There was no sign of Mo, but Dawson was there, sitting back in his chair and looking pleased with himself.

"Just sit down, DI Finch. We'll talk about this later." Randle glared at her until she reluctantly took her seat. She wished Lesley were there.

Beside her Ian stared ahead, refusing to make eye

contact. Rhodri and Connie were behind them, so she couldn't see their faces.

"Right," said Randle. "So the video footage we have doesn't give us anything new and the post-mortems from New Street tell us that the explosive was TATP, which anyone with an internet connection can make at home. On top of that, the witnesses are all traumatised and can't remember anything helpful about this woman except that she had a bruise. Anything useful?"

"The bruise does back up DI Finch's theory that the bomber was coerced," said Detective Superintendent Silton. Zoe gave him a nod of gratitude.

Randle turned to the Superintendent, who sat behind him, facing the room. "Do we have any additional evidence to support that?" he asked.

"She could have been hit, by whoever it was that made her walk in there with a bomb. It's a possibility." Silton held his hands up in a shrug.

Zoe felt her shoulders relax. At least someone was backing her up.

"Is that something Islamist terrorists do a lot?" asked Ian.

Silton frowned. "Plenty of documented cases. But there's no reason to assume this was done by Islamists. No one's claimed it yet. It could be anyone."

"The alternative is far-right groups," said Randle. "They're much less likely to go public."

"It's an option, yes," said Silton. "But in every incident involving one of those groups, there's been a declaration by the perpetrator. They like to shout out their beliefs for everyone to hear. All this woman said was *run*."

"She was wearing a headscarf," said Randle. "So probably Muslim."

Silton stood up. "We have to be very careful about any assumptions we might be tempted to make in this investigation. She might have been wearing the headscarf because she was Muslim. Or she might have belonged to another faith that decreed the covering of the head. Either way—"

"Or she might just have been cold," said Rhodri. Zoe turned in her seat to give him a warning frown.

"That is an option, Constable," said Silton. "Not that I expect someone who's about to detonate a bomb in New Street Station would be too worried about the cold."

"Shh," Zoe whispered to Rhodri.

"Sorry, boss."

Rhodri leaned back. Connie, next to him, had her arms tightly folded across her chest. Her lips were pursed and her forehead deeply creased. *Calm down*, Zoe thought.

"But whatever her motive, you haven't identified our mystery bomber yet, DI Finch?" Randle said.

"Not yet, sir," Zoe replied. 'Still working on it."

He shook his head and turned back to the room. "What do we have from the airport?"

Dawson reached into his inside pocket and brought out a stack of photos. "This."

The photos were passed forward to Randle, who perused them and then handed them to Silton. "A handbag."

"We found it next to a section of wire gate alongside the roadway that had been cut through. Two hundred metres away from that spot there was a plane that had landed just after the explosion, and we've since found out that that this plane has passengers missing."

"What do you mean, missing?"

"Wizz Air flight 375 from Bucharest. The manifest says

a hundred and seventy-one people boarded it. We only have records of a hundred and fifty-eight getting off."

"And that plane was on the tarmac when the bomb went off, DI Dawson?" Randle asked.

"It was, sir."

"So it would have been evacuated. I doubt that every plane's passengers have been accounted for in the panic."

"All the others have, sir."

"And you say there was a damaged gate?"

"Someone had cut through it. With wire cutters. It wasn't accidental damage. Definitely deliberate."

"Any chance they kept wire cutters on that plane? Maybe people escaped, were scared the fire might spread, and wanted to get away from the airport."

Silence descended over the room.

"With respect, sir," said Dawson. "I think that's unlikely."

Dawson sat upright, his back not touching the chair. His breathing was shallow. Zoe had seen him like this when she'd been a DS on his team. For all his bluster back in the office, Randle clearly scared the shit out of him.

"So you think this handbag belonged to one of the passengers?"

"We've got a forensics team going through its contents. There's a postcard from Romania, and a purse."

"Credit cards?"

"Just cash."

"Passport?"

"Nothing."

"Hmm. So whoever owned this bag escaped the plane, but kept her passport with her and didn't own any credit cards."

"Lots of people put their cards on their phone these days," said Rhodri.

"Constable Hughes, you seem intent on regaling us with your knowledge of the world," said Randle.

"Just trying to help," Rhodri muttered. Zoe suppressed a smile.

"Right," said Randle. "We have this bag, a bruise on the cheek of the New Street bomber and some TATP explosive. This is sounding more like a Hercule Poirot story every hour. Does anyone have any concrete evidence? What about the bodies at the airport?"

Dawson nudged Fran Kowalczyk at his side. She cleared her throat. Zoe wondered where Mo was.

"Eighty-six bodies," she said. "Or the remains of them. We've identified fifty-eight of them. We're trying to contact dentists for the rest, but tracking down dentists in Pakistan isn't exactly easy."

"Are the Pakistani authorities working with us on this?"

"Oh God yes," said Dawson. "Foreign Office has stuck its oar in, too. Diplomats coming out of our ears."

There was suppressed laughter on Dawson's side of the room. Randle sent his stare in that direction and it stopped.

"Do we suspect any of the passengers might have planted the bomb?" Randle asked, his gaze on Dawson now.

"We have a potential suspect," said Fran. She was the newest member of Frank's team, only in CID for a few months. Zoe knew what it was like to join DI Dawson's team as a DC and didn't envy her. But she had a quiet calm to her and seemed to be holding her own.

"Go on then," Randle urged. "Don't make us wait all day."

"There was a man with explosives residue on his clothes.

When the bomb went off, he was six rows away from the blast, and most of his clothing remained intact. He was killed by a sharp object piercing his lung. Probably part of a seat. But Forensics found TATP on his sleeves and his hands."

"Could the residue have got there from the explosion?" Randle asked.

"Some of it, yes. But at least half of it was dry. Hadn't been detonated."

"How can that happen, when someone's been right there when the bomb went off?" Zoe asked.

"Residue from explosives handling embeds itself in the folds of the skin. It can be protected by clothing or simply by positioning," Adi said. "According to Sue Turbin."

"Who's she?"

"Fire service investigator."

"She an expert on explosives?" Randle said.

"She is, sir."

"OK. Do we have an ID?"

"Not yet, sir. But we're working on it."

"Good," said Randle. "That's the lead we need to be working on. Zoe, double down on finding out who our New Street bomber was. That's your focus. And Frank, drill down on this suspect on the plane. I want to know who he is, if he was travelling with anyone else, and where he came from. That's all for tonight."

"What about the DCI?" asked Zoe. "Any news?"

Randle frowned. "She's being looked after."

"That's not what I—"

DI Finch, if you need to investigate the health of DCI Clarke, I suggest you make a call yourself. Or just leave her be. OK?"

Zoe glanced at Ian, who shrugged. Randle waved a hand in dismissal and they filed out.

CHAPTER THIRTY-TWO

Sofia walked through the shopping mall, gazing from side to side at the displays but unable to focus on them.

Kyle, another of her boyfriend's men, followed six paces behind, like some sort of unwanted servant. She could feel his presence at her back as surely as if he'd been pushing her along. He'd been in a bad mood since he'd picked her up. She'd overheard him on the phone, laughing, saying he'd done his bit. Of what, she couldn't be sure.

She reached John Lewis and went inside. Maybe she could give him the slip in here, lose herself among the displays. Or she could go into a changing room and find an alternative way out.

It was no help that she'd never been here before. The city centre was out of bounds, Titi apparently insistent that she should go nowhere near the site of yesterday's bomb. This mall, in Solihull, was quiet. Those few who had braved it out looked scared. They stared at her as she passed them, no doubt wondering whether this lone woman would turn out to be a repeat of the one who'd set off the New Street bomb.

She came to the clothes department. Womenswear, it said. There was another door at the far end, a route into a car park.

She glanced round. Even if she gave him the slip, how was she supposed to find Andreea or the children here?

She turned, waiting for Kyle to catch up.

"I want to buy underwear," she said.

His gaze was steady on her face. "Fine."

"This is not something for you to see."

"I'll wait outside."

"No. You wait here." She held out a hand. "Give me card."

Kyle kept credit cards in a leather wallet in the inside pocket of his leather jacket. Company cards, Titi had told her. Kyle was entitled to them as an employee.

She, it seemed, wasn't.

"I'll pay after you've found what you want," he said.

"I buy underwear. I do not want you seeing." She cocked her head. "Spoil surprise."

He smirked. "Go on then. But I'm going to stand at the entrance to the lingerie department. Can't have you running off."

"Why would I run off?" She pocketed the card he handed over and gave him a dismissive look.

He followed her further into the store, to the sign saying 'lingerie'. She had no idea what this word meant.

"Can I help you?" An assistant, a large woman with a bust that Sofia imagined would need the assistance of one of the sturdier items sold here, approached them. She glanced from Sofia to Kyle, her gaze snagging on the tattoo that embellished his neck. "A present for your girlfriend?"

Kyle shook his head and backed away.

CHAPTER THIRTY-TWO

"No," said Sofia. "He is not boyfriend. I wish to try things on."

"Of course. Come with me, we'll get you measured up."

Sofia followed the woman through an archway into a dimly lit room. To one side was a row of changing rooms. At the far end was a door. Sofia stared at it, her heart racing.

The woman steered her into a cubicle.

"Right. Just take off your top and keep your bra on. I'll be back in a tick."

Sofia stood in the tight space, clutching her arms around her body. She shivered.

The woman returned and looked her up and down. "I'm sorry, don't you understand? I can't measure you with your blouse on."

Sofia shook her head. "I need to get away."

"Sorry?"

She jerked her head towards the way she'd come in. "That man out there. He is my boyfriend. He hurt me."

The woman's mouth fell open. She stared at Sofia.

"I need to get away," Sofia said. She pointed towards the door at the far end of the changing rooms. "Can I go that way?"

"That leads to the stock room," the woman said. "And... yes. There's a loading bay. It's a bit of a maze, but you'll end up at the ground floor of the car park."

Sofia nodded, her heart rate picking up. "Please, quickly."

The woman swallowed. "Are you sure?"

"Yes. Sure."

"OK."

The woman pulled aside the curtain to the changing room and led Sofia to the door, glancing back towards where

Kyle would be waiting. She was grinding her teeth. She opened the door and paused to let Sofia through, then followed behind her and closed the door.

They were in a dark room flanked by shelves stacked with boxes of bras and packs of knickers. The woman pointed past the shelves on their left. "Go through there and there's another door. Go down the stairs and then out the fire door. You'll find yourself in the car park."

"You show me way?"

"Sorry, I can't leave the shop floor. I'm the only one on this afternoon. What do you want me to say to your boyfriend?"

"I don't know. Tell him I am sick. That I need to lie down."

"There isn't anywhere to lie down in the changing rooms."

"He does not know that."

"OK." The woman's brow furrowed as she thought about lying to Kyle.

"He will not hurt you." Sofia put a hand on the woman's arm.

"I think I'll get one of the security guards up here, just in case."

"Good. Yes." Sofia gave her a smile. "Thank you."

"Good luck. Look after yourself."

"Thank you."

The woman gave Sofia a push in the small of her back. She needed to get moving. She took a deep breath and hurried past the shelves.

CHAPTER THIRTY-THREE

Zoe had been wanting to do this all day. She'd pushed aside thoughts of her boss while she'd been working on the CCTV and interviewing witnesses. She'd tried not to imagine the comments Lesley would have made at the postmortem. And in the briefing, she'd wished Lesley had been there to challenge Randle. He was being domineering and erratic again, and she didn't like it. It reminded her of the Bryn Jackson murder.

But he couldn't be involved in this one. This was a straightforward terror attack.

Lesley was in a ward with five other women. The curtains around her bed were drawn back and a man and teenage girl sat in chairs beside her. Zoe stopped at the door to the ward and watched. She hadn't known what condition her boss would be in, whether she'd even be conscious, but it looked like she was sitting up and talking. Relieved, Zoe waited, drinking in the sight and not wanting to interrupt Lesley with her family.

Lesley spotted her and waved her in. "Zoe, good to see you. Get in here."

Zoe smiled and approached the bed. She had a chocolate bar she'd picked up in the hospital shop: not much but more to Lesley's taste than grapes or flowers. She handed it over.

"It's a bit inadequate, I know."

"It's bloody marvellous." Lesley tore off the wrapper and bit into the chocolate. Her face dissolved into ecstasy. "You wouldn't believe the crap they give us in here," she mumbled through a mouthful of chocolate.

The man sitting next to Lesley turned and gave Zoe a nod. "Hello." He was thin and grey, wearing a brown suit that was a size too large. Not what Zoe would have expected. She had no idea what she'd been expecting.

"Hello. I'm Zoe, I work for Lesley."

"She's my best bloody DI, is what she is," Lesley said. She brushed chocolate crumbs off her hands and sank into the pillows.

Zoe resisted a smile.

"This is my useless husband, Terry. Terry, give the girl a hug at least."

Terry stood and gave Zoe an awkward hug. She returned it, equally awkward. The girl was smiling up at her.

"I'm Sharon," she said. "I've heard all about you."

"Hi, Sharon." Zoe held out her hand, thinking *I've heard nothing about you*. She knew that Lesley had a family, although exactly how she knew that she couldn't say. But until today, she'd never have been able to name them or say how many of them there were.

"Grab a chair, Zoe," said Lesley. She balled up the chocolate wrapper and chucked it onto the chest of drawers beside the bed. When it bounced off and fell to the floor, she scoffed. "Nurses'll have my guts for that. Terry, pick it up, will you?"

Terry bent to grab the wrapper and put it in his pocket.

Zoe found a chair which didn't seem to belong to any of the other beds and brought it closer. As she sat down, she reached into her inside pocket. "I brought this, too."

Lesley grabbed the envelope. "A get well soon card. How original."

Zoe shifted in her seat. "We thought…"

"Yeah, yeah. Thanks. Ignore me."

"How are you feeling?" Zoe asked.

"I'm right as rain now," Lesley said. She reached up behind her neck, where a thick bandage separated her skin from the pillow. "There was a piece of glass stuck in my brain stem, apparently. Sounds like the sort of thing that'd finish you off, but luckily I got here in time."

A shiver ran down Zoe's back. "I was told you collapsed in the ops room."

"I'm trying to pretend that never happened."

"You were injured, ma'am."

Lesley waved her hand again. "Don't ma'am me here. I'm Lesley. At least till these doctors say I can go back to work."

Zoe nodded. Next to her, Lesley's husband cleared his throat.

Lesley gave him a pointed look. "Terry says I can't overexert myself. He's like my guardian angel, aren't you, love?"

Terry opened his mouth to speak.

"Anyway," Lesley continued. "How's it going without me? They found the sod who did this?"

"I've been given the responsibility of identifying the bomber," Zoe said. "I went to her post-mortem this morning."

"Hmm. How was it?"

Zoe glanced at Sharon. "Nasty. Unlike anything I've seen before."

"Right. And are you any closer to identifying her?"

Zoe shook her head. "She's a nobody. We've got CCTV of her going into the station, talking to a witness, and then... well, you know what she did next." She was aware of Lesley's daughter next to her, her head bent in Zoe's direction. This would be fascinating for a teenager. "We've put out an appeal, used CCTV stills to find out if anyone recognises her. So far, nothing."

"You'll get there. You've only had twenty-four hours. I bet David's like a pig in shit, heading up something like this."

"He's got Detective Superintendent Silton working with him. But yes, it is interesting having him running an investigation again."

Lesley barked out a laugh. "Interesting! I like it. May you live through interesting times, Zoe. Or may you not, as the case may be."

Terry lifted his watch. "I really think..."

"OK, OK." Lesley reached out and grabbed Zoe's hand. "Come back, will you? Bring your DCs. I like them, I think you've got a good team."

Zoe noted that she said nothing about Ian.

"I will, ma'am. And I'll keep you updated on the case."

CHAPTER THIRTY-FOUR

Sofia ran out of the car park. She was on a street, cars passing in front of her. She had no idea where she was.

She ran across the road and paused to look in both directions. To her right was a turn-off. She had to keep moving, to get away from where Kyle might find her.

She ran to the corner and turned left, arms and legs pumping.

At the end of the street was a blank brick building, staring back at her. Dead end.

She ran back the way she'd come then turned left again, heading away from the car park. There was a phone box up ahead.

She yanked the door open and slammed herself into the box, her shoulder hitting the back wall. She winced and rubbed it.

She picked up the phone. Could she make a call with Titi's credit card?

Who would she call anyway?

She pushed the phone against her ear. Her limbs trembled and her chest felt tight. She started hitting buttons. Nothing happened.

There was a sign on the wall behind the phone: dial 999 in case of emergency. She did so.

"Emergency services, which service do you require?"

"I need to find missing woman. Children."

"Are you reporting missing persons?"

"Yes. No. Yes."

"You sure?"

"Yes."

"I'll just connect you now."

The line went quiet. She turned to look back the way she'd run. She hoped Kyle wouldn't hurt the shop assistant. That the security guards would contain him.

"Hello, where are you calling from?"

"I don't know. Solihull. Phone box."

"Can you tell me the number of the phone you're calling from? You'll see it on the phone."

Sofia read out the number from a sticker on the phone.

"OK. What is the nature of your emergency?"

A car came to a stop beside the phone box. A man jumped out. Not Kyle. But a man she'd seen before.

She shrank back into the phone box, hoping he hadn't seen her.

"Hello? Are you still there?"

"I report missing persons."

"More than one missing person?"

"Yes. One woman. Seven children."

"Can you give me their names please?"

Cold air brushed Sofia's neck as the door opened behind her. A fat hand grabbed the phone and slammed it into its cradle. Sofia yelped.

CHAPTER THIRTY-FOUR

"That was a close one," the man said. "We thought we'd lost you."

"Who are you?"

"Never you mind."

"I was making phone call."

"I can see that. Come on, you can make all the calls you like at home."

"Not when Mrs Brooking watches."

"Mrs Brooking has your best interests at heart. Now come on, or the boss'll have my fucking hide."

She felt as if all the air had been sucked out of her. She hung her hands by her sides and walked past him to the car. He looked up and down the street as he opened the passenger door for her. She ducked and he put a hand on her head to push her in. She tensed.

She slumped in the passenger seat. He closed the door, his movements calmer now. She stared ahead as he sat in the driver's seat and started the car, refusing to let him see her cry.

CHAPTER THIRTY-FIVE

THE HOUSE that Sheila's team had been watching was a rundown terrace in Ladywood. One of the windows was boarded up and the front garden was full of litter. Mo spotted rats flitting between piles of rubbish and overspilling bin bags. He shivered.

The streetlamp next to the car was unlit, lending a thick gloom to this part of the street. He wondered if it was a coincidence.

"OK," said Sheila. "Uniform will gain access, then I need you to cover the first floor and I'll take the ground floor."

"No problem." Mo pulled on his stab vest. They were in the back of a black car belonging to the organised crime division. A constable in dark clothes sat in the front.

Four uniformed officers rounded the corner to the side street where they'd parked their van. They kept to the shadows, stealing their way to the target house.

Sheila opened her door. "Let's go."

Mo left the car as the uniformed officers arrived at the house's front door. Two officers had disappeared round the

CHAPTER THIRTY-FIVE

side of the house, forcing open a side gate to cover the back.

"Police. Open up!"

There was no response. The officers stood back and let their colleagues with the enforcer come through. It had the door open in one strike.

The uniformed constables rushed into the building, peeling off and disappearing into darkened rooms. Mo flicked a light switch by the front door but no light came on.

"Nothing," one of the officers called from a back room.

"First floor clear," came a voice from upstairs.

Mo walked up the stairs. They creaked under every step, the carpet threadbare. Damp patches stained the walls. Ahead of him, two officers shook their heads.

"No one here, Sarge."

Mo pursed his lips and went into the front bedroom. The curtains were closed, the room in darkness. He yanked the curtains open to see a bed, neatly made, and a bedside table that held a lamp and nothing more. Behind him was a chest of drawers. He pulled the drawers open: empty.

He scanned the room. There was no other furniture, no wardrobe. He lowered himself to the floor and checked under the bed: clear.

He went into the other three upstairs bedrooms and did the same. All three had their curtains closed. All three were empty. No people, no belongings.

He hurried down the stairs. Sheila was in the kitchen, opening cupboards. Packets of food had been left behind, a half empty bottle of milk in the fridge.

"Rooms down here are all empty," she said. "They're all bedrooms, but none of them occupied."

"They got out," he said.

"They knew we were coming."

"But we only came because Macauley Street cleared out first."

She shrugged. "Maybe they'd spotted us there, decided to move out of the area. Maybe this new lot are pushing them out."

"You got any more on that?"

"Not since we spoke. It makes me nervous though. When these scum try to take each other out, innocent people get in the way."

Mo looked around the room again. "It's so thorough, though. There's not a thing left behind. This didn't happen in a hurry."

"What are you saying?"

"This wasn't a reaction to us. This was planned."

CHAPTER THIRTY-SIX

Andreea stared out of the window. This room had a thin net curtain and a dingy bed against the side wall. There was nothing else.

She watched the street. This was a bad area, the houses run down and shabby. The house immediately opposite had all its windows boarded up and she could see a man selling drugs in an alleyway further along. She still hadn't been told where Sofia was. She hoped she wasn't here.

She'd been brought here from the first building, a hotel they'd told her she'd be living in. It had been a thirty-minute drive in a van similar to the one from the airport. She hadn't recognised the driver, and didn't have the energy to talk to him.

This house was smaller, and shabbier. It smelt of sweat and urine, the nastiest house on a nasty-looking street.

The door opened and a man came in. He was short and heavily built, she remembered him from the airport. He turned to speak to a second man in the doorway behind him.

"This one's got spirit," he said. "A challenge."

The man behind him laughed. "I like them feisty."

The man from the airport turned to her and put a finger to his lips, telling her to be quiet. She stuck her tongue out at him. He gave her the finger and left the room, locking the door with Andreea and the other man inside.

The second man was tall and thin. He looked around fifty. He approached Andreea, smiling.

"So," he said. "What's your speciality?"

"Fighting," she replied. "Strangle chickens."

"Hah!" Flecks of spittle landed on her face as he laughed. "I like you."

He shoved her onto the bed and it bowed under her weight. She sprang up, her fists raised in protection.

"He was right about you, wasn't he?"

Andreea spat in the man's face. His laugh turned to a look of disgust and he grabbed her face with his hand.

"Feisty I like. Difficult gets me pissed off."

She lifted her shoulder, turning to one side and slamming her arm into his chest. He exhaled, winded, and let go of her face.

She jerked out from under him and shoved him onto the bed. She ran to the door and slammed into it.

She turned to him, her back against the wood. She'd heard the lock turn. No one was coming to save her.

She brought her fists up and he laughed. She sneered at him.

He rubbed his arm and stood up. "There's no point in resisting," he said. "They'll only subdue you if you do." He advanced on her. "I suggest you let me get it over with."

She slipped past him towards the window. She tugged on it and it opened a few centimetres.

CHAPTER THIRTY-SIX

"Sorry, darlin'," the man said. "You're not getting out that way."

She jumped onto the bed and reached up to grab his hair. She yanked it down, bringing his head down with it. She leaned over and bit the back of his neck. He shrieked.

He pulled away from her and lashed out to slap her on the cheek. She stared back at him, chest rising and falling.

"I told you to stop it," he said. He lunged at her. She grabbed his nose, sticking her fingers up his nostrils and pulling his head down. She brought her knee up and slammed it into his crotch.

"Fuck!" he groaned. "You little bitch."

She backed away from him, pushing the bed and jumping down to stand behind it. He slammed into it, sending its weight into her legs. She yelped.

He bent over, his hands cradling his balls. She allowed herself a smile.

"You're not getting away with it that easily."

There was a knock on the door. "Five minutes."

"Nearly done," the man hissed. He glared at Andreea. She stared back at him. Her body was full of fire, her muscles taut.

He threw himself across the bed, grabbing both her arms. She pulled back but she was pinned against the wall. He knelt on the bed, the combined weight of him and it pushing her into the peeling wallpaper. She spat. He wiped his face, smiled, then leaned in and licked her cheek.

She screeched. She pulled with her arms, trying to free herself. He shifted his weight to push the bed forward. She pushed down a scream, feeling like her legs might be cut in half.

He pushed one arm up above her head, and then the

other. He snapped his belt out of his trousers and tied her wrists together, then held them to the wall with one hand. He looked into her eyes as he did this, his pupils dilated. She blinked back at him.

She writhed under his weight, but it only made the bed frame dig into her all the more. She couldn't move.

He grabbed her jeans and ripped open the fly. He plunged his hand inside, grabbing at her flesh. She screamed into his face.

"Shush," he whispered as his fingernails dug into her flesh. "You're fun, aren't you?"

CHAPTER THIRTY-SEVEN

Sofia drew her legs up to her chest as she heard the front door slam. It was after 10pm and she'd been watching TV for the last three hours, waiting for Titi to come home.

Mrs Brooking had heated up her dinner and then left for the evening. She'd said nothing about Sofia's escape in John Lewis, although Sofia was sure she knew all about it. Instead, she'd served Sofia's meal – chicken in a butter and white wine sauce – in silence, her mouth tight and her movements quick.

Sofia took a deep breath. She pushed herself off the sofa and walked around it. She wanted to face Titi when he came in, to defend herself.

She waited for him to appear in the doorway. She had no idea if he would be angry at her. Last night he'd been so... loving. Surely he wouldn't begrudge her the need to find her sister?

After five minutes there was still no sign of him. She went into the hallway. His jacket was slung on the floor. She stared at it, her chest tight. She could hear noises from the kitchen. The sound of the fridge opening, of a bottle being opened.

She walked into the kitchen, determined to keep her head high. He sat at the island, swigging from a bottle of lager. He stared at her. He said nothing.

"Hi," she muttered.

He stood up. "*Hi?*"

She shrugged. "You have a good day?"

He put his bottle down on the marble worktop. He clenched his fist and rapped the countertop, almost knocking the bottle over.

She leaned back, just a little. Her mouth was dry.

"You want to know if I had a *good day*," he said.

She forced a smile. "I hope you had good day."

"You *hope I had good day*. When are you going to speak properly, woman?"

"Sorry."

He took a step towards her. She blinked back at him. *Don't flinch*, she told herself. *Don't run away*. She'd done nothing wrong.

He grabbed her wrist. She stiffened as he lifted her arm up between them.

"I am sorry," she whispered. "Please. Do not be cross with me."

"No," he said. "I have *not* had a good day. Things have not worked out the way they were supposed to. And to make it worse," he continued, "you lied to Kyle. You had that woman bring security guards."

"Was not my idea. Hers. Just hers."

He tightened his grip on her wrist. She gasped.

"*Just hers*. And was it *just her* idea for you to creep out of a stockroom and run away through a car park?"

"I wanted to find children. Mrs Brooking says they were never here. They were. You know they were."

He dropped her wrist. She rubbed it.

"I never saw any children," he said.

"But you were here. They were in bed. Last night. When you..."

She thought through the previous evening. He'd never gone into the children's rooms. He'd seen Gabriella, in the kitchen, but for the rest, he'd never laid eyes on them.

But they'd been here. She'd put them to bed. She'd checked on them after Titi was asleep. And they'd been gone this morning. He was the only person who could have made that happen.

"Why did you send them away? Where are they?" She stared into his face. "And where is Andreea?"

"There was an explosion, at the airport. People are still being evacuated."

She shook her head. "I watched the news. Evacuation finished. People missing. From Wizz Air."

He shrugged. "I don't know what you're talking about."

"I was there. I saw them. Your men, they took them off plane. Children, and women. I helped."

He sat down and took a swig from his bottle. "You really need to stop imagining things, woman."

She swallowed. "OK. If I am imagining things, then why was I at airport? To meet Andreea. Where is she?"

"Stop it." He stood up, the bottle still in his hand. He pushed past her, almost knocking her over.

"I'm going to bed," he said. "You can sleep in the spare room."

She ran after him. "Please, honeybun. You must help me.

I am scared for Andreea. She is alone, in strange country. I need to find her."

He let go of the bottle. It smashed on the floor, sending beer everywhere. She yelped as pieces of glass hit her legs.

He grabbed both her wrists. "Let it go, Sofia. If you know what's good for you, you'll shut up and let go of this nonsense. And you'll *never* pull a stunt like that again."

CHAPTER THIRTY-EIGHT

Nicholas was sitting at the dining table in front of his laptop when Zoe came downstairs. There was no sign of Annette, who'd been quiet the previous evening.

"Morning, love." Zoe brushed her hand across the back of his chair. He grunted.

She made a coffee and came back into the room. He was still at the laptop, peering into it.

"Everything OK?" she asked.

"I'm about to press the button," he said.

"The button?"

"The submit button. For my uni application."

She sat down next to him. "What order have you put them in?"

He pulled the laptop away from her. "Don't."

"Don't what?"

"I'm nervous enough as it is. You're making it worse."

"Then why did you bring it downstairs? You could have done this in your bedroom."

"I don't know. I guess… I don't know."

She grabbed the laptop. "Let me look. I'll check it for you."

"No!" He pushed the screen shut.

She stared at him. "Will it have saved?"

"Shit." He shuffled round to the other side of the table and opened the laptop, his eyes wide.

He relaxed. "It's still there."

"Good. You sure it's what you want?"

"Yeah."

"What about Zaf? You still want to go to the same place?"

"Zaf might take a year out."

"What? Since when?"

Nicolas looked at her as if she was stupid. "You *know* since when."

"I thought you were helping him deal with it."

"Not anymore." He slumped in his chair.

"Oh, sweetheart." Zoe moved round to the chair next to him and put her arm around his shoulders, ignoring the shrug designed to push her off. "You'll be OK. He loves you. I saw the look on his face when he found out you hadn't been hurt by that man."

"The Digbeth Ripper."

"You know I don't like using that name."

"It's better than *that man*."

"If Zaf takes a year out, what d'you think you'll do?"

He shrugged her arm off. "I'm not staying here, if that's what you're thinking."

"Maybe a year out would do you good, too. You went through a lot."

The cat jumped up onto the table. Nicholas grabbed her.

"Come here, Yoda." He held her against his chest and scratched under her chin.

"When's the deadline?" Zoe said. "For UCAS?"

"End of the month."

"That's eight days away."

"I know."

"And what happens if you haven't applied by then?"

"You know what happens."

"Sorry. OK, can you save what you've done, come back to it later, or tomorrow? Talk to Zaf, find out what he's planning. The two of you were so set on being at uni together."

"Things change, Mum."

I know, she thought. She pictured her mum, snoring in the spare room.

"I'm happy if you want to stay here. I'm not exactly going to chuck you out."

"I want to go. I want to get away from Birmingham."

"Oh?"

He turned to her. "I was three streets away from here, Mum. When he grabbed us. I got knocked unconscious and woke up in someone's garden. Every time I walk past that street, I think of what he might have done to Zaf."

The man who had taken Zaf, the so-called Digbeth Ripper, had singled out gay men and castrated them. Zoe had found Zaf before he was injured, but it had been close. She felt ice trickle down her back.

"He's locked up, love. He won't be getting out for a very long time."

"That doesn't matter." Nicholas put his finger on the trackpad.

"You don't have to decide immediately," she said. "You've still got a few days."

"I know," he said. "But I've made up my mind."

He clicked the trackpad and leaned back. A confirmation message appeared on the screen.

"It's done," he said.

"You still haven't told me your preferences."

"I'll tell you later." He grabbed the laptop and walked up the stairs, his footsteps heavy.

CHAPTER THIRTY-NINE

"Right," said Randle. "Where are we with these missing passengers? Anyone turned up yet?"

DI Dawson cleared his throat. They were in the briefing room again, Randle at the front with Silton. There were more anti-terror officers today, but still no sign of Mo.

"We've got names, sir," Dawson said. He passed forward a sheet of paper.

Randle surveyed it and passed it to Silton, who raised an eyebrow.

"Seven children, members of a school group here on an exchange with a school in Moseley. And six women. Were the women with the school group?"

"No, sir," said Dawson. "Each of them was travelling alone. But they were seated near each other."

"Hmm."

"Maybe one of them found a way off the plane and the others followed," Zoe said.

"That plane wasn't attacked," Randle said. "They were

evacuated in an orderly fashion, they didn't need to disappear."

"We're sure they're not accounted for anywhere else?" Silton asked. "They haven't got muddled up with records from another plane?"

"Not as far as we can tell," said Dawson. "The airlines checked all their passengers off the planes, they wanted to be sure no one was lost in the panic."

"I think that's exactly the point," said Randle. "Lost in the panic. These women and children probably got off the plane, missed the checkpoint somehow and left the airport."

"Seven children?" Zoe said. "Where would they have gone?"

Randle shook his head. "I don't see how this is related to either of the bombs. These people were on an entirely separate plane. Frank, by all means add this to the mispers file, but don't bust a gut on it. We've got more important things to worry about. Like the man you said had explosives residue on him."

"Yes," said Dawson. "We've managed to identify him."

"Well done. And?"

"His name was Nadeem Sharif. He was British, he'd been to Pakistan to visit family."

"Does he have family here in Britain?"

"A wife and two daughters."

"Talk to them. Find out what his movements were before he went to Pakistan. Be careful, though: the wife could be a suspect."

"You think we should arrest her?"

"We don't have grounds for that yet. But I assume Silton's team will be going into his house, conducting a search for evidence of bomb making."

"I suggest we bring his wife in for interviewing," said Silton. "Treat her as a witness for now."

"OK. What about this handbag you found? Any identifying forensics?"

"We've run prints against the database," said Fran Kowalczyk. "No match."

"Probably just some woman who dropped her bag in the chaos," Randle said.

"It was very close to the gate that was cut," Fran replied. "And not far from the plane with the missing people."

"We're thinking they panicked, got off the plane, and managed to break through the gate," said Dawson.

"With wire cutters?" Zoe said.

Dawson shrugged. "You come up with a better explanation."

"Someone came from outside. Broke through that gate, took them away."

"What?" said Randle. "That's ridiculous. Tell me where we are with the identity of the New Street bomber."

Zoe shrugged. It was a pretty far-fetched theory. "We've had a few more calls from the public but none have been the right woman."

"You've run her against the national DNA database?"

"That was done at the same time as the post-mortem. Nothing."

"Well, keep doing what you are."

What Zoe *was* doing was going around in circles trying to identify a woman who, it seemed, didn't officially exist. She would go back to the witness again: Sameena. Check her account against the CCTV.

"There's also the man who pushed her off the escalator, sir."

Randle sighed. "That's a red herring, DI Finch. Focus on the woman."

"We've got eyes on suspicious individuals around the city," said Silton. "None of them have done anything unusual in the last few days. None of them came into contact with the woman."

Randle flicked off his laptop. "Right, then. You all know what you're doing. Let's hope we have some more concrete evidence by the end of today, yes?"

CHAPTER FORTY

Sofia lay on the bed, staring up at the ceiling. This house was so quiet, the quietest building she'd ever been in. It was a new building, made of concrete. The carpets were thick and she could never hear when someone was moving around. Even the stairs were made of concrete. She knew Mrs Brooking would be downstairs somewhere. Cleaning, cooking, her normal routine. But wherever she was, she was silent.

Sofia heaved herself up and went to the door for what felt like the hundredth time. She turned the handle, slowly this time, and pulled.

Still locked.

Titi had told her not to escape again. It seemed he wasn't taking any chances.

She went back to the bed and perched on its edge. It was warm in here, stuffy compared to the places she'd lived in Romania. She wanted to open a window, let in some air, but all the windows had security locks. To keep burglars out, Mrs Brooking had told her. And now to keep her in.

She walked to the window and leaned her forehead

against the cold glass. She'd heard her boyfriend leave in his BMW this morning. She'd watched him drive off, careful to stand to one side of the window and not let him see her. Now the driveway was empty: Mrs Brooking had parked her blue Fiesta in the garage, like she always did.

Sofia turned to lean against the wall by the window. Her mind felt blank, her body heavy. Was Andreea being held prisoner somewhere like this, too? Had he driven away to wherever he was keeping her, to make sure she couldn't escape either?

And if he didn't want Sofia and Andreea to be together, why had he agreed to pay for Andreea's flight? None of it made sense.

She jumped at a knock on the door. She stepped away from the window.

"Hello?"

"I've brought you some breakfast, miss." Mrs Brooking's voice.

Sofia went to the door. She tried the handle; it was unlocked. Catching her breath, she pulled it open.

Mrs Brooking stood in the doorway holding a tray. The tray was broad, blocking Sofia's exit.

She smiled, looking down at the tray then back at Sofia. It held a teapot, a dinner plate with a bowl placed over it, a glass of orange juice and a second plate with toast.

"I'd rather eat downstairs."

A shake of the head. "My instructions are to bring it to you. You aren't well."

"I'm fine."

"Even so, you should rest." She held out the tray. She knew as well as Sofia did that if she brought the tray in, Sofia would be able to slip past her.

CHAPTER FORTY

Sofia took the tray. It was heavy. "Thank you." She considered dropping it and shoving the housekeeper out of the way. But if Titi had locked her in here, chances were he'd locked the doors to the outside too. She would have to wait.

She nodded at Mrs Brooking, who took a step backwards, her eyes on the door.

"I'll come back to get the tray in an hour."

Sofia shrugged. If she could put the housekeeper at her ease, make her think she was behaving herself, then maybe she would get an opportunity. If the outer doors were locked, Mrs Brooking would have a key.

"Thank you," she repeated. She took the tray into the room, her skin tightening as she heard the key turn in the lock behind her.

CHAPTER FORTY-ONE

RANDLE GESTURED to Zoe to stay behind as people peeled out of the briefing. She ignored the puzzled look Dawson gave her.

"Sir," she said when they were alone.

"I hear you went to see Lesley."

"I did."

"How is she?"

"She's... she's recovering, sir. Better than I expected, to be honest."

"Good. She'll need to take some time off. We'll have to find someone to head up this unit in the meantime. I can't do it forever."

"No, sir."

She had a moment of panic: would he promote Dawson?

"D'you know who you'll be bringing in, sir?"

"Not yet. I'll let you know when I do, don't worry."

"Thank you."

"Good. And another thing."

"Sir?"

CHAPTER FORTY-ONE

"Frank's on the airport, you're on the station. I suggest you stick to your own patch."

"I was just trying to be helpful."

"You haven't examined the evidence and you don't know the context. Stick to your own area of responsibility in future."

"With respect, sir, I did go to the airport during the incident, so I do have some context. You took me there."

"I know I took you. I wouldn't forget a thing like that. But that was different. Incident response and investigation are entirely separate areas of work. Stick to finding out who the New Street bomber was. Your team are working social media?"

"Connie and Rhodri are trawling through all the photos and video they can find. There's a hell of a lot to work through, most of it useless."

"And you're looking at narrowing down to images of the woman just before she detonated the bomb?"

"Not just then. Anything from when she entered the station to when the bomb went off. The building was quiet by then. I don't imagine people would've been recording."

"No."

"And we're trying to trace her steps backwards before she arrived at the station. Identify where she came from, using the CCTV trail."

He frowned. "Any joy with that?"

"We've got her walking past the ICC, then the trail goes cold."

"You have footage of her all the way from the convention centre to the station?" That was a twenty-minute walk.

"We do. I'm trying to find anything from before that, maybe a residential address."

He pursed his lips. "Did she stop on her route to the station? Talk to anyone?"

"No. She's very determined, walks steadily. At that point, she doesn't show any nerves at all."

"Right." He sighed. "Well, carry on seeing if you can get better quality images from the station. Report back to me as soon as you have anything."

"Of course, sir."

"Direct to me. Don't wait for the briefing, this is important."

"I understand."

"Good."

"Is that all, sir?"

"One more thing. You said you're going to visit the witness again?"

"Yes."

"Take Sergeant Osman with you. It's good to have two sets of eyes and ears on this kind of thing."

"I was planning to."

"Good." He nodded dismissal and she left the room. In the team office, Connie and Rhodri had opened another pack of Hobnobs and were both sitting in front of Connie's computer. Ian sat alone at his own desk.

Zoe grabbed a biscuit. "You look as if you've got something."

"I'm not sure, boss," Connie said. "But we've found some video on Facebook that might show the man who pushed her off the escalator."

Zoe glanced at the door. "Our instructions are to drop that."

"I know, boss," Connie replied. "But what if he was

working with her? Don't you think it's worth finding out who he is?"

"OK," Zoe said. "But make sure you work on the images of the bomber, too. I'll need something to take to the next briefing."

"Course, boss," said Rhodri.

"Go on then."

"Sorry?" Rhodri looked puzzled.

"If you're both sitting at the same desk, you can't be working different angles, can you?"

"Oh. Right, sorry, boss." Rhodri gave Connie a shrug, grabbed a handful of Hobnobs and pushed his chair round to his own desk. He sniffed and turned on his computer.

"Right," Zoe said. "Ian, I want you to come with me to see Sameena Khan."

CHAPTER FORTY-TWO

Mo was alone in the team room again, writing up his notes from the raid the previous evening. Dawson had told him he wasn't needed in the briefing, given he wasn't working the terror investigation.

Sheila had made calls to local forces, trying to find out whether the missing women from the brothel on Curton Road might have moved to another patch. There was no sign of them anywhere in the city. Chances were, they would disappear, swallowed up by the city's underworld like so many women before them.

Dawson pushed open the office door and slammed into his chair. "Well, that was a barrel of laughs."

Fran gave him a wary look and went to her own desk, which was as far from Dawson's as it was possible to get inside the cramped office.

"Not making much progress?" Mo asked.

"Your mate keeps butting in with wild theories. Doesn't know when to stick to her own job."

CHAPTER FORTY-TWO

Mo smiled. Zoe could be at her best when she was coming up with wild theories. He made a mental note to speak to her later, find out what she was thinking.

"So I hear your toms have disappeared?" Dawson said.

Mo bristled. The women weren't 'toms', they were prostitutes. Sex workers. Victims.

"The house was empty."

"Looks like your investigation has drawn a blank then."

"I wouldn't say that."

"Have you got any leads right now? Any sign of these women, or the men that DS Griffin thought was running them?"

"Nothing."

"Anything you can be working on once you've finished that report?"

"Not immediately. But that doesn't mean—"

"Right then. I want you with me and Fran, on this airport investigation. There's more to be working on here, and the pressure's on."

Mo sat up. At last he was being involved in the biggest case Force CID had worked for years.

"I'm happy to help, boss."

"You're not *helping*, DS Uddin. You're doing your fucking job."

"Of course."

"Right then. Come on." Dawson stood up.

"Where are we going?"

"To interview the wife of a terrorist. She'll trust you, it'll make it easier."

Fran looked up from her desk, her eyes meeting Mo's. Mo knew why Dawson thought the woman would trust him.

He sucked in a thin breath. "I need to finish this report."

"That can wait."

Mo ground his teeth together. He stood up, ignoring Fran's expression, and followed Frank out of the room.

CHAPTER FORTY-THREE

"Hello, Mrs Khan. I'm sorry to bother you, but we have a few more questions. This is Detective Sergeant Osman."

"Oh." Sameena Khan looked back into her house. "Come in."

Zoe threw her a smile and walked past her into the kitchen. She stopped in the centre of the room, Ian standing next to her.

"How are you?" she asked. "How's Jamila?"

"She's fine. Teenagers, you know. Made of rubber. I'm... OK." Sameena fingered a gold chain at her neck.

"We won't take much of your time."

"It's alright. Do you want a coffee?"

"White, two sugars please," said Ian. Zoe glared at him and he gave her a shrug.

"Black for me, please," Zoe said as the woman turned away and started emptying coffee grounds from a filter machine. At least it wasn't instant.

"Take a seat," Sameena said. She gestured towards the bar stools. Zoe pulled one out and Ian took the one beside her. Sameena placed mugs in front of them and stood opposite.

"How can I help you?"

"We've been watching the CCTV footage from Saturday. When you spoke to the woman."

Sameena's brow flickered. "Yes."

"When you first spotted her, she was coming off the escalators, is that right?"

"Yes. She crashed into Jamila."

"Did you see her trip, or stumble?"

"I…" Sameena looked away. "I'm not sure. The first thing I remember is her coming off those escalators, heading for us. I wasn't really looking at her, I only spotted her out of the corner of my eye."

"Did you notice anyone else on the escalator?"

"I wasn't looking at the escalator."

Zoe sipped her coffee. It was good. "There was a man," she said.

"Well, there might have been," added Ian.

Zoe frowned at him. "Behind the bomber, on the escalator. From the CCTV it looks as if he might have pushed her."

Sameena looked blank. "Sorry. I didn't see anything. I can ask Jamila, if you want?"

"She's not at school?"

"I thought it best for her to stay at home a few days."

"Of course." Zoe looked towards the door.

"I'm not going to call her down now," Sameena said.

"Sorry?" Zoe replied. "You just said you'd ask her."

"I've got her off school because I'm worried she'll be traumatised. I'm not subjecting her to a police interview."

"This isn't an interview, it's—"

"I'll ask her later. I'll call you, if she remembers a man."

CHAPTER FORTY-THREE

"If you could do that as soon as possible, please," Zoe said.

"I'll do my best."

Zoe downed her coffee. She stood up. "Thank you for seeing us, Mrs Khan."

Sameena looked from Zoe to Ian. "There *was* a man, though. Not on the escalator, but I saw her looking at a man, across on the other side."

"You did?" Ian asked.

"Go on," Zoe said.

"She was looking at him. He was looking back at her, from what I could tell."

"How far away were you from this man?" Ian asked.

Sameena shook her head. "He was outside John Lewis. We were next to Caffé Concerto, on the other side."

"So about fifty metres."

"I guess so."

"That's a long way," he said. "In a busy station."

"Can you remember what he looked like?" Zoe asked.

"He was wearing a hoody and a cap. He scratched his neck, and I saw a tattoo."

Zoe's skin tingled. "What kind of tattoo?"

"He was fifty metres away, like your colleague says. I have no idea."

"OK. Anything else you remember about him?"

"He was white. Heavily built. Looked like a nasty piece of work, if you don't mind my saying."

Zoe looked at Ian. He was frowning.

"You say he was standing outside John Lewis?" she said.

"He walked away, went towards the Bullring."

"Did he speak to anyone? Was he alone?"

"I'm sorry, I didn't see any more. He disappeared; it was busy."

"That's fine. You've been very helpful." Zoe jerked her head for Ian to stand up. He finished his coffee and pushed his stool back.

As they left the house, Zoe caught a flash of movement on the stairs. Jamila listening in, maybe? She turned to the girl's mother and pressed her card into her hand.

"If you remember anything else, call me."

"You already gave me one of these."

"I wanted to be sure."

"You don't have to worry. If I remember anything, I will tell you."

"And Jamila?"

"I'll talk to her."

"Thank you."

Zoe hurried to the car. She needed to talk to Connie and Rhodri, tell them to target the spot where the man had been standing.

CHAPTER FORTY-FOUR

The suspect's wife was in her mid-forties, with long dark hair and bulbous shadows under her eyes. Mo gave her a nod and a tight smile as he entered the interview room behind DI Dawson, who didn't make eye contact with her.

A man in a blue suit sat beside her, a blank notepad on the table in front of him.

"You're not under arrest," said Dawson. "You don't need a solicitor."

"Given the nature of the allegations against Mrs Sharif's late husband, my client has asked for legal representation."

Dawson rubbed his nose as he sat down. He eyed the woman. "We didn't say anything about needing legal representation."

"It is my client's right," said the lawyer. Dawson gave him a silent stare.

"In that case," Dawson said, "let's get this on tape."

Mo switched on the recording machine.

"So." Dawson leaned across the table, his hands folded on its surface. "For the tape, present are DI Frank Dawson and DS Mo Uddin." He raised his eyebrows for the woman to continue.

"Aqib Rasheed," the lawyer said. "And my client Aatifa Sharif."

"Thank you." Dawson leaned back. He removed his jacket and placed it over the back of his chair. His eyes on the woman, he pulled up his shirt sleeves. "So, Mrs Sharif. Aatifa. Can you tell me where your husband Nadeem Sharif was on Saturday?"

The woman blinked. Her solicitor put a hand on hers.

"Mrs Sharif has been recently widowed. You know where her husband was on Saturday."

"I want to get it from her."

"He was on a flight home," she muttered. "From Karachi."

"How long had he been in Karachi, Aatifa?" Dawson said.

"Three weeks. He was visiting his grandmother and aunts." Aatifa's voice was low. She sniffed.

"Can you prove this?" Dawson asked.

She frowned and looked at her lawyer.

"We have phone records," the lawyer said. "Calls to Pakistan making arrangements for the trip, and then between Mr and Mrs Sharif while he was there." He slid a sheaf of papers across the table.

"You were well prepared," Dawson said.

"As soon as my client informed me of your suspicions about her husband, I knew what kind of questions you would ask."

"Oh you did, did you?"

The lawyer ignored the question.

"Did your husband talk to you about his trip, Mrs

Sharif?" asked Mo. "Did you speak to his grandmother or aunts while he was there?"

She nodded.

"I've seen the warrant to search Mrs Sharif's house," the solicitor said. "I want to see the evidence behind your allegations."

"We discovered explosives residue on Mr Sharif's skin and clothes," Dawson said. "After the explosion on board the plane he was travelling on."

"Surely any passenger in the vicinity of the explosion might have had residue on them?"

"The residue was present in a form someone could only have if they'd handled the explosives directly."

"And do you have any evidence of where Mr Sharif supposedly got these explosives? How he allegedly got them onto the plane?"

"We have been talking to the authorities in Pakistan. We will have more information soon," said Dawson.

"Well in that case, I suggest you wait until you have more concrete evidence before you hound my client and submit her to an unlawful search of her house."

"Under the 2000 Terrorism Act, we can search the house of any individual suspected of terrorist activity."

"Oh, I know the Terrorism Act, Inspector. You don't spend nine years representing Muslims in this city without knowing how the police like to use it to persecute the community and insinuate that activities—"

Mo placed his hand on the table. His skin felt tight. "Mr Rasheed," he said. "We have forensic evidence linking your client's husband to the explosion on Pakistan Airways flight 546, and the deaths of eighty-six people. You can bang on all you like about persecution of the community, but you can't make that disappear." He turned to Mrs Sharif. "Please, if you have any knowledge of your husband doing anything other than visiting his family when he was in Pakistan, you should tell us. It's in your interest to cooperate with the investigation."

The solicitor turned to his client and whispered in her ear. She nodded.

"So?" Dawson said. "What are you going to tell us?"

"No comment," she said.

Mo eyed the solicitor. He gripped the table with his fingertips. "Can you tell us if your husband had any unusual meetings or was out of the house at times he wouldn't normally be, before his trip?"

"No comment," she whispered.

Dawson shook his head, his mouth tight. He slapped his file closed.

"Interview terminated at fifteen twenty-two," he said. Mo flicked the recorder off. They left the room, Mo feeling heat rising from his stomach.

CHAPTER FORTY-FIVE

Zoe pushed open the door to the team room and walked to the constables' desks.

"We need to find that man," she said.

"The one that pushed the bomber off the escalator?" Rhodri asked.

"The very same."

Ian followed her, closing the door gently. He hadn't spoken once on the way back from Sameena's.

"What do you think, Ian?" Zoe asked. "You were there. You think Sameena might have seen more than she's telling us?"

"No reason to. I think she's doing her best to help."

"You're right." Zoe perched on Connie's desk. "She might not remember everything though." She took a deep breath. "She told us she'd seen the bomber staring at a man. She didn't know if it was the same man we saw push her off the escalator, says she didn't see him."

"Could we try hypnosis, boss?" asked Rhodri.

Ian laughed. "Don't be daft, son."

Zoe turned to him. "It might not be such a stupid idea. If we can't get any images of the man, then maybe Sameena will remember more under hypnosis."

Ian snorted. "You're serious? Get a quack in and put her under?"

"It's been used before."

"They use it all the time in the US, boss," said Connie.

"Yes, and convictions have been overturned because of it. It would never stand up in court," said Ian.

Zoe looked at him. "I'm not saying use it in court. But it might give us something to work with."

"I'd love to see what the DCI would make of the idea," he said.

He had a point. Lesley would laugh in her face. Either that, or give her a bollocking for even considering it.

But Lesley wasn't here.

"It's an option," she said. "I want to exhaust all others first."

"What about Jamila?" Connie asked.

"She wasn't there," Zoe replied. "Well, she was there but she was in her room. Sameena didn't want to call her down, said she'd talk to her after we left."

"That's not what I meant," Connie said. "She could be hypnotised too."

Zoe chewed her lip. "It was her that the bomber supposedly crashed into." She shook her head. "She's a minor. We'd never get her mum's permission."

"An option though, boss, just like with her mum."

"Yeah." Zoe pointed to Rhodri's screen. "How are we doing with finding him or the woman on social media?"

"I've got him on a video from Twitter," said Connie. "It's

not very clear though. And there's no way you can identify him."

"Let's see it." Zoe bent over Connie's desk and waited for the rest of the team to join her.

Connie opened Twitter in her browser and found the tweet. It had been posted by a user called *brummygirrl*, at 2:17pm. Twenty-eight minutes before the bomb detonated. The shot panned across the upper level of the shopping mall, catching the back of the bomber in her green headscarf and then shifting across to the other side of the space. There was a man in a baseball cap and hoody, facing across the empty space towards her. He was side-on to the camera.

"Stop it there," Zoe said. "Can you zoom in?"

Connie pinched her fingers to zoom in but the image just became grainy.

"Anything better?"

"There's this one." Connie flicked to a photo taken from behind the man, showing his back and the side of his head. The image was centred on the bomber and Sameena.

"They were being watched," Connie said. "I think people thought the woman in the headscarf was going to jump."

Zoe shuddered. "They would have thought Sameena was trying to talk her down. Anything else?"

"Nothing useful, boss. The guy was there alright, but he could just have been another random passerby, watching what was going on."

"Except for the fact that the bomber's staring in his direction."

"She could have been staring at anyone," said Ian. "The place is packed."

"That's not the impression Sameena got." Zoe balled her fist on the desk. "Connie, Rhod, I want you to carry on with this. Build a picture of what happened between the two of them, if he gave her some sort of signal. Trace his movements before and after just like we've traced hers. Ian, I want you to check through witness statements. See if anyone mentioned him."

"There were hundreds of people there. Thousands."

"Which is why I want to see if anyone mentioned him, before I take it to the briefing."

"It's a needle in a haystack."

"It's all we have, Sergeant."

Ian rubbed his nose and headed for his desk.

Zoe turned back to the screen. "If he made her do it, if he was working with her, we need to find him."

CHAPTER FORTY-SIX

"You were tougher on her than I expected," Dawson said to Mo as they drove towards the suspect's house.

"She was refusing to cooperate in a major investigation."

"Still. Her lawyer said we were persecuting her."

Mo pursed his lips. "I may be Muslim, but I'm a detective. If the evidence points us to a suspect who also happens to be Muslim, I treat them the exact same way as I would anyone else."

"You think she's a suspect?'

"She might be."

"Phew. And there was me thinking you'd take her side."

Every muscle in Mo's body tensed. There were procedures for things like this, ways of raising complaints. The way Dawson was speaking to him – that kind of thing should have been consigned to the past.

But the DCI was in hospital and the SIO was David Randle. Raising a complaint was not an option. And Mo was used to ignoring things like this. It had got easier over the years, but terror cases always brought it simmering to the surface.

They parked halfway along the street. Outside the house were a squad car, a Dog Unit van and what he recognised as Adi Hanson's car.

"Here we go then," said Dawson. "Make sure you're suited up."

Mo rolled his eyes as he grabbed a forensic suit from the boot. The two of them made their way to the house. Mo scanned the neighbouring houses. Had the neighbours been interviewed?

A curtain shifted in the house directly opposite and a small boy looked out at them. His eyes were wide and his face expressionless. Mo gave him a small wave, at which the boy jerked the curtain shut. Mo shrugged and followed Dawson inside.

Inside, Adi's team were in the dining room at the back of the house. It was a narrow terrace, with a separate living room at the front, dining room at the back and poky kitchen off that.

"No Zoe?" Adi said as they entered.

"Sorry to disappoint," said Mo.

Adi shrugged. "It's fine. This job isn't, though."

"Oh?" Dawson asked. He peered through to the kitchen, where an officer was working with a dog, opening cupboards one at a time and letting the dog sniff inside.

"There's nothing. No explosives residue anywhere, none of the equipment you'd expect. If he made the bomb, then he didn't make it here, or do any preparation."

"We'll need to talk to the wife again," said Dawson.

That'll be fun, Mo thought.

CHAPTER FORTY-SIX

"If he'd been working with explosives elsewhere, would he have brought remnants of it here, on his clothes or skin?"

"We've sent the clothes we found upstairs for analysis," Adi said. "But there's nothing on the carpets, the furniture. This place is clean as a whistle."

"Surely that's suspicious, in itself," Dawson said. "If it's been cleaned too thoroughly…"

"It's just the kind of clean my granny used to get her house up to every Thursday and Friday," Adi told him. "Took her two days, she liked the house to sparkle."

"So Mrs Sharif is a meticulous housewife," said Dawson.

"Or Mr Sharif," said Mo.

"He was away in Pakistan, remember?"

Mo nodded. "True."

Adi stretched his head back and rolled it around a few times. "We'll be done soon. I'll let you know when we get results back on those clothes, but I'm not holding out much hope. Like you say, if he manufactured a bomb then came here, he'd have left evidence."

"He probably manufactured it in Pakistan," said Mo. "No point making it here then taking it on a two-way trip."

"Good point," said Dawson. "I want you to get onto the Pakistani authorities. Find out if they've identified where he was staying. We need those addresses searching."

Mo nodded, not looking forward to threading his way through the inevitable maze of bureaucracy.

"Mind if we go upstairs?" he said. "Have a bit of a poke around?"

"Be my guest," said Adi. "But like I say, you won't find anything."

CHAPTER FORTY-SEVEN

Sofia had given up trying to open the door hours ago. She'd spent the afternoon dozing on the bed, and when she woke she found herself with the duvet wrapped around her and the sky outside the window darkening.

She yawned and dragged herself to the door: still locked. Titi would be home soon. She wondered if Mrs Brooking was still here, or if she'd been left alone here, locked up like an animal.

At least this room had an en-suite. She hauled herself into it and used the toilet, then rinsed her mouth out with cold water. In the mirror her face was blotchy where it had pressed against the pillows. She rubbed at her skin and dabbed water under her eyes to remove the mascara stains.

She emerged from the bathroom to find a tray on the bed: a pot of tea and a plate of biscuits. She ran to the door, tugging on the handle and hammering on the wood.

"You have to let me out! This is imprisonment!"

No answer. She hammered on the door again, giving up when she remembered how fruitless it had been last time.

CHAPTER FORTY-SEVEN

Sofia slid to the soft carpet. *Don't cry*, she told herself. She needed to have her wits about her so she could confront him. He couldn't treat her like this.

She felt a chill shift through her body at the thought of the conversation they would have. They'd never argued before, not properly. She remembered the way he'd looked at her in the kitchen the night before. Would he hurt her, if she defied him?

She pushed herself onto all fours and crawled to the bed. *Stand up*. She tugged at the duvet and lifted herself onto her feet. Should she take a shower, would that bring her back to life?

She was startled by the sound of the lock turning behind her. She spun round to face it, her fists clenched at her sides. If it was Mrs Brooking, she would tackle her. She would fight her way out.

The door opened silently. Her heart thudded against her ribs.

"Sofia, you look like shit."

It was him.

She wiped her face. "You cannot keep me prisoner." Her voice was rough.

He raised a finger to his lips and smiled.

He stepped through the door. She considered rushing him, pushing him back and making her escape. But he was taller than her, and broader. He weighed almost twice what she did.

"Come downstairs," he said. His voice was soft.

"Why?"

"You'll see. I've got a surprise for you."

Sofia pushed her fists into her thighs. A surprise. That

could mean anything. It could mean he was going to apologise to her. That he had a present.

It could mean he was going to punish her.

Either way, she couldn't stay up here.

He turned towards the stairs and beckoned. She walked after him, her legs unsteady. She could smell garlic cooking downstairs. So Mrs Brooking was still here.

Titi walked into the kitchen, not looking back at Sofia. He knew she wouldn't be able to resist following.

Mrs Brooking was at the stove, stirring something in a pan. She turned and smiled at Sofia. "Good evening, miss. I'm making chicken Kiev. I'm told it's your favourite."

She frowned. Chicken Kiev was Russian. *Not* her favourite.

A movement by the door caught her eye. Sofia turned to it, expecting one of her boyfriend's men to jump out at her.

A woman leaned against the doorframe. She was skinny, with pale skin and spiked black hair. She had dark circles under her eyes and her face was bare of the makeup she normally wore.

"Andreea?" Sofia said.

CHAPTER FORTY-EIGHT

Zoe slumped into the sofa and pointed the remote control at the TV. They'd got nowhere with the social media trawl and she'd told the team to go home so they could be back with fresh heads the next day. Ian had still been working through witness statements when she left. He'd told her he'd be going soon but she knew he was always looking for excuses to delay heading home to his wife.

"Zoe. Sweetheart. You're home." Annette came out of the kitchen. She wore a floral apron Zoe had never seen before.

Zoe let the remote drop onto the coffee table. "What are you doing?"

"Cooking tea."

"You don't cook."

"I've been trying."

Zoe stared at her. She pushed away her gut reaction. "What are you cooking?"

"Chops."

"Chops?" Zoe didn't think she'd eaten chops in her life.

"I saw them in the butcher's window, thought they looked nice."

Since when did Annette notice things in butchers' windows? The off-licence was one thing: she'd spot a special offer in there from the other side of Birmingham. But Zoe couldn't recall Annette ever having been to a butcher.

"What about Nicholas?" Zoe asked.

"He's gone out with that Zaf boy."

Good, thought Zoe. She hoped Nicholas and Zaf would be working out their differences.

"So it's just you and me."

Annette nodded towards the armchair. "And her."

Yoda stretched and yawned. Zoe smiled. The cat was getting bigger every day.

"She's wrecking your furniture, you know. I caught her scratching the table leg earlier."

"She's a cat."

"You should get her claws clipped."

Since when was Annette an expert on pet care? She couldn't be trusted with looking after herself, let alone an animal.

"You've been here two nights now."

"That's not much of a welcome." Annette was in the kitchen, calling back to her. Zoe heard a clanging sound as something was dropped.

She sprang off the sofa and ran to see what had happened. Annette was bent over, picking up an empty saucepan.

"You don't have to check on me all the time. You've hidden the booze, I'm safe."

"You went out to the butcher's. Who's to say you didn't go to the off-licence?"

CHAPTER FORTY-EIGHT

Annette stared at her, not denying anything. Zoe leaned in a little and sniffed. Her mum's breath smelled of mints.

"You can't boss me around, Zoe."

"If you insist on staying in my house, I can. If you're around my son."

"He's a good lad. He loves me."

"You're the only grandparent he has."

"Jim not have parents?"

"Jim denied Nicholas's existence till he was eleven. He was hardly going to take him to family get-togethers."

"Poor lad."

Poor lad indeed, thought Zoe. A dad who didn't want to know him, an alcoholic grandmother. Zoe's dad, the only person who might have provided stability, had died while she was pregnant. She sniffed back a tear.

"I miss him too, love." Annette took a step towards her.

Zoe dragged her sleeve across her face. "I don't know what you're talking about."

Annette had made Douglas's last months hell. She'd refused to believe he was dying, she'd drunk herself into oblivion when she should have been accompanying him to hospital appointments, and she'd left Zoe to pick up the pieces after the funeral.

"I'll be upstairs," Zoe said. "Let me know when it's ready."

"Zoe, please..."

Zoe turned away. Part of her wanted to step into her mum's outstretched arms, to pretend none of it had happened.

But she couldn't. She knew from raising Nicholas how much effort it took. You had to be strong, and steady. You had to put the child first. Annette had done none of those things.

And any pretence she made now at remorse wasn't good enough.

CHAPTER FORTY-NINE

"Come in."

Ian pushed his shoulders back and opened the door.

Detective Superintendent Randle looked up. He was in DCI Clarke's office, which he'd commandeered while she was in hospital. A flicker of irritation crossed his face.

"Did DI Finch send you to see me?"

"No, sir." Ian approached the desk, his back straight. He'd spoken to Randle a few times since the Digbeth Ripper case. Since Zoe had demonstrated the contempt she held him in. He'd used an unregistered phone that had appeared in the glove locker of his car one evening: never face to face.

"It's late," Randle said. "I need to get home to my wife."

"I just wanted to know if you need anything more from me, sir."

Randle's lips twisted. His tie had been loosened and his jacket was slung over the chair that Ian stood behind. His shirt was creased and he looked tired.

"I need you to do your job, Sergeant Osman. Come along to the briefings like a good boy, do the jobs you're given."

"If you need me to do any extra jobs, sir. Just let me know."

Randle's gaze flicked past him to the door. He sighed and shook his head. "I suggest you leave."

"Yes, sir."

"Hmm." Randle bent to the file he'd been reading. Ian leaned forward to get a look.

Randle looked up. "What are you waiting for?"

"Sorry, sir." Heat crept up Ian's neck. He tugged on his collar. "Just let me know if you need me, sir."

He pulled the door open, trying not to show his disappointment. As he closed it behind him, he heard Randle mutter *bloody idiot*.

CHAPTER FIFTY

Sofia froze. Andreea stared at her, a smile spreading across her face.

"Andreea!" Sofia shrieked. She ran across the kitchen and threw herself at her sister. Andreea was skinnier than ever, her body stiff and jagged in Sofia's embrace. But she was here, and she was safe.

After a long hug, she pulled back. "Where have you been?" she asked in Romanian.

Andreea's gaze went to Titi. She shrugged. "A hotel."

"A hotel?" Sofia turned to her boyfriend, switching to English. "Why does she not stay here?"

He approached them, smiling as if the last twenty-four hours had never happened. "She's been staying in a nice hotel. Get a flavour of the country. You don't want her invading our privacy do you, my love?" He kissed Sofia on the cheek.

Sofia gazed up at him. "We have plenty room. She can stay here. Until she finds own place. Job."

Andreea had hold of Sofia's hand. "It is OK. Hotel is nice. Do not worry about me." She looked at Titi again. He frowned at her as if in warning.

Sofia looked between her boyfriend and sister. Andreea had a bright red scratch on her cheek and her hair was lank, not gelled like it normally was.

She had to keep Andreea here. She had to make sure no one took her away.

"Did Titi bring you here?" she asked.

"Uh-uh. English," he interrupted. "I don't want to think you ladies are plotting something." He winked.

Sofia felt a flutter in her chest. "No. No plotting." *Not yet.* She tugged Andreea's hand. "How did you get here?"

"He bring me."

"Brought me," he corrected.

"Brought me. From hotel."

"Why did you not tell me where she was?" Sofia asked him. "I could have gone to her while you were working."

He smiled. "A surprise for you."

And it was a wonderful surprise. It really was. Sofia led Andreea into the living room. Mrs Brooking brought a tray of something divine-smelling out of the oven and set it down in front of them.

The sisters sat together on the vast sofa. Andreea's eyes ran across the room as she took her seat. Until two days ago she'd been living at home, in their parents' rundown farmhouse. She would never have seen anything like this.

"Is very nice here," she said. She sounded stiff, formal.

Sofia shrugged. "Is nicer now you are here. Please say you will stay."

Andreea turned to her. "Will you show me around?"

CHAPTER FIFTY

Titi stood up. "I'll come with you."

Andreea wrinkled her nose then smiled. "Yes. Both of you, show me beautiful house."

They walked towards the stairs. Sofia would show her sister her vast bedroom, the soft bed and the walk-in shower. She wouldn't tell her she'd spent the last twenty-four hours in the spare room.

"This is so big," Andreea said. Her voice was tight. Sofia stroked her arm.

"Are you OK?" she whispered. "You seem... different."

"English." Her boyfriend's voice was firm behind them.

"I am happy to be in England," Andreea replied in English. "He says he find me job."

Sofia turned to her boyfriend. "Is that true? Thank you, darling. You give her job in your company?"

He nodded. "I will."

"Then she can stay here. Get a work visa."

Titi shrugged. Andreea stiffened.

What was it they weren't telling her?

"Come and see rest of the house," she said. Titi would bore of this. He would leave them alone, and they could talk.

She led Andreea to the room where she'd been locked up until just half an hour earlier. It was neat and tidy, no evidence of her occupation. The tray had gone and the bedclothes were straight.

"A family could live in this bed," Andreea said. "It is a lovely house for children." She nudged her sister in the ribs. "You could start family."

Sofia blanched. "Children have be—"

"Come on," said Titi. "Dinner's ready." He grabbed Sofia by the wrist and steered her down the stairs. Andreea followed in silence, none of her usual rough edges in evidence.

What had happened to make her sister this meek? And what wasn't anyone telling her?

CHAPTER FIFTY-ONE

Zoe yawned as she dug into her fry-up. Mo sat opposite her, sipping on a mug of tea.

"Not eating?" she asked.

"Catriona says I need to lose weight."

She laughed, allowing herself a glance at his waistline. "You're fine."

He shrugged. "It's not for vanity. She's a doctor, remember?"

Zoe shrugged. "Glad *I'm* not married to her."

"You're OK. With your height, you'll always be slim."

She pushed her stomach in and out, making him laugh. "Maybe I should cut down on the fish and chips."

"And all those packets of biscuits Rhodri brings into the office."

"Yeah. He does like his junk food." She swallowed a mouthful of beans and bacon. "Can't let him eat it all, can I?"

Mo leaned back in his chair, stretching his arms above his head. "So how's your side of the investigation going?"

Zoe chewed, pointing to her mouth to tell him to wait until she could speak. They were in Café Face, their favourite place to meet for breakfast before going into work. It was twenty to eight and the only other customers were grabbing takeaway coffee and toasties. No students coming in to sit down at this time of day.

"There's this man," she said. "I reckon he pushed the bomber off the escalator. Our witness says she was looking at him. I'm wondering if they were working together. Or if he put her up to it."

"You think she was coerced?"

Zoe shrugged. "Could have been. We need to find better video, something closer to her, or to him. I feel that if we work out who he is, it'll be what we need."

"Let's hope so."

"What about you?"

He gulped down a mouthful of tea. "Dawson's got me running around with him. Thinks I'm the perfect person to deal with our Muslim suspect from the plane."

"Typical Dawson."

"He was surprised when I didn't mollycoddle the guy's wife. What am I supposed to do? Her husband detonated a bomb and killed eighty-six people."

"We don't know that for sure."

"He had explosives on his hands."

"He was a victim of the bomb."

"Apparently the residue on him is different. From working with the material, not from being hit by it."

"Yeah. I heard Adi talking about that too. So what happened to your prostitution investigation?"

"It went cold. The brothel we'd been watching was emptied out."

"That's convenient." Zoe scraped the last of her baked beans from her plate and pushed it back. "That was just what I needed."

"I guess they knew we were watching them."

"And they moved everyone out."

"Uh-huh. They didn't do it in a hurry though."

"No?"

"The place was spotless. Nothing left behind, nothing dropped. It was a careful job. Not rushed."

"Didn't anyone spot this?"

"Must have happened when everyone was distracted by the attacks on Saturday."

Zoe nodded and checked her watch. "Better get going. Briefing at eight."

"Yeah." He stood up, leaving a fiver on the table as a tip. "How's things with Nicholas? He's been through an ordeal."

"I'm not sure. He and Zaf, I thought they'd be able to help each other with it. But it seems to be the opposite. Now Zaf's talking about taking a year out and Nicholas can't wait to get to uni and away from Birmingham. And to top it all off, my mum's come to stay."

"Why?"

"Scared, apparently. As if someone's going to set off a bomb in her street in Kings Norton. It was supposed to be a couple of nights, but she's showing no sign of buggering off."

"Maybe it's a chance to patch up your differences."

Zoe pushed open the door to the café. Her Mini was parked directly outside while Mo's car was around the corner. "You know better than to suggest that, Mo."

"It's been a long time," he said. "Almost twenty years."

She turned to face him, hands on her hips. "If you'd gone

through what I did as a child, you wouldn't say that. I don't want her ruining Nicholas's life too."

"OK. I'm not going to stick my oar in. Let's get to work."

"Yes. Let's." Zoe yanked open the door of her car, her chest tight.

CHAPTER FIFTY-TWO

Andreea gazed out of the window of her narrow bedroom. It was cold today, as it always was here, and ice had formed on the glass.

Last night, she'd been spared. Her trip to Sofia's luxurious house meant she didn't have to endure the horrors of the brothel. But she'd heard the other women returning to the hotel in the early hours. They'd been subdued and moved slowly. She'd heard sobbing in the room next door.

The angry man from the van that had brought them from the airport was outside. He stood by a large black car, holding a door open. The skinny woman from the first night emerged from below the window with two girls, both about thirteen years old.

Andreea shifted her weight to get a better view. She hadn't seen children. Were they staying here too?

The woman said something to the man, then held out the hand of the first girl, handing her over to him. He smiled into the girl's face and took her hand. The girl pulled back and the man tightened his grip. Andreea felt her stomach clench.

Who were these children? And where were they taking them?

She thought of the way she'd been treated two nights ago. The man who'd pinned her to the wall, and the four other men who'd come into the room after him. After the second one, she'd lost her will to fight.

She felt her legs buckle. Surely they couldn't be taking these children to men like that?

She stood and placed a hand against the window. The girl got into the car and the second girl followed. The man closed the door and walked round to the driver's seat. He looked relaxed, confident. He spoke to the woman, who laughed and then retreated into the hotel.

Andreea watched as the car drove away.

She might have lost the energy to fight for herself, but she had to fight for those children. She had to get them away from here.

CHAPTER FIFTY-THREE

"OK," said Randle. He was standing at his laptop, photos of the Sharif house on the screen behind him. "So the Sharif house is clean. Which means that he made the bomb elsewhere. Probably in Pakistan. Dawson, where are we with that?"

"It's going slow, sir," replied Dawson. "Authorities over there don't seem to see it as a priority. Inter-Services Intelligence aren't helping at all. I may need to push it further up the food chain."

"I'll talk to the Assistant Chief Constable. Zoe, any further with identifying our New Street suspect?"

Zoe flicked through her notes. "My team are still working on the CCTV, sir. We've got a few images of her, but none that help with identification. And the calls we've had from the hotline have been dead ends."

Randle sighed. "I need you all to do better than this. This is the highest profile case we've had for a decade. If we don't make progress soon, it'll be taken off us."

Detective Superintendent Silton cleared his throat. "You know we want to work in tandem with your people, Detective Superintendent Randle. You have the local knowledge, we have the wider intelligence."

Randle looked at him, wrinkling his nose.

The door opened and Adi Hanson walked in, followed by a woman Zoe remembered from the airport: the fire investigator.

"Mr Hanson, good of you to grace us with your presence. Any news on the forensics from the Sharif house?"

Adi didn't sit down, but instead went to the front of the room. "No. But we do have new evidence relating to our suspect."

Randle stiffened. "Go on."

"After the questions that were raised yesterday about how the explosives got onto his skin and clothes, we decided to run an extra layer of analysis."

The woman who'd entered with Adi interrupted. "We ran a combination of tests that enable us to determine how long the residues had been on his skin. We apply combinations of three different chemicals, and—"

"Spare us the geeky detail," said Randle. "Who *are* you?"

"We met at the airport. Sue Turbin, West Midlands Fire Service."

"The fire investigator."

"Fire and explosives."

"She knows her stuff, sir," said Adi. The two of them exchanged a grin.

Randle sighed. "Just tell us what you've found."

Ian, sitting next to Zoe, sat up in his chair. His hands gripped the seat.

"Sir," said Adi. "What we found is that the residue hadn't

CHAPTER FIFTY-THREE

been on the suspect's skin and clothes for as long as we thought. In fact, they'd been there for a maximum of just a few hours when we took the original samples."

"And when did you take those samples?" Silton asked.

"When the body was still on the tarmac," said Turbin. "Soon after the explosion."

"Hang on a minute," Silton said. "You'll need to be more precise. When exactly did you take the samples?"

Adi inhaled. Zoe watched him, puzzled. He looked at his notes. "Five twenty-five pm, sir. The explosion was at five past four. We took the samples, and they were preserved and sent to the lab. That was over an hour after the explosion. Our analysis shows that the residue got onto the suspect after three pm the same day."

"What does that mean?" said Zoe.

"If he prepared the bomb before arriving at the airport in Karachi, the residue would have been on him for at least nine hours. Longer, if you include travel time. There's no way it was on him for that long."

"So the residue got onto him after the explosion?" Zoe asked.

"Definitely not during the flight," said Turbin. "The explosives were in the hold, no access from the passenger compartment."

"Could he have accessed them after the explosion?" asked Ian.

"He was killed," said Zoe.

"Instantly," said Adi. "His lung was punctured by a section of a chair that sheared off. It would have been quick."

"So someone put the residue on him," Zoe breathed.

Randle took a step forward. "That's a hell of an accusation, DI Finch."

Adi looked at her. He was pale. He scanned the room, his lips moving silently. Then he nodded. "I can't say it was planted, Zoe. But I can say it got there after the bomb exploded. And as we've already established, it didn't get there as a result of the bomb detonating."

CHAPTER FIFTY-FOUR

Zoe left the briefing room, trying to maintain her composure. She ran through the events of Saturday afternoon and evening in her head. Lesley had been called away, Randle had rushed her to the airport, Ian had appeared from nowhere, and they'd gone to the plane. The fire service people had sent them away for a while, and then they'd returned.

At some point during that chain of events, evidence had been planted on the suspect.

Who had had access?

The pathologist, Dr Adebayo. The fire service investigators, and firefighters. Zoe and Ian.

There would be an investigation.

She leaned on the door to the team office. Connie and Rhodri hadn't been in the meeting, the briefings were getting too full and she preferred to leave them working on the case.

Taking a few short breaths, she opened the door and closed it behind her. Ian hadn't left the briefing with her but he would be along shortly.

"Boss? You look like you've seen a ghost." Rhodri stared at her, a half-eaten chocolate digestive in his hand.

She stood by the door, her hand on the handle. "The shit may be about to hit the fan," she told him.

"How so?"

She grabbed the biscuit from him and crammed it into her mouth. "Come into my office, both of you."

They followed her, exchanging nervous glances. As she opened the inner door, Ian appeared. He and Zoe looked at each other.

"Ian, you come in here too."

He nodded and followed the constables into her office. She sat down, not something she normally did when the team were in here. But her legs felt weak. She wished she'd stopped to get a coffee. Anything to hold in her hand, to steady the trembling.

"Right," she said. "Adi Hanson and his colleague from the fire service have uncovered evidence that's going to rip a hole through this investigation. And this team."

Connie put a hand to her chest. Rhodri chewed his lip.

"They have no firm evidence," said Ian.

Zoe clenched her fist on the desk and screwed her eyes shut. "You know how serious this is, Ian. The whole department witnessed that. Why Adi didn't just go to Randle with it, I don't know..."

She swallowed. If Adi hadn't gone straight to Randle, could that mean he knew Randle was under investigation by Professional Standards?

"OK," she said. She forced herself to breathe. "The explosives residue on the suspect at the airport. It turns out it got there after the explosion. Not nine or more hours before,

CHAPTER FIFTY-FOUR

like it would have been if it had transferred to him while he was preparing the bomb."

Rhodri frowned. "So it got on him when the bomb went off. Doesn't that mean he was just a victim?"

Zoe shook her head. "No, Rhod. I wish it was that simple. The condition of the residue means that it was unexploded when it got onto him."

"That doesn't make sense," said Connie. "If it hadn't gone off when he got it on him, it must have got there before he boarded the plane."

"That's what you'd expect, if it was him who made the bomb."

"Unless..." Connie's eyes widened.

"I suggest you leave that thought where it is for now," Zoe said. "There were some pretty serious allegations raised in that briefing. And everyone who had access to the scene will be under suspicion." She looked at Ian, who was holding himself very still. "Including me and Ian."

"What about the Super?" Connie said. "He was Gold Command, wasn't he? Was he on the tarmac?"

"He didn't go anywhere near it." Zoe frowned at the thought of Connie's suspicions immediately jumping to Randle. She gritted her teeth as both of the constables turned their gaze onto Ian.

"I imagine Professional Standards will be talking to us very soon," she said. "In the meantime, we get on with our jobs. This team isn't involved in the airport investigation, so we can continue as we are."

Connie dragged her eyes away from Ian. "You sure, boss? We don't need to—?"

"Carry on, Connie. We have to identify the woman, and

find the man she was looking at. Forget about the airport shitstorm, it won't impact on you."

"We've got news on that, boss," said Rhodri.

"Go on," Zoe said. "Make it quick." Professional Standards could be here any minute.

"A photo of the woman in the headscarf," said Connie. "A decent one."

Zoe moved round to look at Connie's screen. She had a photo of the woman's face enlarged.

"That's excellent," Zoe said. "Where d'you get it?"

"Private Facebook account."

Zoe wasn't going to ask how Connie had accessed a private Facebook account. "It's a selfie."

"Yeah. Looks like the bomber sent it to the account holder."

"How on earth did you find this?" Zoe asked.

"Facial recognition search," Connie said. She shrugged.

"She stopped to take a selfie before setting off a bomb and killing herself?" Ian said.

"It's not from the station," Connie said. She pointed at the screen. "That's the ICC behind her."

"Did we see her stop to take this on her way to the station?"

"I'll see if I can track her route back further," Connie said.

"I'll help," added Rhodri.

Zoe wanted to punch the air. "Good. Follow this up. Find the person whose account this is. Talk to them, if you can. If they know her, they'll be able to tell us who she is."

"Will do." Connie leaned in towards her screen.

"What about me?" asked Ian.

"When Connie gets the details of this account, you contact the account holder."

"OK."

"What happens to us if you're taken off the case, boss?" Rhodri asked.

"There's no reason to think I'll be taken off the case. Or DS Osman."

Ian swallowed and nodded.

"Go on then. Get on with it," she said.

Connie turned and opened the door to the office. Rhodri followed her, his hand on her shoulder. Ian stayed where he was.

Rhodri closed the door. Zoe stood up and opened it. She couldn't have anyone thinking she and Ian were conferring.

"Just carry on with your job, Ian," she said. "You and I should not be talking about this situation. Not alone. Not with the constables, from this point on. Understood?"

"Yes, boss."

CHAPTER FIFTY-FIVE

Titi had stayed with Sofia and Andreea all evening. Holding Sofia's hand, smiling into her face, playing the devoted partner.

He'd been making sure she wasn't left alone with her sister.

At ten pm Kyle had arrived and taken Andreea away. To the hotel, they'd said. Andreea's face had been pinched as she'd left, but she'd said nothing about the hotel.

Titi had let Sofia back into the master bedroom afterwards. She'd told him she wanted to watch some TV before going to bed, and he'd been asleep when she'd slipped under the thick duvet beside him.

She'd woken after barely four hours sleep and lain awake next to him, listening for signs of him waking. When he'd done so she'd closed her eyes and tried to slow her breathing.

Now she was in the boot of his car. She'd crept downstairs while he was eating breakfast – no sign of Mrs Brooking, thank God – and gone to the car on the driveway, hiding in its vast boot.

CHAPTER FIFTY-FIVE

She lay in the darkness, her body jolting as he drove. She could hear him on the phone, shouting at people, complaining. Someone wasn't dead, and apparently he wasn't happy about it. He'd done everything he was supposed to do, right down to the distraction and the work on the body. She didn't understand her boyfriend's business. Maybe she'd misheard.

She held herself stiffly, careful not to hit the sides. It was cold and musty, two pools of red light showing from the rear lights. She had to hope he wouldn't open the boot when he got to work.

The car became still. She heard him slam the driver's door, then silence. No hum of traffic, no distinct voices. She had no idea whether this was because she was somewhere quiet, or because the car was soundproofed.

But she couldn't stay here. He might come back and open the boot, or he might just drive her home. And she was freezing.

Titi had said he was going to give Andreea a job. Maybe she would be here, at his workplace. He'd told her he ran an importing business, which was why he'd been in Bucharest.

She put her ear to the roof of the boot. There was no sound, nothing at all. She listened for a few minutes until her neck became sore.

Move, she told herself.

The car had back seats that flattened down. Maybe she could push one of them out of the way and get out through the gap. She couldn't find a way to open the boot from inside, so that was her only hope.

She leaned her shoulder into the seat and shoved, revealing a crack of light. She pushed her fingers up into the gap at the top of the seat, feeling for a catch that would release it. When she finally found it and squeezed, the seat sprang away from her and she crashed forwards, letting out a muffled cry.

She flattened herself on the seat, not daring to look up.

Slowly, she turned towards the front seats. They were empty. She let herself breathe again.

She felt dizzy. She lay still for a moment, willing the spinning in her head to stop. She sat up, peering over the windowsill.

She was in a driveway, in front of a red brick building. *Hotel Belvista*, the sign said. The building was large but shabby. Two windows were boarded up and weeds grew through cracks in the tarmac.

She looked up at the building. Did her boyfriend work here? Was Andreea inside?

She'd pictured him in a smart office, surrounded by lush indoor plants and hardworking staff. She hadn't imagined anything like this.

She had to get away from the car, before anyone spotted her.

She put a hand on the door handle. It pulled and the door sprang open. She drew it back, anxious to avoid any sudden movements.

Slowly, she eased her legs out of the car boot and into the back seat. She wriggled through the open door and onto the ground outside. There was a lump of dog shit lying on the ground six inches from her face. She swallowed, trying not to retch.

She reached up into the car and pushed the seat back. It clicked into place. She pushed the door closed, biting her lip as it clunked shut. She crouched on the ground, facing away from the dog shit, breathing heavily.

CHAPTER FIFTY-FIVE

The car was twenty metres from the building. She couldn't go in the front door.

She shuffled along the side of the car and looked round it. There was no movement behind the dirty windows, no one outside. Where was Titi?

She had to hope there would be an entrance at the side or the back of the building.

She crouched low and said a prayer to herself in Romanian. She clenched her fists, pushed herself up and started to run.

CHAPTER FIFTY-SIX

Zoe left the police station, avoiding the eyes of people she passed. She had no idea how widely news of the new evidence had travelled, and how many people knew she'd been at the airport.

She walked towards her car, keeping her footsteps light and her pace steady. She wanted to turn her head, to see if she was being watched.

At last she reached her car. She dived inside and started the engine.

She hadn't told the team she was going anywhere. She didn't have anywhere to go. Leaving here would look suspicious.

She turned the engine off and grabbed her phone. She had no idea if he would pick up.

"Zoe."

She felt her body relax. "Carl. I thought you wouldn't take my call."

"We can't talk like this, Zoe. You know that."

CHAPTER FIFTY-SIX

"So you've been told about the allegations of evidence being planted."

"I have, yes. And someone from Professional Standards will be interviewing you. Not me."

"No." There was no way they'd let a detective inspector from PS interview his own girlfriend. "Are we OK?" she asked. "Surely you don't think I have anything to do with this?"

"You should know better than to call me like this."

"I'll come to yours tonight. I can tell you my suspicions."

"No. *Christ*, Zoe. This has to be done properly. We can't see each other until this is out of the way."

She sank into the seat. "I thought you'd say that."

"Sorry. I'll miss you."

"Me too."

"My colleague DS Layla Kaur will interview you. You met her when we interviewed DS Osman, when his children were missing."

There was a pause. Zoe heard muffled conversation.

"I'm with her now," Carl said. "She's a good detective, professional, fair. She'll do her job."

"OK. Take care, Carl."

"I will." He drew in a breath.

"What?" she asked.

"Nothing, Zoe. Hang up and go back inside the building."

She turned in her seat to see a car pull into the car park. Two people were inside: a woman at the wheel and Carl in the passenger seat. His eyes snagged on Zoe as the car passed but he didn't acknowledge her.

She stared after the car as it parked, her heart thumping.

She watched them leave the car and walk to the main door. She ducked down in her seat. She shouldn't be doing this, watching them from her car, hiding.

She opened the car door. She waited until they were out of sight then walked after them to the door, her thumbnail firmly digging into her palm.

CHAPTER FIFTY-SEVEN

Rhodri leaned across the desks. "What d'you think?"

Connie looked up at him, her face hot. "Shush."

"D'you think it was him?" Rhodri glanced at Ian, who sat at his own desk, clicking his mouse but his eyes not focused on his screen.

"I don't think anything, Rhodri," she said. "I wasn't there, remember?"

"Yeah, but..."

She glared at him. "He's your sarge, Rhod."

Rhodri looked at Ian, his face expressionless. Connie thought back to the kidnapping case, the way she'd found Randle's number in Ian's phone. An unregistered burner phone.

And the Super had been involved in ACC Jackson's murder. The DI had suspected him at the time. She'd said nothing since.

Could the sarge and Randle have been working together, to fake the evidence at the airport? If so, why?

Connie shook her head. She was imagining things. It

would be a mistake. A forensics error. The idea of someone in Force CID being involved in a terror attack was ridiculous.

The door to the office opened and a woman stepped in. She was short, with dark skin and black hair in a pixie cut. Connie sat up straight.

The woman held up her ID. "I'm DS Kaur from Professional Standards. I'm looking for DI Zoe Finch."

Connie glanced across at Rhodri. He shrugged. Ian stood up from his desk, wiping his hands on his trousers. He held out a hand but the woman didn't take it.

The door opened again and a man came in. DI Carl Whaley, Zoe's handsome boyfriend. Connie felt the breath catch in her throat. She looked at Rhodri: *where's the boss?* He looked blank.

"Sorry, I was just outside." Zoe stood behind the two PS officers in the doorway. "You're looking for me."

Carl gave Zoe a nod. "DI Finch, we'd like you to come with us." He turned to Ian. "And you too, DS Osman. We need to speak with you in connection with the incident at Birmingham Airport on Saturday."

Rhodri's eyes were wide. Connie frowned at him, wanting to tell him to stop staring.

"Of course," Zoe said, her eyes on the female DS. "Ian?"

Ian grabbed his jacket and walked to the door. Zoe turned back to Connie and Rhodri.

"Keep working on the ID of the bomber and her suspected accomplice. Leave me a voicemail if you find anything."

"Yes, boss," Connie and Rhodri muttered in unison.

Zoe nodded. She gave them a tight smile and followed Carl out of the room.

CHAPTER FIFTY-EIGHT

Mo and Dawson returned to their office in silence. Fran was waiting, her eyebrows raised at Mo. He didn't know what to tell her.

"Well fuck me sideways with a coal shovel," Dawson said, breaking the silence. Fran gave him a disdainful look.

Mo nodded. Zoe had been at the scene, she was one of the people who'd had access to that body. She would be questioned. He stared out of the window, his mind racing.

Dawson clapped his hands. "Well wake up, then."

"What happened?" asked Fran.

"What happened, *boss*, is what you mean," said Dawson.

"What happened, boss?" Fran's voice was thin.

"Our suspect is probably no longer a suspect. Looks like someone planted the residue on him."

"They did what?"

"We don't know anything yet," said Mo.

"Hmmph," replied Dawson. "It doesn't look good for your mate."

Mo took a deep breath and let it out again. *Don't react*, he told himself. *Don't give him the pleasure.*

Dawson slumped into a chair. "That isn't our problem for now. So what else do we have?"

"The suspect could still have..." Mo began. They'd dragged that man's widow in for questioning. They'd humiliated her in front of her solicitor. And all because of evidence that most likely had been planted.

This was going to have repercussions he couldn't begin to imagine.

"He could have nothing," Dawson said. "You gave his widow a hard time for no reason. Pleased with your attitude towards Muslim terror suspects now, eh?"

"Her religion had nothing to do with it," said Mo. "Her husband was a viable suspect."

"Well, not any more. So what else do we have?"

Mo walked to the board at the end of the room. It was filled with photos from the scene. To be honest, it was a mess, and not much help. But in the middle of it was something that had been nagging at him.

He grabbed a photo. "The gate."

"The gate?" said Fran.

"The one that someone cut through with wire cutters. Why? If they were trying to get at the plane, that would be a way to do it."

"OK." Dawson clicked the top of his pen. "Good. What else?"

Fran joined Mo at the board. She grabbed another photo. "The handbag. It was by the gate. Whoever cut the gate might have dropped it."

"You think a woman did this?" Dawson said.

CHAPTER FIFTY-EIGHT

"More than one person did this," said Mo. "You don't pull off a crime like this alone."

"And there's no reason why one of them couldn't have been the owner of this bag," added Fran.

"So she's clever enough to pull off a bombing on an aeroplane, make us all think the thing was put there in Pakistan, but she's dumb enough to forget her Gucci handbag?" said Dawson.

Mo shrugged. "You never know. Where's the bag now?"

"Evidence store," said Fran.

"Let's get it back. Give it to the FSUs, check it for prints, fibres, DNA."

"You reckon the idiot woman who dropped this bag's in the database?" said Dawson.

"It's worth a shot," replied Mo.

"It is indeed. Fran, make the call."

CHAPTER FIFTY-NINE

Zoe sat across the table from DS Layla Kaur and a male detective she hadn't met before. They were in Lloyd House; she'd been brought here in a squad car while Ian had gone in Carl's car.

"DI Finch," Layla said.

"DS Kaur."

"You're not under caution. We're interviewing you as a witness for now."

Zoe nodded. She knew how quickly that could change.

"I need you to run through the events of Saturday with me. From the moment you arrived at the airport, to when you left. Who you saw, who you worked with."

"D'you mind telling me who your colleague is?"

Kaur looked at the man next to her. He was middle-aged, with thinning hair and pale skin.

"Detective Superintendent Rogers," he said.

Zoe stiffened. Carl's boss: she'd heard about him, although Carl had been careful not to give much away.

Calm down, she told herself. *Cooperate*. She'd done nothing wrong. She had nothing to be afraid of.

"I was driven to the airport by Detective Superintendent Randle. We arrived at four twenty-one pm."

DS Kaur raised an eyebrow and wrote in her pad. Zoe wondered whether Randle would be questioned. He'd not gone near the tarmac, not once.

"We went straight to the ops room, where we were briefed by DCI Donnelly, who was Silver Command. Then I—"

DS Kaur raised a finger. "Wait. Tell me who else you spoke to at the ops room. Who was there?"

"I don't know all the names. But there will be a log. We had to sign in and out. The people I spoke with were DCI Donnelly, as I've mentioned, and there was a woman from airport security, I'd need to refer to my notes to recall her name. At the aeroplane I spoke to Dr Adebayo, and officers from West Midlands Fire Service."

"We'll need names."

"Like I say, everyone will have been logged – but yes, if you let me go to my desk and fetch my notes—"

"You can do that afterwards. Tell us what happened after you were briefed," said Detective Superintendent Rogers.

Zoe looked at him. "Detective Superintendent Randle told me to go to the plane. He wanted me to work with the fire service to preserve evidence. Then DS Osman arrived."

"He came after you?" Kaur asked. "He wasn't driven there by Detective Superintendent Randle?"

"He told me he'd had a call. That he'd been on a shopping trip with his family and come straight to the airport. He said that explained why he got there so quickly."

"DS Osman is part of your team, is that right?"

"He was assigned to my team in November last year."

"So why didn't you contact him and give him the order to come to the airport?"

"To be honest, at that stage I didn't know what the situation was. I didn't even know there'd been an explosion when Randle told me to get in his car and come with him to the airport."

"So he knew but you didn't?"

"I'd been at the Force CID office in Harborne police station with my supervising officer, DCI Clarke. She was called away to the New Street bomb. At that point all I knew was that a bomb had exploded at the station. I knew nothing about the airport."

"OK. So you arrived at the airport, you were briefed, and you left the ops room to go to the site. Did DS Osman accompany you?"

"He did. I asked him to help me secure the crime scene."

"It was still an active rescue operation at that point, is that right?" asked Rogers.

"It was. I was hoping – well, I'd been told – to do what I could to prevent that rescue operation destroying evidence."

"Did you have access to the bodies that were being brought off the plane?" he said.

Zoe closed her eyes, running through the events of Saturday afternoon in her head. It had all happened so fast.

"I spoke to Dr Adebayo, the pathologist. She was already at the scene. I saw her again the next day when she performed the post-mortem on the New Street bomber and on Inspector Jameson."

"That's not pertinent right now." DS Kaur flipped over a sheet of paper and continued to write.

"Will Dr Adebayo be interviewed as well? She isn't a police officer."

"DI Finch," said Rogers. "Did you see Dr Adebayo or anyone else placing anything on one of the bodies?"

"I saw Dr Adebayo working on the bodies. She was instructing her team to match personal belongings to the bodies, as part of the identification effort."

"Did you see any of the pathology team leave anything on the body of" – DS Kaur flipped her pad back a few pages – "Nadeem Sharif?"

"At that point I didn't know who Mr Sharif was. We hadn't identified him as a suspect. So I'm afraid I can't tell you if I saw anyone with that body."

"You know what he looked like," Kaur replied. "Did you see anybody tampering with a body that fitted his description?"

"The man had been killed by debris from the crash. He sustained disfiguring injuries. I don't remember seeing him, but I'm not sure I would have remembered. Especially as I wasn't looking for his face in particular."

"Did you see DS Osman doing anything unusual?" Rogers asked.

"Sorry, what do you mean by unusual?"

"Touching any of the bodies, placing anything at the scene."

Zoe shuffled her feet beneath the table. "DS Osman and I weren't together all of the time. I went to the plane. I tried to get access, but it was impossible. Then I returned to the location where the bodies were being placed. He was..."

She felt ice run down her back.

"Go on," said Rogers.

"He... I need to make sure I'm remembering this

correctly. He was crouched over, near the bodies. I didn't see him touch any of them. I didn't see him place anything at the scene."

"So you saw him crouched next to the bodies. Did he spot you watching him?"

"I wasn't watching him. But yes, he saw me approach. He walked to where I was standing and I brought him up to speed with my progress on the plane, or lack of it."

"Did he behave suspiciously?"

Zoe tried to cast her mind back to Ian's face when she'd approached him on the tarmac. "No," she said. "He was just looking at the bodies, talking to Dr Adebayo. It was a crime scene, he was part of the investigating team."

"Except it wasn't an investigation at that stage," Rogers said.

"We knew it would be. The sooner you can start collecting evidence, the better."

"I don't need you to tell me how to manage a crime scene, DI Finch."

"That wasn't my intention."

Zoe sat back in her chair. She wondered what Carl was asking Ian.

She knew Ian was bent. She knew he had connections with organised crime, and that he'd had work done on his house as payment. She knew Carl had given him a deal that let him keep his job in return for spying on Randle.

But this was a terror attack. Why would Ian be involved in this?

"Are you sure you didn't see anything else untoward?" DS Kaur asked. She'd closed her notepad and was looking into Zoe's eyes, her gaze steady.

Zoe nodded. "I'm sure."

CHAPTER SIXTY

Sofia crept along the rear corridor of the hotel, her footsteps quiet and her movements small. She'd found an unlocked basement window at ground level and slithered in through it, terrified there would be someone inside waiting for her.

She'd landed in a laundry room, washing machines humming and steam rising at the windows. She'd taken a few minutes to catch her breath and calm her racing mind, then headed out into the corridors.

The hotel was quiet. She could hear faint voices on the floor above but there was no one down here.

Still, she had to be careful. The basement could be the busiest part of the building, where staff offices were, maybe kitchens.

She came to a flight of stairs. They were covered in a dark red carpet worn by many years' worth of footsteps. She could smell cooking, but nothing that made her want to eat.

She placed a foot on the bottom step. The surface beneath the carpet was concrete: silent. She walked up to the half landing, her movements steady. She hardly dared to breathe.

She stopped to look up and round the bend in the stairs, towards the ground floor. She was facing the main door to the hotel, where her boyfriend had presumably gone in.

If he found her here, what would he do? Could she pretend Andreea had invited her?

No. He'd been with them all night. And she never went out without one of his men driving her. She couldn't be here.

She had to be quick. She tiptoed up the rest of the stairs and pulled herself round to the next flight. It would be safer on the upper floors, less likely that Titi had an office up here.

At the first floor she stopped. She could hear women's voices approaching.

She froze as she heard a mobile phone ring along the corridor. She pushed herself into the wall, her chest rising and falling. She stared in the direction the sound had come from.

A woman came out of a door, a phone clamped to her ear. She shoved it into her pocket as she saw Sofia. "What is it?"

Sofia's throat was dry. "I'm looking for Andreea," she said in Romanian.

The woman smiled. "She's out. Working."

"Oh." Sofia felt the anticipation drain from her body.

"She'll be back later tonight. You want me to give her a message?"

"Tell her Sofia was here. Tell her I need to speak to her."

"You won't get much chance to speak to her, *iubită*. They work her hard. They do that with the new ones."

"What work does she do?" Sofia looked along the corridor behind her, scared Titi might hear her.

"Same as all of us. *Hospitality*." The woman's face was hard. She was young, in her twenties. She'd be pretty, if she didn't look so angry.

"She works in the hotel?"

The woman laughed. "You're not from around here, are you?" She cocked her head. "Come to think of it, who are you?"

"Sofia. I'm Andreea's sister."

The woman's eyes widened. "You need to get out of here. Now."

"Why?"

"Just go. I can't have them finding me with you."

"I don't understand…"

The woman put a palm on Sofia's chest and pushed her backwards. "Cristina!" she called. "Daria! Help me get rid of this bitch."

Sofia stared back at the woman. "You don't know me. What did I do to you?"

"You damn well know what you did. You ruined your sister's life, and all of ours, is what you did. Now get out, before I scream the place down."

CHAPTER SIXTY-ONE

Zoe walked back into the team room, her body full of tension.

"Boss," said Connie. She exchanged glances with Rhodri. "It's good to see you."

"Thanks." Zoe blew out a short breath. "How are you getting on with our mystery man and woman?"

"Are you alright, boss? They don't think you—?" said Rhodri.

She waved a hand. "Let's not talk about it. I'm here, and we've got an investigation to focus on. How are you getting on?"

Connie grinned. "Good news. I've found the woman this account is registered to."

"Go on."

"She's Romanian. Name of Ana-Maria Albescu. She came to this country three months ago."

"And she's a friend of the bomber?"

"They were sharing photos. I guess they must have been."

CHAPTER SIXTY-ONE

"Excellent work, Connie. We need to track her down."

"She was fined two weeks ago for soliciting."

"She's a sex worker?"

"She was picked up on Macauley Street."

"That's the street Mo's been watching."

"You think it was the sarge who picked her up?"

"Can you check the records?"

"Yes." Connie stuck her tongue out as she checked the system.

"No, boss. She was arrested by PC Battar. Not DS Uddin."

"OK. But if she was working Macauley Street…"

"You got an idea, boss?" said Rhodri.

"I might have. But I need to talk to Mo."

Zoe turned on her heel and all but ran out of the door.

CHAPTER SIXTY-TWO

Zoe crashed into Mo coming out of his office.

"Zo. Everything OK?" He looked worried.

"We've got a lead on the New Street bomber that I think's connected to your prostitution investigation."

"Slow down. What?"

"Were you aware that one of the women working Macauley Street was fined two weeks ago?"

"Local uniform stopped a few of them. We had to speak to their station, tell them to leave it alone."

"An Ana-Maria Albescu. She was a friend of the woman who set off the New Street bomb."

"What? How?"

Zoe shrugged. "It might be irrelevant. But it's the best chance we've got of identifying our bomber."

"OK. You want me to look into it?"

She hesitated. She'd been given the job of identifying the suspect. But if PS thought she'd been involved in planting evidence...

"Let's go together," she said.

He sighed. "I can't. Not now. I'm off to the airport with Fran."

"Of course. Sorry."

"We're looking into the gate that was cut though. Dawson reckons whoever did it might be involved in the attack."

"But the bomb was already on the plane."

"I need to talk to Adi and the Fire Service people, check there isn't a chance it was planted later."

"That would change everything."

"It might mean that whoever placed the bomb also planted the evidence on Sharif," Mo said.

Zoe felt her spirits lift. "You're right." It was a long shot, but it was a possibility.

He nodded. "I've got to go. Let me know how you get on with Ana-Maria, yeah?"

"Yeah. And you with the airport."

"Let's hope so."

She watched him leave then headed back to the team room.

"Connie, what address did Ms Albescu give when she was fined?"

"27 Curton Road, boss."

"Shit."

"What?"

"That's Mo's brothel. The one that was emptied." Zoe threw herself into Ian's chair. He still wasn't back from his interview with Carl.

"We have no way of finding her," she sighed. "*Damn.*" She punched the desk.

"It's OK," said Connie. "I've got her phone number."

"You've got what?" Zoe stood up. She went to Connie's desk. Rhodri was next to her, grinning.

"She's a bloody genius, boss, isn't she?"

"Sometimes she is Rhod, yes. How long have you had this for, Connie?"

"I got it while you were with the sarge just now."

"Good. Give it to me."

Connie read out a number and Zoe punched it into her phone.

"Stop," said Connie.

Zoe hung up. "What?"

"She's a sex worker. She won't talk to you."

"So how am I supposed to get hold of her?"

"I'll track down the phone provider. See if we can get an address."

"That'll be Curton Street."

"It might be registered to her pimp."

"Or it might be unregistered."

Connie shrugged. "It's worth a go."

"How long will it take?"

Connie glanced at her watch. "It won't be today."

Zoe gritted her teeth. So close...

"Right," she said. "Rhodri, you come with me."

CHAPTER SIXTY-THREE

"Where we going?" Rhodri asked as he buckled his seatbelt.

"Curton Street."

"But the sarge said it was empty."

"It's the only lead we've got. I want to check it out. Call Sheila Griffin, find out if we can get access."

"Boss." He pulled his phone from his pocket.

It was almost dark and the streets were busy: rush hour. Nicholas would be home already. Zoe hoped he planned to go out, spend time with Zaf instead of his alcoholic grandmother.

Rhodri sniffed. "No answer, boss."

"Probably for the best," Zoe said. "Leave it."

"Er, OK. Watch out!" Rhodri threw a hand up as Zoe almost hit a car that had pulled out of a side road. She gritted her teeth as it braked and she wove around it. She glared at the driver. "People need to look where they're going."

"You *are* driving pretty fast, if you don't mind me saying."

"We're in the middle of a terror investigation, Rhodri. I need to drive fast."

"Maybe put the lights on?"

She shook her head. "It isn't an emergency."

He turned to look out of the windscreen, saying nothing. She slowed a little.

The brothel was quiet, curtains open and no movement in the windows. Zoe pulled up across the street and sat low in the driver's seat.

"What now?" asked Rhodri.

Zoe looked up and down the street. An elderly couple shuffled along the opposite side carrying shopping bags. They paused while the woman put one of her bags down, rested then picked it up again. Other than that, there was no one around.

"Let's take a look," Zoe said.

"We haven't been given access."

"I'm not going inside."

She opened her door and hurried across the street, stopping behind a hedge. Rhodri was still in the car. She waved to beckon him over.

"Come on," she muttered. "We're only taking a look."

After a few moments of looking up and down the street, he left the car and joined her. He looked nervous, his eyes darting between the houses.

"What next?" he asked.

"Follow me."

She rounded the hedge and walked to the house's front corner, stopping next to the wall where no one inside would be able to see her.

"It's empty, boss. No one's going to see us."

"They might have come back. No one's been here since Sunday night."

"OK."

"Now shush."

She rounded the side of the building. There was an alleyway between this and the next house, with a gate blocking their way. Quietly, Zoe tried the latch. It opened.

"People really should be more security conscious," she muttered. Rhodri nodded, his eyes wide.

They crept along the alleyway. It was dark with litter piled up at the sides: beer cans, crumpled newspaper, cigarette butts. At the end were two more gates. One to the brothel's back yard, and the other to the neighbour's.

Zoe pushed at the gate to the brothel's side. It opened. She shook her head.

"Maybe uniform bust it open when they searched the place," Rhodri said.

"Fair point."

The yard was full of junk. An old pushchair rusted against the wall. Bin liners were piled up, along with the rotting remains of a wooden bed.

"They emptied the inside, but not all this," she said.

Next to them was a window into a back room. Zoe darted past it and into the corner where the wall to the main house met the wall to the kitchen, jutting out at the back. Her breath misted in front of her.

No lights shone from the windows, no sounds came from inside.

"Let's try the back door," Zoe said.

Rhodri frowned at her but said nothing.

She approached the back door and was about to put a

hand on it when it moved. She sprang back, crashing into Rhodri.

"Quick," she hissed. She ducked down and dashed past the door, careful to keep low. Rhodri scuttled after her and they rounded the back of the house, flattening themselves against the kitchen's back wall.

"Someone's in there," Zoe whispered. "The door moved."

"Sure it wasn't the wind?"

She shook her head. "No wind. Look." She blew out and her breath misted in front of her face, moving forwards.

She heard the door opening around the corner. She pushed past Rhodri and peered around the corner into the side yard.

A man emerged from the door, his back to them. He walked towards the gate and the alleyway beyond. It closed after him, on a spring.

"Come on," she whispered. She crept out from their hiding place, pausing to look into the kitchen. No movement. She pulled the gate open, hardly breathing. The man had left the alleyway.

They ran to the front of the house, their footsteps light. The man paused on the pavement to light a cigarette. For a moment the lighter illuminated his face. He was white, with a face that looked like it had seen hard times, and a twisted nose.

"I know him," Zoe breathed.

Rhodri nodded. "Kyle Gatiss."

"Let's follow him."

CHAPTER SIXTY-FOUR

THE MAN WALKED along the street to a black car. He pulled a key fob from his pocket and the indicator lights flashed. He got in the driver's side.

The car was a Mercedes, new-looking. It didn't fit around here.

"D'you think there's anyone in there with him?" Rhodri asked.

"With a car like that, could be any of them. Or could just be him. Come on."

They ran to Zoe's car.

"Watch him while I turn around," she told Rhodri. He turned in his seat.

"He's moving," Rhodri said. "Headed the other way."

"Right." Zoe yanked hard on the steering wheel. "Good job this thing's manoeuvrable."

She sped out of the parking space and turned the car in a smooth arc.

"Nice," said Rhodri.

Zoe patted the steering wheel. "Who needs a response vehicle when you've got Longbridge's finest?"

"They don't make them in Longbridge anymore."

"No."

The Mercedes was at the other end of the street. Zoe slowed as it turned out of the street, then sped up.

"Shall I call for backup?" Rhodri asked.

"Not yet. We're just observing."

They pulled out of Curton Road and followed the car towards the inner ring road, Zoe careful to keep a few cars between her and her target. Her car stood out, a British racing green Mini. But at least it didn't look like a typical police vehicle.

The Mercedes took the tunnels under the Bristol Road and Pershore Road and turned onto the Alcester Road, heading south.

"Where d'you reckon he's going?" asked Rhodri.

"No idea."

"But we're going to find out."

"We are, Rhodri. Just be patient."

"Did the sarge know Gatiss was involved with that brothel?"

"Good point. Call him."

Rhodri grabbed his phone, his eyes on the road and the car they were following.

"Sarge, sorry to disturb you."

Zoe glanced at him as he waited for Mo to reply.

"We've just left the house on Curton Road you told us about," Rhodri said. "Kyle Gatiss was inside. We're following him. Currently on the Alcester Road, driving through Moseley."

CHAPTER SIXTY-FOUR

Zoe heard Mo's exclamation down the line. She smiled. So he hadn't known.

"Yes, Sarge... Yes, we'll let you know. He's just turned off Wake Green Road... Hang on, he's stopping."

They were in Hall Green, on a wide street of large shabby houses. Zoe slowed as the Mercedes turned into a driveway. She drove past it as he stopped, pulling up a couple of houses further along.

"The Belvista Hotel," she said. Rhodri repeated the name into the phone then shook his head at her.

She nodded. "Ask him if he needs me to call Sheila."

"He says he'll do it. Wants us to watch and sit tight."

"OK."

"He says he means it, boss."

"Tell him to stop giving me orders."

Rhodri reddened. "Did you hear that, Sarge?" he said, his eyes on Zoe. She smiled.

"He says it's just advice, boss."

She grabbed the phone. "Thanks for the advice. We'll be careful."

"They could be armed, Zo," Mo said. "You don't go in there without backup."

"And right now, we have no reason to go in there anyway."

"No. Report back to me or Sheila and we'll decide what to do. Probably put surveillance on the place."

"A woman from that brothel knows the New Street bomber," she said.

"All the more reason to be careful."

Zoe sighed. "Alright. I'll call you later."

He made a humphing sound and hung up. Zoe opened her car door.

"What are you doing?" Rhodri asked.

"We can't see anything from here." She leaned back into the car, raising her eyebrows at him. "It's OK. We'll just observe."

She walked along the street, glad of the darkness and the heavy clouds. A light drizzle had started to fall and the street was deserted. The hotel was in darkness, the Mercedes parked next to a battered Renault.

She looked at the building. It was run down, windows boarded up and weeds growing in the driveway. She didn't imagine it did much trade with holidaymakers.

Rhodri was behind her. "Should we stop here?"

"Yes. This is a good spot."

He breathed a sigh of relief.

"Stay behind this wall," she told him. "Keep an eye on that Merc."

He nodded. She leaned forward, trying to get a better view.

The front door to the hotel opened and the man emerged. He was lit by a lamp over the doorway, his features unmistakeable. Zoe had come across Gatiss before. He was part of the organised crime group they'd targeted in the Canary investigation into child abuse, and he was connected to Trevor Hamm, who she believed Randle was working for. They'd never managed to pin anything on Gatiss. Maybe now they would. Or on his bosses.

He held a woman by the arm. She was short with sleek dark hair, expensively dressed. She didn't look like a woman Zoe would expect to see working here.

The woman jerked out of his grip and shouted at him. She had an Eastern European accent.

Gatiss growled at the woman and pushed her down the

CHAPTER SIXTY-FOUR

steps leading from the hotel. He grabbed her wrist and pulled her to the Mercedes. Zoe shrank back, holding her breath.

Gatiss opened the back door to the car and shoved the woman inside. He slammed the door shut and got into the driver's seat.

"What now?" said Rhodri. "We follow him?"

Zoe pushed her thumbnail into her palm. They could stay here, find out if the woman who'd received that photo was inside. Or they could follow Gatiss and see where he took them.

"Come on," she said. "Quick."

CHAPTER SIXTY-FIVE

"You cannot treat me like this," Sofia growled from the back seat.

Kyle looked at her in the rearview mirror. "Put your seatbelt on."

"Where are you taking me?"

"Home, of course. The boss has been wondering where you'd got to."

She sneered at him, full of contempt. She'd fled from the woman who she'd spoken to, the mad woman who accused her of ruining her own sister's life. She'd found a place to hide in the hotel, a laundry cupboard in the basement. Twice someone had come in and she'd had to cover herself with linen.

She'd waited for hours, trying to ignore the fact she needed to use the toilet. When the light from the high basement window had darkened, she'd emerged, looking for Andreea.

There had been no sign of her sister. And when she'd run outside, there'd been no sign of Titi's car.

CHAPTER SIXTY-FIVE

She'd gone back into the hotel, heading upstairs and standing outside the door that the woman had come out from. She was scared to talk to the women in this place. When they'd started to emerge from the rooms and clatter downstairs, she'd hidden again in a bathroom. She'd left the door open a crack, keeping an eye out for Andreea. Eventually she'd decided she had to leave, to get back to the house before her boyfriend missed her. As she descended the stairs, she'd been confronted by Kyle standing at the front door.

One of the women had spotted her, and a phone call had been made.

"You're gonna be in so much trouble." Kyle gave her a hard smile in the rearview mirror. "It'll be like Irina all over again."

"Who is Irina?"

"Was. She died."

Sofia felt a chill flood through her. "Tell me, who is Irina?"

"Ask Trevor." He adjusted the rearview mirror. "*Shit*."

"What?"

"Hold on." The car accelerated and she felt herself pinned to the seat. She grasped the leather, her heart racing. Kyle's eyes flicked between the road ahead and the mirror.

Sofia turned in her seat.

"Stay down," he said. He jerked the steering wheel and they turned sharp left, into a quiet road full of modern houses.

"Where do we go?"

"Shut up." He sped up, throwing the car around a bend and then another. After they'd taken four turns at speed, he slowed. His eyes were on the mirror.

She turned to look out of the back window.

"I said stop that. Keep down." Kyle's voice was harsh.

Sofia's breath was shaky. "What happened?"

The car pulled to a halt. Kyle sat with his fingertips on the steering wheel, his eyes on the mirror. His pupils were dilated.

"I lost them," he said.

"Who?"

"Never you mind." He indicated to pull out and started to drive, at a steady pace this time.

CHAPTER SIXTY-SIX

"Where is he?" Zoe yelled. She turned her head from right to left, scanning side streets as they passed them. "What happened to him?"

"We lost him, boss."

She slapped the steering wheel. "Damn."

Rhodri shuddered. "Sorry."

"Not your fault. Seems my Mini isn't all that surreptitious after all."

"What now?"

"I need to tell Mo about the hotel. They'll clean it out, now we know we're onto them." She gave the wheel a heavy whack. "*Shit*. And we don't know if the owner of that Facebook account is in there. Connie can follow that up, see if she can get an IP address or something."

She dialled Mo and got his voicemail. "Mo, it's Zoe. Call me back, it's urgent." She slumped in the seat. "I'm pissed off about this."

"Yeah."

"Where d'you think he was heading?"

"He could have taken us the wrong way."

"Yeah." She stared ahead. The rain was picking up, spray rebounding off the road. "We're in…"

"Edge of Solihull," Rhodri said.

"Not too far from the airport."

"No."

They came to the M42. To take Rhodri back to the station, she'd have to double back at the roundabout. For the airport, it was a left turn.

"Call Connie, will you, Rhod?"

He nodded and picked up his phone. "Con, it's Rhodri… yeah… sorry. Look, I'm out past Solihull with the boss…"

Zoe turned left, heading for the airport, as Rhodri filled Connie in. When he hung up, they were leaving the motorway again.

"She's going to see what she can find," he said.

"Good." She eyed the clock. "It's getting late. We'll see if we can find DS Uddin, then I can drop you home."

"I'm the other side of the city, boss. It's OK, I'll stick around."

"Fair enough." Her phone rang: Mo.

"Mo, are you at the airport?"

"We left about an hour ago. I've just got home."

Zoe gritted her teeth. "I need to talk to you."

"Of course, everything OK?"

"It's just… Gatiss, and the brothel. There's more going on than we realise here."

"Fine. Come over."

"I will."

CHAPTER SIXTY-SEVEN

"Get upstairs, now!"

Titi stood in the hallway to the house. His face was red and a blood vessel throbbed on his temple.

Sofia forced herself to stand tall in front of him. He couldn't talk to her like this.

"I am hungry," she said. "Where is Mrs Brooking?"

"Mrs Brooking has gone home for the night, and a bloody good job too. I don't want her knowing what you've done."

Sofia shook her head. "I did nothing wrong."

He clenched his fist and she flinched. "Go on then. Go in the fucking kitchen. Get yourself some food, if you're so hungry."

She looked up the stairs. Perhaps she would be better off up there. She could lock herself in the bathroom.

He looked past her to where Kyle stood on the doorstep, his expression unruffled. Kyle had seen this kind of thing before, she realised.

"Kitchen!" he hissed. Sofia walked past him and opened the fridge door.

She gazed into it, her mind dull. There was a plate covered in clingfilm: for her, or for Titi? What would he do, if she ate something Mrs Brooking had left for him?

Trevor was talking to Kyle in the hallway. Getting a report on what she'd done, she assumed. She stepped towards the doorway, her senses on fire. She heard the word 'police'.

Her mouth fell open. Kyle had been trying to lose a police tail?

She hurried to the far side of the room and leaned her face on the glazed doors to the garden. It was dark outside, faint LED lights illuminating a path that led down to a pond.

Were the police watching Kyle? Or her boyfriend? Did it have anything to do with Andreea's disappearance?

She heard a plate being slammed onto the marble worktop. She turned to see Titi peeling the clingfilm off it. He wrinkled his nose and pushed the plate away.

"You can have this," he sneered. She approached him, her arm outstretched for the plate.

As she was about to take it, he grabbed her hand. She yelped.

"How did you get there? Who took you?"

"No one. No one took me."

He shook her hand. She gritted her teeth. His fingernails dug into her flesh.

"I hid. In car."

"Which car? My car?"

She nodded. Her chest felt tight.

"You hid in the car when Kyle was driving."

"No. When you were driving. Please, Titi. Not Kyle's fault."

"Don't fucking call me that." He glared at her. "When?"

"Morning. When you leave for work."

He let out a breath. "No wonder Mrs Brooking couldn't find you." He jerked her hand up to his face. "You stupid woman, what were you doing?"

"I wanted to find Andreea."

"You know where Andreea is. I brought her here, last night. We had dinner, it was very civilised. You should be grateful."

"Yes. I am grateful. Very grateful. It was good to see her."

He let go of her hand, pushing her into the worktop. She fell against it, winded.

"Titi? Trevor?"

"What?"

"Where is she? Why you not let me see her?"

"She's busy." He leaned towards her, hot breath gusting into her face. "Don't you understand that, or d'you think every woman sits on her arse all day doing fuck all except shopping and touching up her nail varnish?"

"You like me to shop. You give me money. I get job, if you prefer."

"What job would *you* do?"

"I am trained barista. I get job in coffee shop."

He laughed. "Don't be ridiculous. You stay here, where I can keep an eye on you."

She forced out a breath. "Yes. Sorry."

"Sorry." He turned away from her. "That's all you seem to say lately. Maybe I'll just send you back to Romania."

She thought of what Kyle had said in the car: Irina. Trevor's dead – what? His girlfriend? His wife? She stepped towards him. She put a hand on his back. It was hard.

"No. Please. I like it here."

He turned to her, his eyes narrow. "Maybe I'll put you to work, like your sister. See how you like that."

She shrugged. "I want you to be happy, honeybun. I do what you want."

CHAPTER SIXTY-EIGHT

"See you in the morning, Rhod."

Zoe drove away from Northfield station. She'd left Rhodri to get the train across town and was heading to Mo's.

She hit hands-free and dialled Ian. She hadn't heard from him since he'd gone for his interview with Carl. Maybe he was back at the office, with the constables. She should have gone inside. She was his line manager: she owed it to him to check how his interview had gone.

"This is DS Ian Osman. I can't take y—"

She hung up. Where was he? It was almost seven, maybe he'd gone home.

She called the office.

"Boss, everything OK?"

"Connie, you still there?"

"Still trying to match that Facebook account to the address Rhodri gave me. What's up?"

"Is Ian there?"

"Haven't seen him since... well since he went with DI Whaley, boss."

"Hmm. OK, thanks. You get off home, I don't want you working too late."

Zoe's own interview had taken just under an hour. In the meantime she'd been to the brothel, driven out to Hall Green, and followed Gatiss to Solihull. She'd taken a detour via Northfield station and was now on the Bristol Road.

Three hours, almost four. If Ian still wasn't finished, did that mean he was in custody?

She hit the hands-free button.

"You know we can't talk right now," Carl said.

"Who's to say I'm calling about the investigation?"

"I know you, Zoe."

"OK. Two things. First, are we still going for a curry tonight? And second, has Ian been arrested?"

"First: no, have you seen the time? And second, what makes you think that?"

"He hasn't come back into the office."

"I'm not telling you anything about his interview, or about the investigation, Zoe."

"Just tell me what time his interview finished. I'm his line manager, you need to keep me informed."

"As you're also a subject of this investigation, we informed your senior officer."

Lesley was still in hospital. "David Randle," she said.

"Yes."

Zoe gripped the steering wheel. "Just tell me what time you let Ian go, and I'll get out of your hair."

"Four thirty pm."

"And he was free to go?"

"He was."

"OK." She hesitated.

"I'm not answering any more questions."

"Sorry. Shall we do that curry tomorrow, then? I can't stand another evening in the house with my mum."

"She still there?"

"God knows how I'm going to get rid of her."

"I'm sorry, but you know this is tricky for me. I've already had to talk to Detective Superintendent Rogers about a possible conflict of interest."

"It was interesting meeting him," Zoe said.

"There you go again. I'm not talking about the investigation with you. I shouldn't have taken this call."

"You couldn't resist me."

Zoe could hear the smile in his voice. "Maybe not. I'm sorry, Zoe, but I think we should keep away from each other till this is concluded."

"How long will that be?"

He sighed. "Again with the questions. I'll see you around, Zoe. I'll miss you."

"Yeah. Me too."

She turned off the Bristol Road and through the maze of houses that led to Mo's nondescript modern home. When she arrived, she parked and sat in the car for a few minutes, staring ahead into the night. The rain had stopped and streetlights reflected off the wet road. She could smell damp: it was getting into her car somewhere. Something for her to deal with when this case was done. She hoped that would be soon.

She heaved herself out of the car and pulled on a smile as she approached Mo's front door. He opened it, a tea towel in his hand and a smile on his face.

"Come in. I made biscuits."

"Biscuits? You only just got in from the airport."

"Fiona and Isla nagged me until it was easier to just do it

than it was to argue with them. Come on, you can dunk one in your coffee."

Zoe grimaced. The coffee Mo and his wife Catriona kept in was way too good to be ruined by dunked biscuits, even homemade ones.

She followed him into the bright kitchen. The worktops were littered with the detritus of baking. Flour dusted the surfaces, a rolling pin stuck out of the sink, and two trays of biscuits sat on a wire rack. Zoe leaned in and sniffed.

"Gingerbread. Not bad."

Mo nodded. "Nothing but the best here."

Catriona came in, her youngest daughter clinging to her arm.

"Hey, Cat, hey, Isla," Zoe said. The girl gave her a shy smile.

"Don't mind me, I'm just getting this one to bed. She won't go without a biscuit. And if she has one, her sister has to have one too."

"They're still hot," said Mo.

Catriona laughed. "What does that matter, when you're ten?"

She grabbed a couple of the biscuits and handed one to Isla, who shovelled it into her mouth then gasped at the heat.

"Serves you right," said Mo. He kissed his daughter on the cheek and watched as her mum took her out of the room.

Zoe leaned on the kitchen island. Mo brought the coffee maker out of a cupboard and started spooning coffee into the top.

"So," he said. "Tell me what happened at the brothel."

She recounted the events of the evening to him: checking the brothel with Rhodri, Kyle Gatiss coming out, following him to the Belvista Hotel, the woman he'd brought out, and then losing him on the way out of the city.

"Where d'you think he was going?" Mo asked.

"Maybe another brothel, maybe a safe house. Maybe Hamm's got a new place, or one of the other bastards he's in league with. Fancy houses out that way, their kind of thing."

"Robert Oulman lived in Solihull," Mo said.

Oulman was one of the three men they'd arrested as part of the Canary investigation. A businessman who'd been involved in abusing children.

"He's in prison," Zoe said.

"Yeah. What about this Facebook account? You think the woman could be in the Belvista hotel?"

"She could be. Maybe it's where the women who were in Curton Road are based now. Place looked big enough."

Mo nodded. "I'll ask Sheila to check it out. Dawson wants me focused on the airport."

"What's new there?"

He handed her a mug of coffee. Zoe sipped, enjoying the smoothness slipping down her throat.

"That bag they found near the gate," Mo said. "DNA analysis is due back tomorrow morning. The prints didn't give a match but you never know. And we've got CCTV. The camera inside the airport on that spot had been tampered with, but we managed to get something from a nearby house."

"Oh?"

"It's not clear, and trees obscure most of it. But it looks like a group of people left the airport not long after the explosion and got out via that gate. Two vans left the scene, both with people in."

"Who?"

"We can't tell. But there were people missing from that Wizz Air plane. Women and children."

Zoe felt a chill grip her. "Where did they go?"

Mo shrugged and stared back at her. "Seven kids, and six women, and we have no idea."

She shook her head. She knew this already. She'd been at the briefings.

"I still don't get how they were there at the right time though," Mo said.

"Maybe it's unrelated. Maybe they were going to get them off that plane, and the explosion just made it easier."

"It's a hell of a coincidence."

"What about the location of the explosion? Did Adi have anything more on that?"

"Definitely in the hold."

Zoe stared up at the ceiling. "So not planted by someone who cut through the fence then."

"Nope," Mo replied.

"So who?"

CHAPTER SIXTY-NINE

Zoe kicked her front door shut with her foot. She'd had a text from Nicholas saying he was going out with Zaf, so she'd stayed at Mo's to eat dinner with him and Catriona. It had been an awkward meal: she'd wanted to talk about the case but Mo and his wife had a rule of never talking shop at dinner.

She walked into the living room and dropped her bag on the floor. Two people sat on the sofa.

"What are you doing here?" she asked.

Jim glanced at her mum and stood up. "I wanted to talk to you."

She shook her head and walked past him to the kitchen, where she switched the kettle on. Inspector Jim McManus: Nicholas's dad. He ignored her and her son when it suited him, but liked to poke his nose in when it didn't suit her.

"Is this about the Digbeth Ripper?" She stood with her back to him, watching the kettle. She didn't want to drink instant after the premium roast she'd enjoyed at Mo's, but didn't have the energy to set a proper pot going.

"He told me he's scared. Being in Birmingham. Wants to go to university as soon as he can. Did he tell you he's applied to Stirling?"

She turned to him. "That wasn't on his list."

"You saw his list of preferences?"

"He wouldn't show me. *Damn*. He changed them."

"Stirling's a long way away," Jim said.

"It's his life," she said. "If he wants to go to Scotland, then good for him." She had no idea what the Psychology course at Stirling University was like, Nicholas hadn't even been to an open day there.

"Did he put that first?" she asked.

"That's what he tells me."

"He might just be trying to piss you off. I'll talk to him when he gets home."

"Where is he? I've been here a couple of hours, and he hasn't returned my texts."

"He's out with his boyfriend."

"Zaf? Is that wise?"

Zoe stared at him. "Zaf is a great kid. He loves Nicholas." She ignored the look of doubt that crossed Jim's face. "I can't think of anyone I'd rather have him going out with."

Jim raised his palms. "Alright, alright. But maybe hanging around with the other kid who was attacked just brings back memories."

"Zaf isn't the *other kid*. He's Nicholas's boyfriend. He's the brother of one of my officers."

"I did wonder how they met."

"Well, now you know." The kettle clicked behind her. Zoe turned to it and poured water over the coffee granules.

Jim leaned against the fridge. The kitchen was tiny,

barely enough space for the two of them. "I heard what happened."

She sipped her coffee. "Be more specific."

"The airport thing."

"The airport thing," she said. "You mean the Professional Standards investigation into whether a member of Force CID planted evidence."

"Not just Force CID."

"Half of Birmingham could be involved in this one."

"But you don't think so." He folded his arms across his chest.

"I'm not talking about this with you, Jim."

"Zoe. I know you struggle for cash, with being a single mum. If you decided to take some money, it wouldn't be all that sur—"

She threw out her hand and clamped it over his mouth. "Don't you say another word. I would never take dirty money, Jim. If you don't know that about me, you know nothing. Have you told Nicholas you think I might be capable of this kind of thing?"

He pulled her hand off. "Course not. And I don't really think you..." He shook his head. "Let me know if you need financial help, yes?"

She put down her coffee before she was tempted to throw it in his face. "I think you should leave now. I'll tell Nicholas you were looking for him."

"Zoe, don't be—"

"This is my house, and I want to go to bed. Just leave, before I do something I regret."

He cocked his head at her. She wanted to punch him. But he was the father of her son, and a police officer. She clenched and unclenched her fists, her gaze steady on his face.

"Fair enough." He turned and walked out of the kitchen, crashing into her mum who was standing on the other side of the doorway.

Zoe glared at her. "What are you doing there?"

Annette blushed. "Just coming to make myself a cocoa."

"Since when did you drink cocoa?" Annette's idea of a nightcap was something considerably stronger.

Annette shrugged. "Sorry." She shuffled back into the living room. Zoe gave her a *stay there* look while she showed Jim to the door.

When he'd gone, she went into the living room. Her coffee was still in the kitchen. She didn't want it.

"He seemed like a good man," Annette said. "Cares about Nicholas."

"You have no idea what he cares about, Mum. There's a reason I've kept the two of you apart all these years." She couldn't be bothered explaining any of this to her mum. "I'm going to bed."

CHAPTER SEVENTY

Zoe walked into the briefing room to find Ian sitting at the back.

"Where did you get to yesterday?" she asked, trying not to sound as if she was accusing him of something.

"You wanted me to find the account holder, the woman who got that photo. I went to the address."

"You spoke to Connie?"

"Got it off the board. Everyone had gone by then."

Zoe frowned. "When was this?"

He shrugged. "Just before seven. The address was in Ladywood, Curton Road. It was empty, all dark."

Where had he been, then, in the hours after his interview with Carl had ended?

"I already went there, with Rhodri," Zoe said. "I tried calling you."

"Sorry. Low signal."

"You should have called me back."

"Boss, I was knackered." He lowered his voice. "Alison

laid into me when I got home, I missed a special dinner for the kids. I was distracted."

She sniffed. "How is Alison?"

"OK. Ollie's better than he was, he's back at school full time."

"That's good. Is Alison working again?"

Ian nodded, then pointed as the door opened and Randle came in. The room had filled up while they'd been talking. Mo was at the front with Dawson and there were more people Zoe didn't recognise from the anti-terror unit. Sheila Griffin was behind Mo, making notes on a pad.

The door opened again and Lesley walked in. A ripple ran through the room.

Lesley walked towards Randle, gave him a curt nod, and sat down beside him. She had a dressing on her neck, much smaller than the one she'd been wearing when Zoe visited her, and carried her head stiffly. Her eyes looked glazed.

Zoe wished she wasn't back here, so far away. She waited as Lesley's eyes roamed the room then landed on her and stopped. Her boss gave her a tight smile and she smiled back.

"How are you?" Zoe mouthed. Lesley shrugged.

Randle stood up. He turned to Lesley, a smile on his face.

"Before we start, I'd like to welcome DCI Clarke back. The doctors didn't want her coming back so soon, but well..." he turned to the room, "... you know Lesley."

Applause broke out. Lesley acknowledged it with a tight smile and a nod of her head. "Let's just bloody get on with it, eh? Got some terrorists to catch."

A ripple of laughter. Lesley widened her eyes and the room went quiet. As Randle turned on his laptop, she leaned behind him and shook hands with Detective Superintendent Silton.

CHAPTER SEVENTY

"Right, folks," she said. "Bring me up to speed."

Randle leaned towards Lesley and whispered in her ear. She nodded and sat back in her chair, crossing her legs. She gave Zoe a nod.

"Zoe, let's get this out of the way," said Randle. "How are we doing with identifying the New Street bomber?"

Zoe cleared her throat. "We found a selfie that she sent to a friend via Facebook. She took it on her way to the scene."

"On Saturday?"

"It was sent at two fifty-three pm."

"When did you find this?" Randle asked.

"Yesterday afternoon."

"And you're only telling us now?"

"We spent the rest of yesterday following it up. We traced the account holder to a brothel on Curton Road that DS Uddin's been investigating along with DS Griffin from the Organised Crime division."

"Did you speak to her?" asked Lesley.

"No, ma'am. The brothel was cleared out a few days ago."

"Any idea why?" Randle asked.

Zoe looked across the room at Mo.

"No idea," Mo said. "But they didn't leave in a hurry. It was planned, thorough."

"Because they knew you were watching them," Randle said.

"I believe if that had been the case, they would have been less neat. They didn't leave in a hurry."

"And there *was* nothing left behind," said Zoe. "No personal effects, no clothing. But when DC Hughes and I went to the site yesterday, we saw a man there."

"Who?" asked Randle. He leaned forward.

"Kyle Gatiss," Zoe replied. "If I may?"

Randle nodded and Zoe went to the front of the room. She held up a photo of Gatiss that Connie had printed.

"Kyle Gatiss, twenty-eight years old, no permanent residence. He was a person of interest in the Canary investigation, although we didn't find grounds to prosecute. He's a known associate of Trevor Hamm, Jory Shand, Howard Petersen and Robert Oulman. Oulman is currently serving a prison term. Shand and Petersen got suspended sentences, but Hamm is – well, we were unable to prosecute him either."

"You think Hamm was behind the brothel?" Lesley asked.

"It makes sense. We've suspected him of being involved in organised prostitution before."

"We don't have firm evidence though," said Randle. "Just one of his associates being sighted at a house that DS Uddin was watching."

"We followed him, sir," Zoe said. "To an address in Hall Green. The Belvista Hotel."

"So?"

Zoe shrugged. "It's just a theory right now, sir. But there may be a woman in that hotel who knew the bomber. We need to find her, and speak to her, if we're going to find out who was behind the attack."

"It's all very tenuous," said Randle. He looked at Silton, who nodded.

"The bar is high in a case like this," Silton said. "By all means observe the hotel, but you won't get a warrant to go in."

Zoe's shoulders dropped.

CHAPTER SEVENTY

"We've got information that might change your mind," said Dawson.

Randle turned to him. "You're working the airport."

"Yes, sir. There's a gate that was cut through with wire cutters, near the runway."

"A long way from the plane with the bomb," replied Randle.

"Now we know that our original suspect isn't in the frame, we've been focusing on this gate. We think someone connected to the explosion gained access this way, or used it to leave the scene."

"Go on."

"We've obtained camera footage, from a nearby house. The CCTV from the airport had been tampered with."

"Suspicious in itself," said Lesley.

"Let's not jump to conclusions," said Randle.

"The video shows people leaving the airport via that gate," said Dawson. "Twenty minutes after the explosion. We think it accounts for the missing women and children from the Wizz Air flight."

"Hang on," said Silton. "The Wizz Air flight was from Romania, not Pakistan."

"I know, sir," said Dawson. He pulled at his tie. "But those people are still missing. And we've got images of people we think might be them leaving the area in a van."

"Show us," said Randle.

Dawson nodded at Mo, who approached Randle with a USB stick. Randle took it off him and plugged it into the port on his laptop.

The room sat in silence as they watched indistinct images of unidentifiable people, largely concealed by trees. They seemed to be climbing through something and then getting onto two vans, which drove away.

"These images are crap," said Lesley. "They aren't solid evidence."

"No," said Mo, "but we also have forensics."

Lesley turned her gaze on Adi. "Come on then, Adi. Complete the picture."

Adi walked to the front and brought up a photo on the screen.

"This is the gate that was cut through. There was little in the way of forensics on it, we tried to identify the brand of cutter but the cuts were too rough. And the tarmac in the area meant no usable footprints. It had been dry, so no mud transferring from footwear."

"Something gives me the feeling that's not all you've got for us," said Lesley.

Adi nodded. He clicked the mouse and another image came up. "This handbag was left near the gate."

Lesley raised an eyebrow. "A terrorist who drops her handbag?"

Dawson raised a hand. "Wait till you hear this."

Adi glanced at him. "We found fingerprints on the bag, but none of them matched anything on file. But we did find some hair inside, and we've analysed the DNA."

"Well, put us out of our misery, then," said Lesley. Beside her, Randle was quiet. Ian shuffled in his chair.

"There are two distinct sets of hair," Adi said. "One from a woman with short dark hair, and the other from a man, with light brown hair. The woman was nowhere in the database. But the man was." He brought up a close-up of the hair follicle and pointed at it. "This hair belongs to Trevor Hamm."

Someone at the back whistled. Zoe exchanged glances with Mo, whose eyes gleamed. It still didn't make sense, but the forensics wouldn't lie. They had a link between the New Street and airport attacks. Zoe clenched her fist on her knee: this was the breakthrough they needed.

"Sir," she said, looking at Randle. "Does this change my chances of getting a warrant to search that hotel?"

"I can't tell you that yet, DI Finch."

"But—"

"Don't rush me. We still don't understand if there *is* a link between the Wizz Air flight and the Pakistan Airways flight."

"There's something else, sir," Sheila said.

Randle stared at her. "What?"

"A man we were tracking, who we suspected might be behind a new gang. Umar Abidi. Pakistani national, working through members of the community in Birmingham. We found out this morning he was on the flight."

"The one from Karachi?"

Sheila nodded. "We've been working with Pakistani intelligence, as far as we can. He was on it, but he's disappeared."

"You think Abidi had something to do with the bomb?"

"Not with planting it, sir. But he could have been the intended target."

"A whole plane, for one man?"

Sheila looked drawn. "The international gangs can be brutal."

"So where is he now?" Randle leaned forwards.

"Like I say, gone. Probably back to Pakistan."

Randle shook his head. "Follow it up. Find out where he is. And keep me informed, yes?"

"Sir." Sheila looked at Mo. "But the two groups, they could have been working together. Trevor Hamm would have wanted Abidi out of the picture."

"You think Hamm's capable of something like this?"

"Honestly, I don't. He's too small-time for that kind of thing. But he could have been working with whoever was behind it."

Randle stood up. "All of you, carry on as you are and wait for further instructions."

Zoe watched as Lesley sat back in her chair, her face pale. She looked tired. She turned to Randle. Was she going to challenge him?

Zoe waited but Lesley said nothing. Randle strode out of the room, Silton at his heels.

The room was abuzz, people discussing the consequences of what they'd just heard. Lesley stood up.

"Oi! Calm down everyone, and show some bloody professionalism. You heard what the man said. Get on with it."

Zoe walked to the door with Ian, who wasn't meeting her eye. He kept tugging at his fingernails.

Connie was in the corridor, shifting from foot to foot, biting her lip.

"Boss!" she cried when Zoe emerged.

"You've heard," Zoe said.

"Heard what?"

"Come on. I'll fill you and Rhodri in."

Connie shook her head. "No, it's not that. I've got something you want to see. We've got the man on camera. Close up."

"Which man?"

"The man who shoved the bomber off the escalator."

CHAPTER SEVENTY-ONE

Sofia had spent the night in the same bed as Trevor. She slept badly, flinching every time he moved.

At last he woke and left the bed. She stared up at the dark ceiling as he showered in the en-suite. When he emerged, she turned towards the window and pretended to be asleep. She only allowed herself to breathe again when he'd gone downstairs.

She was a prisoner here. This house was luxurious, she'd been overwhelmed by the soft carpets and plush curtains when she'd arrived. Mrs Brooking cooked her delicious food, even if it wasn't always the kind of food she really wanted, and did all the washing and cleaning. Trevor gave her money to buy clothes she would never have dreamed of wearing at home.

But none of that changed the fact that she couldn't leave. Yesterday she'd had to hide in the boot of a car to do something as simple as look for her sister. When she'd questioned Trevor about the children on Sunday, he'd locked her in the spare room.

He had her passport. He had her credit cards. She was trapped.

She smelled cooking from downstairs: Mrs Brooking making Trevor his favourite breakfast of eggs and bacon. It would kill him one day, all the greasy food he ate. She sniffed the air, pushing down the nausea in her stomach.

The front door slammed. Sofia turned to look up at the ceiling, her heart pounding. She slid out of bed and went to the window. This room was at the back of the house, overlooking the long garden and the pond full of koi carp. The window was locked.

She pressed her ear to the glass and heard a car engine. Trevor was leaving. He was going to work.

What now? Could she get past Mrs Brooking, escape from here? If she did, where would she go?

She couldn't do anything in her nightdress. She walked to the bathroom and turned on the shower, glad of the hot water on her skin. She closed her eyes as it washed over her, trying not to cry.

She could see her sister's face in her mind. At home, when she'd told her she was leaving for England. That she'd find a way to bring her here, too. Two nights ago, across the table at dinner. Andreea was feisty, rebellious. She fought with their dad non-stop. At dinner on Monday she'd been subdued. She'd sat with her hands in her lap, barely speaking unless she was asked a direct question. She'd kept glancing at Trevor the way a frightened dog looks at its owner.

What had Trevor done to her, to make her like that?

Sofia stepped out of the shower. She pulled on jeans and a sweater and crept downstairs. She had to get past Mrs Brooking. She knew the city was to the north, she'd paid attention when Kyle had driven her places. The airport was

CHAPTER SEVENTY-ONE

the other way, not far. Could she run there, get herself a plane ticket? Could she tell the authorities she'd been kept prisoner?

They'd never believe her. If they saw this house, if they spoke to Trevor. Mrs Brooking would back him up, so would Kyle.

She was never leaving.

Sofia lowered herself to the bottom step, her head in her hands. She wanted to die.

She jerked her head up as the front door opened. She leaned back, nervous.

It was Trevor. He grunted as he saw her on the stairs.

"What are you doing there?"

"Nothing." She stood up. "Is everything OK?" Trevor never came home this soon after going to work.

"Come with me," he said. "You can see your sister."

CHAPTER SEVENTY-TWO

Zoe followed Connie along the corridor, pushing past the people who'd spilled out of the briefing room.

"Do you recognise him?" she asked.

Connie looked back at her and nodded.

"Who?" Zoe asked.

"You should see for yourself."

Zoe jabbed her fingernails into her thigh, frustrated. She passed Mo, who gave her a puzzled look.

"Connie's found something," she said. "Come on."

"I've got to follow up the airport lead," he said. "Dawson wants me questioning people."

"This won't take a minute."

Mo looked up and down the corridor. Dawson was nowhere to be seen.

"OK then," he said. "But make it quick."

Ian gave him an irritated look, which Zoe chose to let go. Ian was jealous of Mo. He knew as well as she did which sergeant she'd rather have on her team.

They hurried into the team room. Rhodri was at the board, pinning up a photo. He stood back, grinning.

"Boss."

Zoe nodded at him, and approached the board. She took down the photo.

"Where did you get this?" she asked.

"The hotline," Connie said. "A woman sent it in."

"Why did she wait this long?"

"She was using a film camera. Only just had it developed."

Zoe stared at the photo. "Who uses film these days?"

"She's a professional photographer," Rhodri said. "She said this was from a RAW file, whatever that is."

"It means it's uncompressed," said Connie. "Easier to blow it up as big as we need."

Zoe nodded. She handed the photo to Mo.

"He gets around, doesn't he?" she said. Mo passed the photo to Ian, who looked at it but said nothing.

The photo was of a man on the escalators. He stood behind the woman in the green headscarf, his eyes on the back of her head, his expression intense.

He wore the grey hoody and black baseball cap they'd seen in the CCTV images, but the quality of this photo meant they could see his scarred cheeks and the nose that had clearly been broken more than once.

Zoe looked up. "Now we'll get our warrant," she said.

She pinned the photo to the board and eyed it. "Kyle Gatiss, you have been a busy boy."

CHAPTER SEVENTY-THREE

Zoe hurried back to the briefing room. The corridors were quiet now, people busy with their separate parts of the investigation.

She threw the door open to find Lesley sitting alone at the front, her hands clasped between her thighs.

"Boss?" Zoe ran towards her. "Are you OK?"

Lesley looked up. "Zoe." She drew her hands up and shook them out. "I'm fine. What's up?"

"There was a man, at New Street Station. He was behind the bomber on the escalator, he shoved her off it."

Lesley raised an eyebrow. "And you've just identified him."

Zoe slumped back. "How did you know?"

"I don't get to do this job without knowing when a member of my team's so excited she looks like her knickers might fall off. Who is he?"

"Kyle Gatiss."

Lesley nodded, her eyebrows raised. "The same Kyle Gatiss you saw at the brothel."

CHAPTER SEVENTY-THREE

"The same Kyle Gatiss who works for Trevor Hamm."

"It's a link, Zoe, but not the strongest one. The brothel, for starters..."

"Someone was living there who knew the bomber."

Lesley raised a hand. She winced. Zoe leaned in but Lesley waved her away.

"You've got a Facebook account, and a selfie. That's not enough."

"Ma'am. I'm sure if we bring him in for questioning, what he says'll help us connect the two attacks."

Lesley shook her head. She stood up. "He'll get lawyered up. That Startshaw bugger. And he'll say nothing. You can't bring him in, it'll just scare them off."

"What, then?"

"The woman with the Facebook account. She might just talk to you, if you can track her down."

"She gave her address as Curton Road. She isn't there anymore."

"But you think she's at this Belvista place."

"It's a possibility."

Lesley sat down again. She took a few deep breaths. "Shit, Zoe. I probably shouldn't be here."

"Ma'am?" Zoe stared at her boss, her skin cold. It wasn't like the DCI to show weakness.

Lesley screwed her eyes shut then opened them again. "Forget I said that." She looked into Zoe's face. "You tell no one, alright?"

"Of course I won't. How can I help?"

"Walk with me, back to my office. If I need support, I'll put a hand on your shoulder. Don't do anything obvious, just take my weight if I need you to."

"No problem."

Lesley gave her a thin smile. "Thanks." She stood and walked to the door. "There, that wasn't all so bad."

Zoe followed her boss to the door and opened it. She walked along the corridor towards Lesley's office, hoping Randle wouldn't be in it. Twice, Lesley slowed and placed a hand on Zoe's shoulder. "Keep walking," she hissed. Zoe walked slowly, careful not to make it obvious she was helping her boss. The strength she'd built up through years of karate made it easy to bear Lesley's weight.

As they approached Lesley's office, Ian appeared from round a corner. He had his phone in his hand, held out as if he were in the middle of a call. He gave Zoe a wary look and nodded at the DCI.

"Sergeant Osman," Lesley said. "I trust you've been behaving yourself."

He stiffened. "Yes, ma'am."

Lesley chuckled. "Don't let me keep you from your work."

They reached the office and Zoe opened the door. David Randle was behind the desk, his hands clasped behind his head. He looked deep in thought.

"David," Lesley said.

Randle stood and rounded the desk. He grasped Lesley's arm and a frown crossed her face.

"Lesley, take a seat. I'm worried about you."

"Don't be." Lesley lowered herself into her chair. "Good to have my office back." She gave Randle a pointed look.

He nodded. "Of course. I'll let you get settled in. I'll be back in half an hour or so, I can brief you."

"See you then."

Randle raised an eyebrow at Zoe as he left the room. Lesley leaned back in her chair.

"Right." She opened a drawer. "Let's hope he hasn't nicked my fucking biscuits." She brought out a pack of shortbread. "Pah. All that's left." She looked at the door. "Not much I can do though is there, DI Finch?"

"Ma'am."

Lesley held out the packet and Zoe took a biscuit. She watched as Lesley ate two then wiped crumbs off her hands.

"Right," Lesley said. "Let's work out a plan of attack. We need to get you into that hotel to talk to your Facebook woman."

"Ana-Maria."

'That's the one. D'you know what she looks like?"

"'Fraid not."

"Surely her account has got photos on it, selfies?"

"Nothing."

"Well that's odd for starters. You sure Connie can't dig anything up?"

"With respect, ma'am, it's a private account."

Lesley waved a hand, sending a biscuit flying into the corner. "I know, Zoe. Procedure, by the book. That's me." She fingered the back of her neck. "That was before." She sighed. "OK, you don't need a warrant to knock on the door. You can ask if anyone knew the bomber. Take a photo with you. No one's going to tell you the truth, but you might spot something. These missing women and children, for starters."

"The hotel's big enough for them to be living there."

"And if Hamm's got them, they need getting out of there as soon as possible."

"I'll talk to DS Griffin. She can put surveillance on the house."

"Do that. But don't wait. If there's kids in there, we need

to get them out as soon as we can." Lesley closed her eyes. "Poor buggers."

Zoe nodded. She knew from the Canary case what happened to children that these men got their hands on. Four days had passed: plenty of time.

"I'll keep you posted, ma'am."

"You do that." Lesley flashed her a weary smile. "It's good to be back, Zoe."

CHAPTER SEVENTY-FOUR

The Hotel Belvista was a large but shabby building on a wide road in Hall Green. It looked more dilapidated now, in daylight, than it had when they'd followed Gatiss here.

Zoe knew that being alone with Ian wasn't wise, given Carl's investigation. But after his disappearing act yesterday, she wanted to keep an eye on him. And the constables had social media feeds to trawl through. So she'd insisted he come along with her.

Zoe knocked on the front door and a woman in her fifties with dyed red hair and grey roots opened the door.

"Yeah?" She had a strong Scottish accent.

Zoe held up her ID. "DI Finch and DS Osman. We're trying to identify this woman." She showed her the picture of the bomber.

The woman didn't look at the photo. "Never seen her in my life."

"She's a suspect in a murder inquiry," Ian said. The woman gave him a look of contempt.

"You deaf or something? I don't know her." She started to push the door closed.

"Let them in," said a male voice out of sight behind the door. The woman turned.

"They're police," she said. "Looking for some woman. Nothing to do with us."

"No reason we can't help them with their enquiries."

The woman gave Zoe and Ian a long look then pulled the door open. "Come in."

"Thank you."

Zoe walked past the woman, expecting to see the man waiting for them. The hallway was empty.

There was a double flight of stairs ahead, one set leading up and one down to a basement. She could hear women's voices from upstairs.

She turned back to the woman. "We believe that someone who knows this woman lives here. Are you sure you don't recognise her?"

"Positive." The woman ignored the photo once again. "Wait there."

The woman walked down the stairs to the basement, her footsteps heavy. Zoe watched her disappear then looked back at Ian, who was examining the hallway. It was a narrow space, with no natural light and a smell of boiling cabbage mixed with sweat.

"Doesn't look like we're going to get much help here," Ian said.

"They let us in, didn't they? Let's see what happens."

The woman trudged back up the stairs. She sniffed. "Follow me."

Zoe gave Ian an *I told you so* look and followed the

woman along a corridor. She took them into a dingy living room lined with threadbare armchairs. A gas fire was turned off in the corner. Zoe shivered.

"Wait here." The woman left the room.

CHAPTER SEVENTY-FIVE

TREVOR SAT in the back of the car, holding Sofia's hand. A man she didn't recognise was driving. Not Kyle, not Adam.

He stroked the skin on the back of her hand. "It's going to be alright," he said to her. His voice was low.

She stared back at him, her stomach clenched. She nodded. If she spoke, she'd cry.

They drove along country lanes, ones she recognised from the times Kyle or Adam had driven her into the city centre. After fifteen minutes they were in the city, houses and shops rising up around them. Sofia gazed out of the window, wondering if she'd be allowed to go shopping again. Her trips into town had been an opportunity to get away from the monotony of the house. But now Trevor didn't trust her...

Or maybe he did, if he was taking her to Andreea. Maybe she'd be allowed to bring her sister home. Or at least visit her.

She looked across at Trevor. He was muttering into his phone, his face creased with anger. He snapped something she didn't understand and shoved the phone into his lap. He stopped stroking her hand and grabbed it. She tried to pull it away but he only tightened his grip.

Her throat was tight. She stared at the man in the front. This was no happy reunion. Trevor didn't trust her, and she shouldn't trust him.

So if he wasn't taking her to Andreea, where was he taking her?

They turned into a wide road with large houses that made her think of some of the wealthier areas of Bucharest. The houses were broad and tall, but not as smart as Trevor's mansion in the countryside.

The car slowed and they turned into a driveway. Trevor put a hand on the door handle. Sofia opened her door and stepped out.

There were two cars in the drive ahead of them. A blue Volvo and a green Mini. Sofia wondered whose they were.

The door to the house was shut. It looked the same as it had yesterday, except today the sun was shining. She hoped that was a good sign.

She heard Trevor's voice from the car. "Back here, now!"

She turned.

He was staring ahead, at the cars. He stepped out of the car, standing between the car and the open door.

"Is she here?" Sofia asked. "Andreea?"

"No. Get back in the car."

Sofia took a look up at the house. There was movement on the second floor, a window reflecting sunlight as it closed. She swallowed.

If Andreea wasn't here, then this place would lead her to her. She walked to the door and turned back to look at Trevor.

Trevor was inside the car. He'd closed his door. The

driver was out of the car, advancing on her. He had his arms in front of him, like he was about to grab her.

Sofia ran to the door and slammed into it. It opened and she fell through, almost crashing onto the floor.

The hallway was empty. Sofia regained her balance and ran up the stairs, calling Andreea's name.

CHAPTER SEVENTY-SIX

Zoe walked to the far end of the room and pulled the curtain aside, rubbing the dirt off her hands onto her jeans immediately afterwards. They were in a corner room, windows facing the side and back of the house. At the back was an overgrown garden, rubbish bags piled up to one side and the concrete of what might once have been a patio cracked and pockmarked.

"Nice place," she said. "Can't imagine they get many tourists."

"No." Ian sat in one of the armchairs, releasing a cloud of dust. "Christ."

Zoe wandered round the room, taking in its details. There were two cheap looking pictures on the wall that reminded her of her mum's house, and a chest of drawers under a window. She pulled out a drawer: it was empty. There was no TV, no sign of anyone spending time in here.

"This is ridiculous," she said. They'd been waiting fifteen minutes. She approached the door.

Her phone rang. "DI Finch."

"Zoe, you need to get back here." It was Lesley. "Detective Superintendent Rogers wants to talk to you again."

A stone sank in Zoe's stomach.

"And if you've got Ian with you, bring him too."

She turned to Ian and placed a hand on the phone. "Professional Standards want to talk to us again."

He paled. "What about?"

She removed her hand from the phone. "D'you know what it's about, ma'am?"

"That's not the sort of thing you ask Professional Standards, DI Finch. Just get back here. I'll talk to Dawson, get someone from his team to go to the hotel."

"Yes, ma'am."

Zoe hung up and went to the door. She turned the handle. "*Shit.*"

"What's up?" Ian said.

"They've locked us in."

"Here." He came up behind her and grabbed the door handle, turning it a couple of times. He put his shoulder to the door and gave it a shove.

Zoe raised an eyebrow at him. "See? Locked."

"Hmm." He retreated to his chair and sat down, slowly this time.

Zoe banged on the door. It rattled on its hinges.

"We could bust it down easily enough, if we wanted to," Ian said.

"Well let's."

"Why don't you try knocking first?"

She banged on the door again. She put her mouth close to the wood, careful not to make contact, and called out.

CHAPTER SEVENTY-SIX

"Hey! Unlock this door!"

Ian laughed. "You think that's going to make any difference?"

She walked to his chair. He picked at his fingernails. "You don't seem very bothered by this," she said.

He shrugged. "Maybe they don't want us poking around the place while we wait."

"They've imprisoned us, Ian. It's an offence."

He shook his head and leaned back, then shifted forward. "Let's just wait."

"No." Zoe returned to the door and rattled it, hoping the hinges might give up. The door loosened but didn't give. She pounded on it again. She didn't call out: no point.

She heard someone running past.

"Let us out!" she called. "We've been locked in."

The footsteps slowed then picked up pace.

"Stop!" Zoe called. "Let us out!"

There were more footsteps, coming from along the corridor. It sounded like an avalanche of feet making their way down the stairs, heading out of the building.

She turned back to Ian. "They're clearing the place out."

"Like they did the Curton Road house."

"Except this time it sounds like they're in a hurry."

He looked back at her, his face calm. From upstairs, now, she could hear shouts: confused, afraid and angry.

"We need to get out of here before they remove any evidence," she said. "Help me with this bloody door."

"Why don't you just phone for backup?" he asked.

"Oh yeah," she replied. "Sorry we can't come and talk to Professional Standards but we've been locked in a room. No chance."

"Fair enough."

Ian pushed up from his chair and stood beside her. The two of them leaned into the door, pushing as hard as they could.

CHAPTER SEVENTY-SEVEN

Sofia buried herself in the cupboard she'd hidden in the day before, listening for signs of Trevor or his driver coming after her.

After a few minutes, she relaxed. They hadn't followed her.

She pushed the door open a crack and listened. She could hear people running, thundering footsteps on the floors above her. Women were shouting in Romanian.

Sofia's stomach fluttered. She pushed the door open and slid out. She was in the laundry room, washing machines rumbling away next to her.

She heard someone run past the door and shrank back. The footsteps didn't slow or stop.

Maybe Andreea would be here this time. Maybe Trevor hadn't been lying about that.

She opened the door to the corridor, holding her breath. The corridor was quiet. She checked in both directions then ran towards the stairs.

A woman came out of a door and ran towards her, gesticulating. "Come on!" she said in Romanian. "We have to leave."

Sofia followed the woman up the stairs to the ground floor. Women were running down the stairs from the upper floors, tumbling out of the front door. They carried boxes, bin bags, bedding. It was like an evacuation.

"Where's the fire?" she asked.

A woman turned to her. "No fire. Police."

"Police?"

She ran with the women out onto the driveway. Trevor's car had gone. The two cars she'd seen when she arrived were still there.

She looked back at the house. Women continued to pour out of the door. Were the children here too? There was no sign of them.

She grabbed the nearest woman by the arm. "Have you seen seven children? Between ten and twelve years old, four boys and three girls."

The woman gave her a hard look. "They've gone."

"What do you mean, they've gone?"

"She took them, just a few minutes ago."

"Who did?"

The woman turned to another woman. She muttered something to her and the second woman laughed.

"Crazy woman," said the second woman, tall with blonde hair piled on top of her head and a bruise on her arm.

"Yeah, with mad black hair and holes in her tights," said the first woman.

Sofia felt tears come to her eyes. "What was her name?"

"Don't ask me. Never spoke to her, she was nuts."

"Where did she take them?"

The woman with the bruise leaned in. "There's a rumour."

"What rumour?"

"She was taking them home. Back to Romania."

"That's stupid," Sofia said. How would Andreea take a group of seven kids home?

The woman shrugged. "Just what I heard."

"She told me she was going to the airport." Another woman, wearing a red hoody with a hole in the sleeve, turned to them. "Good luck to her, is what I say. No kids should have to do this."

"Do what?" Sofia asked.

The red hoody woman looked her up and down. "You're her, aren't you?"

"Come on, ladies! All in the vans." An older woman with dyed red hair was sending the women towards two dark vans that had pulled up on the pavement. The same ones from the airport?

"Do any of you have any money?" Sofia asked the women. "Do you work here?"

The woman with the bruise laughed. "You really are her, aren't you? You need to leave us, before someone hurts you."

Sofia frowned. Why would they want to hurt her?

The woman she'd spoken to yesterday pushed through the crowd. "You're back. I told you to get lost."

"She's looking for money, Ana-Maria."

"She's got a sense of humour. Get lost, if you know what's good for you. Go back to your precious boyfriend."

"Do you work for him?"

"Yes, we work for him. On our backs. What d'you think we do?"

Sofia stared at the woman. She'd suspected Trevor was

exploiting the women, but maybe by making them work in a clothes factory or a shop. Not as prostitutes.

"I'm sorry," she breathed.

"Sorry," barked the woman in the hoody. "Well that makes it alright then."

"Oi, get a move on!" the woman by the vans shouted. The women turned towards her.

"Don't go with her," Sofia called after them. "You can get away. You can overpower them."

The woman called Ana-Maria turned to her. "They've got our passports, *iubuta*. What are we supposed to do?"

CHAPTER SEVENTY-EIGHT

The door fell open on the third attempt. Zoe ran out into the hallway, looking up and down to see who'd locked them in.

"What'd she do that for?" Ian panted. "It's not as if we couldn't have called for help."

Zoe ran to the main door. It was closed but not locked. Outside, the driveway was empty, just her and Ian's cars standing in front of the building.

In the entrance hall, a sponge bag had been dropped by the door and a chair had been pushed over.

She considered calling out, then thought better of it. Ian opened a nearby door.

"There's an office in here," he said. "No one about."

Zoe followed him in. The office held two shabby desks and three chairs that looked like they might fall apart if she sat on them.

Ian opened the drawers to one of the desks. "Search through that paperwork," Zoe said.

"We don't have a warrant," Ian replied.

"They locked two police officers in while they made off. We have grounds for search, Ian. Just empty the drawers, tell me what you find."

He put up his hands. "Fair enough. But where is everyone?"

Zoe picked up the phone on the desk and got a dial tone. "I thought you might be able to tell me that."

Ian looked her in the eye. "No idea, boss."

She held his gaze. "I'm going upstairs, see if anyone's around. You search this floor. If you see the woman who locked us in, arrest her."

"I'll start with this lot first." He piled files on the desk and opened the next drawer.

Zoe looked at the stairs. Up or down? She'd heard feet above her head, when they'd been in that sitting room. She took the stairs two at a time, emerging onto a narrow corridor with doors leading off on both sides. At the far end was a fire escape.

She opened the first door. It led to a narrow bedroom containing a single bed and a scuffed chest of drawers. The duvet was crumpled and the drawers hung open.

"Someone left here in a hurry," she muttered. She pulled on gloves and checked the drawers: not quite empty. A t-shirt had been left in the top one and a pile of knickers in the one below.

Zoe dropped to the dusty floor and looked under the bed. There was a holdall. She pulled it out: empty.

She left the room and opened each door in turn. All of the bedrooms were similar: featureless rooms with nothing on the walls and single beds. If they were running a prostitution operation from here, this wasn't where the customers were coming.

CHAPTER SEVENTY-EIGHT

At the end of the corridor, she pushed the fire exit. It didn't budge. She leaned into it and pushed again. It was locked.

She ran downstairs. Ian was working through the ground floor, opening doors and checking rooms. She found him in a dining room.

"There's no one here, boss."

"Anything useful in the office?"

"Accounts, records of guests. All looks above board."

"It's a front. Has to be. Keep looking."

"I am. Have you called this in? We need Uniform looking for whoever left here."

"Apart from that woman, we don't know who any of them are or what they look like. We didn't see any vehicles."

"There were a lot of footsteps. They must have had a fleet of cars, or a minibus."

"I'll call it in. Can't see it doing much good." She grabbed her phone and called the operator at Harborne.

"Amanda, it's DI Finch. I'm with DS Osman at an address in Hall Green. Sixteen Jarman Road. A group of people left here in a hurry, and we need to track them down. Can you alert any cars in the area?"

"Do you have a description?"

"Mostly women, probably young. Travelling in a group. One of the women was in her fifties, with dyed red hair."

"I'll pass it on."

"Thanks."

Zoe shook her head at Ian as she hung up. "An unknown number of unknown people, travelling in one or more unknown vehicles. That's going to get us laughed at."

"Worth a try."

"Yeah." She eyed him. How many people had known

they were coming here? How many knew they'd traced Kyle Gatiss here?

Gatiss might have seen them. There had been a roomful of people in the briefing this morning. One of whom might have planted the evidence at the airport...

Zoe watched Ian as they passed through the downstairs rooms. He didn't seem nervous or guilty. She knew he had to maintain his cover while he was working for Carl, that he'd have to convince Hamm and his associates that he was bent. But this...?

"I'm going to take the other side of this floor," she said. "See if there are any more offices past that sitting room."

Ian nodded and Zoe walked out of the room. As she turned into the dingy hallway, she spotted movement further along. Someone was going into the sitting room they'd been trapped in.

Zoe looked back at Ian.

"Ian," she hissed. She gestured for him to follow her, and crept along the hallway. The door to the sitting room was open.

"Who was it?" Ian whispered.

"A woman," she replied. She raised a finger to her lips.

Zoe slid round the doorway, one arm raised in front of her and the other hand hovering near the handcuffs on her belt. A woman was stood at the other side of the room, looking away from her.

"Police," Zoe said. "Stay where you are."

The woman turned to her. She was young, with smooth dark hair. She wore a white cashmere coat.

"Do not hurt me," she said. She had an Eastern European accent. "I am looking for Andreea."

CHAPTER SEVENTY-NINE

The woman stared back at Zoe, her face pale. It was the woman she'd seen being shoved into the Mercedes by Kyle Gatiss. She smelled of expensive perfume and her hair was neatly styled. She didn't belong in a place like this.

"Who are you and what are you doing here?" Zoe asked.

The woman stared at her. "I do nothing wrong."

"Do you live here?"

"No. I look for sister."

"Your sister? Does she live here?"

The woman shrugged. "I think so." She backed away from Zoe, her eyes wide.

Zoe took a shaky breath. "Slow down. I'm not going to hurt you." The woman looked terrified. She pushed her hair back and Zoe noticed a bruise on her wrist. "Tell me your name and your sister's name."

"My name is Sofia Pichler. I am looking for Andreea, my sister. She took children."

"What children?"

"Children, from airport."

Zoe looked back at Ian. He frowned at the woman.

"You know about the children at the airport?" Zoe said.

The woman shrugged. "I know they disappear. They say Andreea took them."

"From here?"

The woman nodded.

"Do you know where she took them?"

The woman backed away again. Zoe put her hands by her side. "I'm not going to hurt you. You can relax."

"You arrest me?"

"That depends."

"On what?"

"On whether you've broken the law."

The woman gasped. "I help, with children. Is that broken the law?"

Zoe looked at the woman. She seemed innocent enough, with her immaculate hair and clothes. But it could be a front. For all Zoe knew, this woman could be running the operation.

Zoe took a step forward. "I'll need to take you to the police station," she said. "You'll be questioned about the brothel that's been operating from this building, and the missing children."

"You arrest me?"

"No. But you will be under caution."

"I do not understand."

"We'll get you an interpreter."

Zoe looked round. Ian had gone, and that was enough to have her worrying about what he might be doing. She motioned to the woman to sit down. "Wait here."

"I need to find Andreea. She is in danger."

"Why do you think she's in danger?"

"Because she took children. They will be looking for her."

"Who will be looking for her?"

A shrug. "Men."

Zoe sighed. "Sit there."

She left the room and closed the door. In the corridor, she called for Ian. He emerged from a room at the back of the building.

"This woman's going to have to be taken to Harborne," she said. "I can't get any sense out of her."

"You'll want to see this," Ian replied.

Zoe's hand was on the doorknob. She knew that if she left the woman, she would escape. In search of her sister.

"Bring it here," she said.

Ian twisted his lips in annoyance then disappeared into the room. He returned with an A4 brown envelope.

Zoe took it off him. It was full of passports. She clenched her fists, her head light.

"Shit," she said.

"They're all Romanian," he said. "Women."

Zoe searched through them. Sofia Pichler, the woman had said. No sign of a passport for her here. But there was an Andreea Pichler. She glowered at the camera, her eyes almost obscured by tousled black hair.

"We need to find these women," she breathed. Ian nodded.

"Stay here." She put a hand on his arm. She wasn't letting him out of her sight.

She took out her phone again.

"Amanda, put out a call. We need a squad car to take a witness to Harborne nick. Sofia Pichler. Tell DCI Clarke, she'll need to be interviewed as soon as she arrives."

"The car is four minutes away, ma'am."

"Good." Zoe clutched the passports under her arm. "Ian, come with me."

CHAPTER EIGHTY

Zoe watched the two uniformed officers bundle Sofia into the squad car. Ian stood next to her.

"Right," she said as the car pulled away. "We need to find her sister. And those kids."

"And all the other women who've disappeared."

"How many of them are there?" she said. "Judging by the contents of this envelope, at least twenty women. And there were seven children missing. They can't be all that hard to miss."

She walked to her car and turned back to Ian. "Come with me."

"I'll take my car, we can cover more ground."

"No, we go together."

"Boss, I think it's best if—"

"Just get in my car, Ian," she replied in a tone that brooked no dissent. In just the few minutes he'd spent without her in the hotel, she'd wondered what he was getting up to and how much damage he might be doing. She wasn't taking any more risks.

He slid into the passenger seat and buckled up. "That means leaving my car here."

"You can get a lift back later."

"Hmm."

"Right," she said. "We've got two groups of people. The children are the priority."

She started the car, waiting for a familiar VW Polo to enter the driveway before moving off.

She wound down her window.

"Adi."

"Zoe, good to see you."

"You too, Adi. Start with the office to the right of the front door. There's another one at the back. We need documents proving they were trafficking women from Romania. And check prints for a match with that handbag."

"Will do." He closed his window and parked.

She hit hands-free on her phone.

"Rhodri, I need you to keep in contact with control. Tell me if anyone spots a group of women or a single woman with seven children, in the Hall Green area."

"Are they already looking?"

"They are."

"Righto."

"Thanks."

She looked at Ian. "Where would you go, if you were her?"

"The airport?"

"You think she'll even know where it is?"

"It's well signposted when you get onto the main roads."

"She won't have transport. Road signs won't be relevant."

"She might be walking."

"With a bunch of kids? It's seven miles to the airport."

"If that's where she's going."

Zoe sat back in her seat. She dragged her fingers through her hair. "Think."

She pulled herself upright and headed for the road. "Let's start driving anyway. No use sitting here."

She waited as a bus passed, buffeting the car. She turned to Ian.

"She'll have got a bus. Find out where that one goes."

"The number six." He got his phone out. "Into Solihull."

"Where there's a terminal. Buses to the airport."

"You think she had the money?"

"She could have stolen it." Zoe swallowed. "She could have earned it."

"OK. Follow that bus, then."

"Too slow." Zoe pulled out into the road and overtook the bus, forcing a car coming the other way to swerve. The driver honked the horn at them.

"I'll put the lights on," she said. The cars in front moved out of the way.

"Right," she told Ian. "You keep your eyes on the pavements, in case she is on foot. And if we spot a bus, we stop it."

CHAPTER EIGHTY-ONE

Mo was starting to feel like he'd knocked on every door in Birmingham, and now it was getting dark. He stamped his cold feet on the ground as Fran rang the doorbell of their eleventh target. It was a wide bungalow with garden gnomes adorning the front path and a Neighbourhood Watch sticker in the front window.

A man in his sixties answered the door, arm encased in an oven glove. Mo could smell roasting meat. He held up his warrant card.

"Sorry to bother you, sir, my name's DS Uddin and this is DC Kowalczyk. We're speaking to people who might have seen anyone leaving the airport on Saturday evening, after the explosion."

The man sucked his teeth. "Nasty business, all that. Traumatised my dogs."

Mo nodded. "We believe two vans left the airport by a gate further along Elmdon Lane" – he pointed in the general direction – "and we're hoping someone might have seen

CHAPTER EIGHTY-ONE

them. I know you'll already have been asked if you have CCTV on your house."

"I don't know anything about CCTV," the man said, "but I did watch the whole thing." He met Mo's gaze. "Just wanted to know what was going on. So I could look after my dogs. Not being voyeuristic, or anything."

Mo smiled. "Of course not. We'd be grateful if you could tell us what you saw, Mr…"

The man sniffed. "The name's Eccleston. Come on in, it's bloody freezing out there, if you'll excuse my French."

"Thank you." Mo exchanged glances with Fran. He hoped this wouldn't take too long.

The man led them into a sitting room at the front of the house with two brown sofas that had suffered considerable dog damage. A chocolate Labrador lay curled up on one of them.

The man ruffled the dog's ears. "Saw the whole thing, I did. Horrible business. I took photos too. D'you want to see them?"

CHAPTER EIGHTY-TWO

Connie peered over the computer screens at Rhodri. "Everything OK?"

"The boss is at the hotel with the sarge. Asked me to talk to control, check if they've tracked down the women and kids."

"They're not at the hotel?"

"They buggered off, apparently."

"There are some nasty bastards out there."

Rhodri blew out and a lock of hair bobbed in front of his face. "Yeah." He leaned back in his chair, hands behind his head. "It's frustrating, being stuck here."

"It's fine," she said. "They need us following up evidence, talking to other units."

He grimaced. "Dogsbody work."

"Don't go doing anything daft, Rhod."

"I won't." He sighed. "Better make the call. Tell you what, I'll walk down there."

She smiled. "You do that. I'm just checking some prints."

CHAPTER EIGHTY-TWO

"Oh yeah?"

"That woman that just came in, the Romanian one. See if she's on the database."

"Sounds like fun."

"Police work isn't always fun, Rhod."

He raised an eyebrow. "Back in a tick."

Connie watched him leave the room, then returned to her screen. She was checking to see if there was a record of the woman in the HOLMES database, and if she might be associated with the organised crime group DS Uddin had been investigating.

So far, there was nothing.

A thought hit her. She switched to another part of the system. She ran an analysis, then stared at the screen, her fists clenched.

She picked up the phone to call the boss just as the door opened.

She straightened in her chair. "Ma'am."

"Oh do sit down, Connie. I need to sit down too." DCI Clarke sat at Rhodri's desk and rubbed her eyes. She was pale.

"Are you alright, ma'am?"

"I'm bloody tickety-boo. Why does everyone keep asking after my health?"

Connie opened her mouth to answer, then thought better of it.

"Right," said the DCI. She stood up. "Come with me. You're going to help me interview Sofia Pichler."

"Me, ma'am?"

"Yes, you. Zoe and Ian are out, and I trust you. Your colleague is nowhere to be seen, so you drew the short straw."

Connie brushed crumbs off her trousers and stood up. Rhodri was going to hate her. "I've just discovered something that might be useful when you're interviewing her, ma'am."

"When *we're* interviewing her, you mean. What's that?"

"Her fingerprints. They match the ones we found on the bag that was dropped at the airport."

CHAPTER EIGHTY-THREE

Zoe drove as fast as she could without making it impossible for Ian to scan the pavements. There were no buses.

"They don't run very often, do they?" she said as they squeezed through a traffic jam that was bunching up to give them a way through.

"I think we're off the route," he replied. "Haven't seen a bus stop for a bit."

"Damn. Tell me how to get back on it."

"Will do." He held up his phone, the other hand on the doorframe to steady himself as she jerked out of a bottleneck.

Her phone rang.

"DI Finch."

"Boss, it's Rhodri. I've got something from Control."

"Go on."

"A commotion's been reported in Solihull. At the bus interchange."

"What kind of commotion?"

"Someone trying to get a bunch of kids onto a bus without paying, boss. A fight's broken out."

Zoe thumped the steering wheel. "A fight?"

"The person trying to get onto the bus is Eastern European. Someone decided to have a go at her."

"Where's the interchange?"

"By the rail station. Station Approach."

"Thanks." She turned to Ian. "Get directions." He nodded and peered into his phone. "Quickly," she snapped.

"Er…" said Rhodri.

"What else?" Zoe asked, speeding past a line of cars that was pulling onto the pavement for her.

"Connie's disappeared."

"What? She's probably gone to the loo."

"She's not in there. Apparently."

"OK." Zoe clutched the steering wheel. The last time Connie had gone AWOL had been during the search for her brother Zaf. She'd joined forces with Nicholas and hacked his attacker's social media accounts.

But that time, she'd been told to go home by Ian.

"She'll be back soon," Zoe said. "It's not like Connie to disappear in the middle of a job."

She caught Ian's raised eyebrow and gripped the wheel tighter. *Shut up.*

"OK, Rhod. Just keep in contact with Control. Tell me if anything else comes up. What was Connie working on?"

"Hang on." There was a pause. "Fingerprints, boss."

"Whose?"

"The woman you found at the hotel. Sofia Pichler. From what I can see on Connie's monitor, her prints match that bag. The one at the airport."

Zoe grinned at Ian. "That links the Belvista to both

attacks. Rhod, we need to find out everything we can about the Hotel Belvista. Who owns it, who's been staying there. Talk to Adi. Make sure he's keeping any documents that have been left behind. We want a paper trail on that place."

Zoe smiled. She liked paper trails. Lesley liked procedure, and Zoe liked to winkle out evidence hidden in accounting documents and contracts.

She slowed as they approached the station. She remembered something. "Rhodri. Are you still there?"

"Still here, boss."

"Ask Adi to check the phone in the hotel's office. Dial 1471, find out the last incoming caller."

They'd cleared the place out, which meant they'd been tipped off.

"There she is," said Ian. A crowd of people had spilled off a bus and into the road, a spiky-haired woman at the centre. Two uniformed officers approached her. "Come on." He grabbed his door handle.

"And check the number you get against phone records," Zoe told Rhodri. "See if you can match it."

"Will do, boss."

CHAPTER EIGHTY-FOUR

Connie slid into the interview room behind the DCI, trying to project confidence. She'd done this with the sarge and the DI before. She knew how to handle herself in an interview.

But the DCI was in an even more prickly mood than usual, and Connie was wishing someone else had been there when she'd walked into the office.

The woman sat alone on the other side of the table. The DCI nodded at her. The woman sniffed. She had shiny, almost-black hair and dark brown eyes that were rimmed with red.

"Please, have you found my sister?" she asked.

"Our officers are out looking for her," the DCI replied. "Don't worry."

"I cannot help worry. I know if they find her, they might..."

DCI Clarke leaned forward. "What might they do, Sofia? And who is it you're scared of?"

CHAPTER EIGHTY-FOUR

Sofia shook her head. "Is fine. What do you need to know?"

Lesley sat down and gestured for Connie to do the same. Connie gave Sofia a nervous smile as she took her seat. The woman frowned back at her.

"Right." The DCI placed her elbows on the table and steepled her fingers. "You've been offered legal representation but turned it down. Is that correct?"

"I do nothing wrong. I do not need lawyer."

"As long as you understand that you are entitled to one."

The woman nodded.

"Detective Inspector Finch found you at the Hotel Belvista. We have reason to believe an organised crime gang is operating out of that hotel. Specifically, that it's running a prostitution operation and is connected to or behind the attacks on New Street Station and Birmingham Airport on Saturday."

The woman's eyes widened. She straightened in her chair.

Lesley opened a file and took out a photo of a pale blue handbag. The woman gasped. Connie watched her; she looked shocked and puzzled.

"My bag. Thank God. Do I get it back?"

The DCI snorted. "It's evidence in a terror inquiry. So no, you don't get it back."

The woman frowned.

"We found this bag at Birmingham Airport, near a gate which had been cut through. We have CCTV images of people leaving the airport from that location and driving away in vans. Were you in one of those vans?"

Sofia nodded. "I look after children."

Connie felt her stomach hollow out. "Where are they?" she whispered. "Did you hurt them?"

The DCI waved a hand and Connie swallowed.

"Which children are you referring to?" the DCI asked.

"From plane. I was told to bring eight children from plane. I get it wrong, I bring seven. We take them all to my home."

"Your home is the Belvista hotel?"

"No. Home is..." Sofia blushed. "I do not have address. Is in countryside, near airport."

"Who do you live with, Sofia?"

"Boyfriend."

"And did your boyfriend tell you to bring these children home with you?"

"No. He was angry about it. Next morning, children were gone. I think he took them to hotel. Which is where Andreea must have found them."

"Andreea is your sister."

"She is. I am scared for her. I saw her Monday night, she wasn't herself."

The DCI flattened her hands on the table. She gave the woman a reassuring smile. "The more you can tell us, the better able we will be to protect your sister. Do you have any idea where she is?"

Sofia shook her head. She sniffed and rubbed under her eye. "They say she took children. That is all I know."

"Who said this?"

"Other women. In hotel."

"Where are these women now, Sofia?"

"I do not know. They leave in vans. Same vans from airport."

CHAPTER EIGHTY-FOUR

Lesley turned to Connie to check she was making notes. "Can you describe these vans, please?"

"Black vans. Volkswagen. I remember because my friend Mihai had Volkswagen van in Bucharest."

"Did you see the registration plates?"

"Sorry."

"OK." The DCI turned to Connie. "Give that to Control. They're looking for two black VW vans with women on board."

Connie stood up.

The DCI turned back to the woman. She hesitated a moment, leaning back in her chair. Her eyelids fluttered and she took in a sharp breath.

"Ma'am?"

The DCI frowned. "I'm fine, Constable. Sofia, we're going to pause this interview while we pass on what you've told us to other teams. But before we do, can you tell us if you recognise this man?"

She pushed a photo of the man from New Street Station across the table.

"That is Kyle."

Connie bit her lip.

"Kyle who, Sofia?"

"Sorry. Just Kyle. He drives me places."

"And how do you know Kyle? Is he your boyfriend?"

"No." Sofia wrinkled her nose. "He work for him."

"Who is your boyfriend, Sofia?"

"I call him Titi."

"Is that his real name?"

"No."

"What do other people call him, Sofia?"

Connie felt her heart pick up pace.

"Men call him boss. No name. Mrs Brooking, she call him Sir. But his name is Trevor."

CHAPTER EIGHTY-FIVE

Mo and Fran waited as Mr Eccleston went to fetch his camera. The house was quiet, the only sound the dog snoring on the sofa.

"Here we are," the man said. "Sorry I haven't transferred them off my camera yet." He held out a digital camera.

Mo fiddled with it. "I'm sorry, Mr Eccleston, can you show us how to get to the photos you took on Saturday night?" He didn't want to accidentally delete anything.

"We can just take the memory card," Fran said.

"I want to check them first," Mo told her. She nodded.

"Here." Mr Eccleston pressed a few buttons and an image showed on the camera's display. It was the view from the front of the house, the road backed by privet hedges. Behind the hedges was a faint glow.

"You were taking photos of a terror attack?" Fran asked.

The man blushed. "I thought they might be useful for the police."

Mo raised an eyebrow. "How come you didn't tell us about these before?"

"I've been away. I was visiting my mother from Sunday to yesterday."

"So you haven't spoken to any of our officers?"

"Just you."

Mo held out the camera. "Take us through the rest of the photos, please. Be extra careful not to delete any."

"Don't worry, you have to hit three buttons before the damn thing'll let you remove them." The man took the camera and started scrolling though pictures.

"Slow down," Mo told him. "And let us see." He shuffled next to Eccleston to get a better view. On the sofa, the dog stretched and yawned.

"Sorry," Mr Eccleston said. He pressed the button to advance to the next photo and waited.

"You don't have to wait. Just move between the photos slowly and stop if I ask you to."

The photos advanced. The photographer had moved towards the airport and the view was no longer from the front of his house. Advancing through the photos was like watching a stop-motion film of the route from here towards the gate that had been cut through.

"You think they got through the gate at the end of the road? That's how they did it?" the man asked.

"Carry on with the photos, please," Mo told him.

As the images neared the gate, the glow shifted to the left of the shot and became brighter. The plane was ablaze now, and the photographer was approaching it.

"Did you go as far as the airport?" Mo asked, hoping the man hadn't decided to trespass in search of better shots.

"No," he said. "There were vans blocking the way." He scrolled forwards until two vans appeared in shot, each parked at right angles to the gate and the road.

CHAPTER EIGHTY-FIVE

Mo felt Fran tense next to him. "That's them," she breathed.

He nodded. "Keep going," he said, his eyes on the camera. They would need to take the memory card to the station and get these blown up.

The vans receded as the photographer moved backwards, away from them.

"You backed off," Mo said.

"I heard shouting, in a foreign language. I didn't want to get involved."

"Did you recognise the language?"

"No idea. Sorry."

The sound of barking came from another room. "That's Ella. I need to let her back in. D'you mind?"

"We won't take up much more of your time."

The man sniffed and sped up, scrolling through the rest of his photos.

"How many did you take?" Fran asked.

"My camera's got an auto setting. Means you don't miss the best shot. About two hundred, I suppose."

"How did you get such clear shots at dusk?"

"I upped the ISO. Makes things a bit grainy, but good enough if you balance it with the shutter speed." He continued scrolling through the photos.

"Stop," said Mo.

"Hmm?"

"Pause the photos right there."

The sound of barking intensified. "I really need to let her in. Mrs Barrow next door, she complains..."

"Fine," said Mo. "Leave the camera with us." He took it off Eccleston and held it gingerly.

"It's that button there," said Fran.

"I know." Mo pressed it and the photos advanced, more slowly this time.

The vans turned in the road, heading towards the photographer. As they approached, the angle shifted as if the photographer were moving out of the road, standing aside. The photos continued, the front van filling more and more of the image.

Mo held his breath. The registration plates were indecipherable on this screen, but they'd be able to get them back at the office.

As the van passed the photographer, the angle changed again, the lens pointing into the vehicle. A man sat in the front seat of the first one, his eyes ahead on the road. "How come they didn't stop and take his camera?" Fran said.

"Maybe they didn't notice him. It looks like they had enough on their hands at the time."

Mr Eccleston returned with a second Labrador on a short lead. He hoisted the lead and led the dog to the sofa where it joined its companion. He eyed the camera. "Everything OK?"

"Fine." said Mo. He flicked to the next shot. "We'll need to keep this," he said.

Eccleston sniffed. "You *will* return it? I've got a trip to Morocco coming up."

"We'll return the camera once we've copied the contents of the drive." Mo passed the camera to Fran, who looked at the screen then back at him.

In the photo, the man in the van faced the photographer, a frown on his face. His face was clearly distinguishable. He had thinning red hair and narrow eyes.

"Let's go," said Mo.

CHAPTER EIGHTY-SIX

Zoe jumped out of her car and ran after Ian towards the group of people at the bus stop. She held up her warrant card.

"Force CID," she told the two uniformed officers at the edge of the crowd. "This woman's connected with an investigation."

"What do you need us to do?" asked one of the officers, a young woman.

"Make sure she doesn't get away. Get those kids. We need to take them to safety."

"They're on the bus," replied the other officer, an older man.

"OK. Ian, you go with PC" – she eyed the male officer's badge – "PC Hines here, round up the kids and find somewhere safe for them to wait. We'll need a van to take them to the station."

"Boss." Ian rounded the crowd and made for the bus, PC Hines at his heels.

"Right," Zoe said, turning to the female officer. "PC

Ellers. The woman's name is Andreea Pichler. I'm expecting her to run. We have to corner her, get her into your car. OK?"

"Ma'am."

"You go that way."

PC Ellers nodded and started to circle the crowd. At its centre, a man with thick grey hair was shouting at Andreea. She screamed back at him in Romanian. A middle-aged woman carrying a briefcase was trying to intervene, to talk to both of them.

Zoe approached Andreea, who hadn't spotted her. She stared at the man, her eyes full of fear and hatred. He spat back at her, telling her to *fuck off home*.

Zoe looked across the crowd to see PC Ellers opposite her. To Zoe's right was the bus, a barrier. As long as Andreea didn't manage to push through the crowd, they'd be able to grab her.

If Andreea was grabbed by police, the grey-haired man would feel vindicated. The thought left a bad taste in Zoe's mouth. She'd have to leave the two constables to deal with him.

Andreea was just a few feet away. She was thin, with black hair that spilled over her eyes. She wore a long shirt at least two sizes too large with ripped jeans. Her skin was pale and there were bruises on her wrists.

Zoe was about to lunge for her when a car screeched past the bus and came to a halt in front of it. Someone at the edge of the crowd screamed and Andreea's gaze shifted from the grey-haired man to the car.

A man got out of the car. Andreea's eyes widened and she pushed the grey-haired man back, sending him staggering into the crowd. The man from the car ran through, pushing people aside to get at Andreea.

CHAPTER EIGHTY-SIX

The man was short, with ruddy skin and thin red hair. If he was part of the organised crime gang, she hadn't come across him before.

The bus door opened and Ian stepped out, a girl aged about twelve behind him. She was crying. Andreea looked round at the girl, then Ian, then back at the man from the car. She yelled something in Romanian, leaped over the grey-haired man, now on the ground, and ran.

"PC Ellers!" Zoe cried as she sped after Andreea. The young woman dashed past the bus and across the road, heading away from the car. The man jumped back into it and revved the engine.

Zoe picked up pace, arms and legs pumping to catch up with Andreea. Andreea ran diagonally across the road, making for the main road beyond. PC Ellers was ahead of Zoe, talking into her radio as she ran.

At the junction Andreea paused and looked from side to side. The road was quiet. She turned right and continued running. The car reached the junction and threw itself round the corner, chasing her.

Without turning, Andreea ran out into the road. A bus appeared, coming the other way. She stared at it: her escape.

The car accelerated.

"Stop!" PC Ellers shouted. She stood on the pavement, gesticulating at Andreea who was halfway across the road.

Andreea turned to see where the voice had come, just as the car reached her. She screamed.

"No!" Zoe ran after her, joining PC Ellers in the road. Andreea had disappeared behind the car.

As they reached the car, PC Ellers placed a hand on its rear wing. The car revved again and sped away, leaving Andreea lying in the road.

CHAPTER EIGHTY-SEVEN

"You drive," Mo said. "I need to make a call."

Fran nodded and got into the driver's seat. They drove away from the airport as Mo dialled Sheila Griffin.

"Mo, how are you getting on?"

"We've got a photo of a man who was driving one of the vans on Saturday. Leaving the airport."

"D'you recognise him?"

"I was hoping you might. Where are you?"

"I'm at the Hotel Belvista," Sheila said. "Can you send it to me?"

Mo put the camera in his lap and took a snap of the photo with his phone. He emailed it to Sheila.

Five minutes later they were on the Coventry Road and his phone rang: Sheila.

"That's Adam Fulmer," she said. "He was one of our targets on Canary. Disappeared about four months ago, we figured he'd gone abroad."

Mo thumbed through the rest of the photos. In the back

of the van were blurred figures he couldn't make out. Women, children, or both?

"He was driving a van away from the broken gate at the airport on Saturday," he told her. "We believe the missing women and children were inside. Where can we find him?"

"Last we saw of him was last September, in Curton Road," she said. "And that's still empty."

"Damn." Mo exchanged a look of frustration with Fran. They were driving through Small Heath, heading back to the office.

"I'll see if I can find any evidence of him having been here," Sheila said.

"Give me the address."

Sheila told him where the hotel was and Mo gestured for Fran to turn around when she could.

"I'll see you there," he said.

Fifteen minutes later, they pulled up outside the hotel. Ian's car was in the driveway along with Adi's Skoda and a couple of others he didn't recognise.

Mo got out of the car while Fran found a parking spot further down the road. He found Adi in an office to the right of the entrance, piling files into boxes.

"DS Uddin." Adi smiled. "You got Zoe with you?"

"Sorry to disappoint."

"Only I've got something for her."

"You can give it to me."

"I think this one is just for her."

Mo narrowed his eyes at the forensics manager. Adi liked to play favourites among the detectives, especially the female ones. "Just tell me, please."

"Sorry. Way too sensitive. She send you?"

"No. I'm meeting DS Griffin here."

Adi shook his head. "Haven't seen her, sorry. She might be that-a-way" – he gestured behind him – "there's another office".

"Have you found evidence of women and children being kept here?" Mo asked.

Adi nodded. "Zoe found an envelope full of passports. And we've got plenty that they left behind. They were in a hurry this time."

Mo showed Adi the camera. "I'm looking for this man. Any evidence of him being here? His name's Adam Fulmer."

"Nothing here, sorry. But we'll keep looking."

CHAPTER EIGHTY-EIGHT

Zoe fell to the ground, placing her fingertips on the side of Andreea's neck. She lifted her hand, willing her own heartbeat to stop thudding in her ears.

PC Ellers was behind her, talking into her radio.

"Urgent ambulance required, and vehicles to pursue a dark blue Lexus." She read out the registration number of the car.

Zoe eased Andreea onto her back. The bus that had been approaching when Andreea ran across the road had stopped a few feet away, cars lining up behind it. The driver got out.

"Is she alright?" he asked. "That car, it came from nowhere—"

"Please stand back," PC Ellers said. "We need everyone to stay clear."

Zoe's vision blurred as she bent over the young woman. Her mouth was open, her black hair obscuring her eyes. She placed her hands on Andreea's chest and pushed down, counting to thirty.

Andreea didn't move.

Zoe pinched her nose. She covered her mouth with her own and pushed out two sharp breaths.

She straightened up, her eyes on Andreea's chest. No change. She started the compressions again. She was aware of PC Ellers standing over her, of the crowd staring.

She heard an engine behind her: a police van. From the corner of her eye she saw Ian approach it with PC Hines and a group of children. She squeezed her eyes quickly shut then opened them again.

"Come on," she muttered. She bent over Andreea and breathed into her mouth. The woman's body was still, unyielding.

She sat up for thirty more compressions. Andreea's body shifted beneath her hands but there was no breath.

She felt a hand on her back. She shook it off and bent to continue the CPR.

"Ma'am. Ambulance."

Zoe felt a rush of air as two green-suited paramedics swooped in. She staggered to her feet and backed away, her eyes not leaving Andreea.

She thought of Sofia's face in the hotel: *where is my sister?* How had these two women got mixed up in all this? What was their role in abducting those children?

One of the paramedics stood up and turned to her. He shook his head.

PC Ellers was right next to her. Zoe let the constable take her weight as the energy left her.

CHAPTER EIGHTY-NINE

Zoe turned back to where she'd left her car, her footsteps heavy. She needed to pull herself together. They still had to track down the driver of that Lexus. Find him, and they'd find whoever had set those bombs. And Kyle Gatiss: she still needed to locate him.

"Are you OK, ma'am?" PC Ellers asked.

Zoe nodded. "Thanks for your help. I can't stay: you can finish off here?"

The woman nodded. PC Hines had already fetched police tape from his car and cordoned off the section of road where Andreea lay.

Zoe passed the bus that Andreea had been trying to enter. It was still at the stop, the crowd dispersing. The man who'd been shouting at Andreea sat on the grass next to the pavement, crying. Zoe stared at him. If he hadn't got involved, where would Andreea be now?

Two uniformed officers were shepherding the children onto a police van. They clung to one another, sobbing and shivering. Zoe approached them.

"It's going to be OK," she told them. "We'll call your parents. The school. You're going home."

The children stared back at her, faces blank. She had no idea if they could understand her. And even if they could, what had they been through since Saturday? Would they be able to trust anybody in this country?

She turned towards her car and stopped.

It was gone.

She turned back to the bus. Had Uniform moved it out of the way?

She approached one of the constables.

"There was a green Mini parked here. Do you know where it's gone?"

"A Detective Sergeant took it. He showed me his ID, I assumed it was his. He asked to borrow my phone, too, but he only used it for a moment."

Ian. What was he doing?

Zoe's phone rang.

"DI Finch."

"You sound glum." It was Adi.

"My car's been nicked. Well, not nicked exactly..."

Ian, I'm going to bloody kill you, she thought.

"What can I do for you, Adi?"

"You asked me to check the last call to come into the hotel."

"You did it?"

"I dialled 1471. Low-tech approach, but it gave me a number."

"Go on." She grabbed a pen and wrote the number down.

"Both your sergeants are here, by the way."

"Both?"

"Yeah. Mo and Ian."

"What?"

"Mo's looking for some bloke from a photo. And Ian... I'm not sure what he's doing. He's disappeared upstairs."

"Is Mo with you?"

"He is."

"Hand the phone to him."

There was a pause and then Mo's voice came on the line. "Zo."

"What's Ian doing?"

"Says he's checking the bedrooms. We're looking for anything that might lead us to the missing women and children."

"I've got the children. They're safe."

"All of them?"

"All of them."

"Thank God for that. What about the women?"

"Uniform are looking for two VW vans," she said. "No sign of them yet. What's this about a man in a photo?"

"We found some guy who took photos at the airport on Saturday. Got shots of the vans leaving."

"Describe the man to me."

"Sheila says his name's Adam Fulmer. He's got red hair, a weaselly face."

Her shoulders slumped. "Red hair?"

"Thin on top."

"He was driving the car that hit Andreea."

"What car?"

"He killed her. If it is him."

"So he's a murder suspect now. I'll tell Sheila."

"There's already an all units call out to find him."

"Right," Mo said. "Sheila says he was a suspect in Canary."

"I don't remember him."

"He disappeared four months ago. Sheila thought he'd buggered off abroad."

"And now he's back, and he's given us another link."

"Don't count your chickens just yet," Mo said. "He might disappear again."

"We'll find him. Mo, did Ian come in my car?"

"Hang on a minute. Looks like it, I can see it outside."

"The bastard."

"You didn't let him drive it?"

"No I bloody well didn't."

"Shall I tell him to come back and get you?"

"No. You keep an eye on him for me, will you? Don't let him leave with my car."

"Will do."

"Thanks."

She hung up and eyed the phone number Adi had given her, the number that, she suspected, had been used to warn the hotel that they were coming. It was a mobile number.

She plugged the number into her phone. As the call connected, a name came onscreen. Her jaw tightened.

"Boss?" came the voice at the other end.

She closed her eyes. "Ian."

CHAPTER NINETY

Zoe climbed out of the squad car. She'd spent the journey on the phone: one call to Carl, and the other to the DCI. Lesley had told her to get back to the office immediately, but she wasn't missing this for the world.

"Thanks," she said to the driver as she closed the door. Her car stood in the hotel's driveway, blocked in by another squad car. She took a deep breath and looked up at the building.

As she approached the front entrance, two uniformed officers emerged. Between them, and handcuffed to one, was Ian. Zoe took a step back to let them pass.

Ian glared at her as he passed. She looked back at him, hiding her anger.

Ian had lied to them all. To her, and to Carl. He'd made them think he was working for Professional Standards, when in reality he was still working for organised crime.

She turned at the sound of a car pulling up at the kerb. Carl emerged, DS Kaur behind him. Zoe allowed herself a smile.

Carl approached Ian. He looked at the uniformed officers. "Have you read him his rights?"

"We have, sir," the one handcuffed to Ian replied.

"Good." Carl looked at Ian. "You lied to me, DS Osman. You put the lives of your colleagues and the general public in danger. You won't get away with this."

"I was working for you," Ian hissed. "Keeping them sweet."

Carl raised an eyebrow. "We'll see." He looked over Ian's shoulder and caught Zoe's stare.

She felt her chest clench. The investigation into the planting of evidence on Nadeem Sharif still wasn't over. She knew there would be more questioning. She might even be suspected of working with her DS. She gave Carl a tentative smile.

He returned the smile and turned to the car. Ian was being guided inside.

Zoe watched as Carl slid into the back next to Ian and they drove away.

CHAPTER NINETY-ONE

SOFIA WAS IN AN INTERVIEW ROOM, Connie sitting on a plastic chair outside it, having been assigned to keep an eye on her.

"How was she?" Zoe asked. "When you interviewed her."

"The DCI'll have a better idea, boss. But I think she just got mixed up with some very nasty people."

"She admitted to helping take those kids off the Wizz Air plane."

"She was scared. She thought she was rescuing them."

"Hmm."

Zoe gazed at the interview room door then turned towards Lesley's office. The DCI was behind her desk, stockinged feet up on its surface. She was on the phone.

Lesley raised a finger as Zoe walked in: *hush*.

"Where are they now?" she asked. She nodded as the caller replied.

"Bring them here," she said. "I want to interview them myself."

She hung up. "We got them."

"Fulmer?" Zoe asked.

"And Gatiss. An unmarked response vehicle found the vans and followed them to an address outside the city, in Dorridge. There was a woman there, a Margaret Brooking. She's in custody along with the woman from the hotel. Fulmer showed up in the Lexus a few minutes later, walked right into it all and had the cuffs on him before he realised what was going on. They've found some of the women, too, we're not sure how many are still missing."

"What about Hamm? What about Shand and Petersen?"

"No sign of Hamm. Petersen was at his niece's wedding and Shand was in London."

"That doesn't mean they're not involved."

"No. But let's start with what we actually have, eh?"

"Hamm has to be behind all this. Sofia gave us his name."

"We've got links between them all," Lesley said. "But it's not enough."

"This is ridiculous," Zoe said. "Hamm killed his wife..."

"Irina's death was ruled misadventure."

Zoe raised an eyebrow. "He was the man who provided the kids in Canary, and now he's taken advantage of a bomb on a plane to traffic women and children."

"Not to mention the New Street bomb. Please tell me you've identified that woman?"

"We're talking to the woman she sent the selfie to, Ana-Maria. But she's terrified, won't say a thing."

"So was she put up to it by Hamm, or the Pakistani gang that put the bomb on the plane?" Lesley asked.

"If she was one of the women from Hamm's brothel, we have to assume he was behind it. An extra distraction. Maybe he was paid to do it, by the Pakistanis."

CHAPTER NINETY-ONE

Lesley whistled. "Trevor Hamm. He *has* moved up in the world. Scuzzy fucker."

"Surely we have grounds to prosecute him now?"

"Even for the things he *is* guilty of, we have to convince the CPS. And *they* have to convince a jury."

Zoe dropped into a chair. Lesley winced and fingered her neck.

"But before all that," Lesley said. "We have to find him."

Zoe sat up. "I've got an idea."

CHAPTER NINETY-TWO

Zoe opened the door to the interview room. She forced herself to slow down. Her present adrenaline-fuelled state wasn't what was needed right now.

Sofia looked up at her. "You find Andreea?"

Zoe swallowed the lump in her throat. She took a seat next to Sofia.

"Sofia, I'm very sorry."

Sofia's eyes widened. She started shaking her head. "You lose her!"

"Andreea is dead, Sofia. I'm so sorry."

Sofia yelped. She leaned back in her chair, staring at Zoe. "You lie! She has run away!"

"I was with her when she died. She was hit by a car. I tried to save her, but it was too late. I'm so sorry."

"No! What car? How she hit?"

Zoe wanted to grab the other woman's hands, to take her in her arms. Sofia stopped moving and stared into Zoe's eyes, her face full of hope that she might be imagining this.

CHAPTER NINETY-TWO

"Some men were chasing her," Zoe said. "Men who we believe were working for your boyfriend, Trevor Hamm."

"Which men?"

"A man called Adam Fulmer. Do you know him?"

"Adam." Sofia collapsed into herself. "I know him. Why he hit Andreea?"

Zoe leaned forward. "I don't think it was deliberate. He was chasing Andreea, trying to catch her before we did. She ran into the road."

Tears ran down Sofia's face. "No. She cannot be dead. She only just arrive in England. She rescue children."

"We have the children. They're safe."

"All of them?"

"Yes." Zoe grabbed Sofia's hand. "And that's thanks to you and your sister."

Sofia's brow furrowed. "Tell me where Andreea is. I want to see her."

Zoe shifted her seat closer. "I know this is hard for you to hear, but Trevor is responsible for her death."

Sofia stared at her, her eyes filling. "No. He cannot be. Was accident."

"We need to find him, Sofia. He hurt a lot of people. Killed people. Including Andreea."

Sofia shook her head. "Titi is good man. Never kill."

Zoe sighed. This woman was the best link they had to Hamm. She had to get through to her.

"I can take you to your sister."

"You can?"

"Yes."

Sofia's head sank into her hands. "Thank you."

Zoe nodded, her jaw firm. She let the young woman

collapse into her arms, her body shaking. "Of course you can see her."

CHAPTER NINETY-THREE

Zoe stood in the kitchen, staring out of the window that gave onto a brick wall. She turned as Lesley came in.

"How is she?" the DCI asked.

"In a bad way. She holds herself responsible."

"She was the one who took up with Trevor Hamm. She's partly liable."

"There's no criminal liability on her part, ma'am. She was taken in by him, just like the other women were."

Lesley pulled a face. She gestured at the kettle and Zoe stood back to let her fill it.

"I came to tell you they've checked, and they've got all the women now," Lesley said. "Some of them ran. Looks like they thought our officers were with Hamm and his men, and took off as soon as the vans got stopped, but they've been tracked down."

Zoe felt relief course through her. "How many women?"

"Eighteen. Plus Sheena McDonald, who we already arrested. She claims she owns the hotel."

"Really?"

"That's what the paperwork says. And she's going along with it."

"She's not the person behind all this."

"She's no innocent victim, Zoe. She kept those women and kids locked up. She coordinated their movements, worked with the men to take them to locations around the city where they would meet customers."

Zoe shivered. "The children have only been here four days. Please tell me they hadn't got to that stage."

"We're still trying to work that out. They're all minors, and none of them speak English. We need to contact their parents, and take things from there before we can conduct any interviews."

Zoe thumped the wall.

"I know," Lesley said. "But we got them out. You tracked Andreea down, and you got those kids to safety."

"It doesn't feel like it. Not till we find Hamm."

"I thought you had a brilliant idea."

The kettle clicked and Zoe poured two cups of coffee. "Have you got any biscuits?"

"In my desk."

"I think a pack of them might help me with this."

CHAPTER NINETY-FOUR

Zoe placed the packet of digestives on the table and put a coffee in front of Sofia.

"I thought you might need this."

"Thank you." Sofia wiped her eyes and sipped the coffee. "When will I see Andreea?"

"I've spoken to the pathologist. We can go now, if you'd like?"

Sofia put down the coffee. "Please."

"Why don't you bring those biscuits?"

Sofia frowned at the biscuits then picked them up. The woman was thin, not as thin as her sister but she looked like she didn't eat properly. Zoe imagined Trevor Hamm insisting she stayed skinny, like all his women.

They got into her car and pulled out of the station car park, heading for the hospital and the morgue in its basement.

"Where will I go?" Sofia asked. "Afterwards."

"Your home is that house in Dorridge, yes?"

"Dorridge. I do not know name, but it is big house in countryside. Trevor's house."

"Our forensics team are there. We'll find you somewhere to stay, don't worry."

"I want to go home."

"I'm sorry, it's just not—"

"No. To Romania."

Zoe nodded. "Of course. Do you have money, for a ticket?"

The woman shook her head. "He have passport too."

"I'm sure something can be worked out."

"Where we go?"

"To the hospital. Andreea is there."

Sofia sniffed.

"I was hoping you might be able to tell me something," Zoe said.

"Yes."

"Where can we find Trevor, if he isn't at the house?"

Sofia stiffened. "I do not know."

"If he's not at home, and he's not at the hotel, surely there must be somewhere he would go."

"He not tell me much."

"Do you have his mobile number?"

"Only his men. I call Kyle if I need lift anywhere. Trevor call me from phone that does not leave number."

Damn. Zoe had been hoping a little kindness might encourage Sofia to give her boyfriend up.

"I am sorry. I want to help."

"That's OK." Zoe pulled in at the hospital, not envying Sofia for what she was about to do.

CHAPTER NINETY-FIVE

Zoe sat in the modern interview room on the fifth floor of Lloyd House. She'd put on her best shirt and jacket for this, and brushed her hair.

Detective Superintendent Rogers and DS Kaur sat opposite her. They had a file open in front of them. Next to Zoe was Inspector Jane Keele, her Federation rep.

"We've spoken to the other professionals who were at the airport when the bodies were being brought off the plane," said Rogers. "We have a statement from Dr Adebayo saying she saw DS Osman tampering with one of the bodies."

"Tampering?" Zoe asked. "How, exactly?"

"You told us in your earlier statement that you didn't see him doing anything untoward."

"No," she replied. "I saw him near the bodies, and I assumed he was examining them. But I didn't see him touch any of them."

"You're sure about that?"

"Positive."

Rogers folded his arms across his chest. "Sergeant Osman

is a member of your team, DI Finch. We have the pathologist saying she witnessed him touching one of the bodies, yet you say you saw nothing. You also say you weren't aware of him making a phone call to the address at Jarman Road when your unit was on its way to raid that address."

"We drove there separately. I think he made the call on the way."

Rogers cocked his head. "That's very convenient."

Zoe felt her pulse race. "Not for me it isn't, sir. With respect, do you think I enjoy calling Uniform in to arrest one of my own team? And DS Osman would have taken steps to ensure I didn't see him doing anything untoward. He knows that I know about his previous illegal activity."

"He claims he was working undercover the whole time, that he did the bidding of the organised crime group in order to gain their trust. Did you see any evidence of that?"

"I was aware of DS Osman's work, and the fact that he was working with officers from Professional Standards. I didn't get involved in that, and I didn't consider it my business to interfere."

"So you turned a blind eye to your own team member working with the organisation you were investigating?"

"With respect, sir." Zoe licked her lips. "At the airport we believed it was a terror attack. We had no idea that organised crime were involved in this, and so it didn't occur to me that Ian might be involved. And far from turning a blind eye, I was the one who called him in."

DS Kaur passed a document to Rogers. He eyed it.

"This is the phone record from DS Osman's police issue mobile phone on Wednesday. Do you recognise this number here?" He pointed to a line and turned it towards Zoe.

"I assume that's the hotel."

"No. This one is the hotel." Rogers pointed to the line immediately below it.

Zoe shook her head. "Then I have no idea what that number is."

"It's an unregistered mobile phone. We were able to identify the mast that number was using at the time of this call, and it was in Harborne. Near to the Force CID offices." He blinked at her.

"I'm not sure what you're implying." Zoe glanced at her rep.

"Could DS Osman have called you before he called the hotel?"

"DS Osman and I were both in Harborne station at that time. But we spoke face to face. If he wanted to tell me anything, he could have done it there, or at the hotel when we met. I can't see any reason he would have tried to call me, and that isn't my phone number."

"You don't use an unregistered mobile number for personal activity?"

"No, sir."

"Very well." Rogers pulled the file back across the table. "You're free to go."

Zoe felt her stomach relax. "I'm not under suspicion?"

"We don't have any evidence to suggest you were working with DS Osman."

"That's because there isn't any."

"But you've been close to a lot of this kind of thing, DI Finch. You've worked closely with DS Osman, and we believe you might be hiding information about another colleague."

"Which colleague?"

"I'm not in a position to say. But you seem to attract this

kind of thing. Is that a coincidence, or should we be worried?"

"It's a coincidence, sir."

"Very well. Keep your nose clean from now on, will you?"

"Of course, sir."

Zoe stood and waited to be dismissed, then hurried down to the basement car park, her heart pounding against her ribcage. She couldn't believe that by investigating her suspicions about colleagues, she'd brought herself into the line of fire.

She approached her car and pressed the button on her remote. The indicator lights blipped and a figure appeared from behind a pillar.

"Bloody hell, Carl, you startled me."

"Sorry. Didn't want Rogers thinking I was chasing after you."

"Do they think I'm involved, Carl? Do *you* think I'm involved?"

He shook his head. "You know I don't think that, Zoe."

"But what about your boss? Does he think I'm bent? Am I going to have to keep looking behind me, in case I've got PS on my tail?"

"Not if you've got nothing to hide."

She clenched her fists. "You know I've got nothing to hide."

"Exactly." He took a sharp breath. "So are we going to get that curry sometime then?"

She put a hand on her car. "Not just yet, Carl. Some other time."

She yanked the door open, gunned the gas and drove off before she had the time to change her mind.

CHAPTER NINETY-SIX

Zoe walked straight through the team room and into her office, her feet heavy. Connie and Rhodri looked up from their desks and exchanged worried looks.

Zoe sat in her chair and spun it round so they couldn't see her face. She wanted to punch the wall, or scream.

Not if you don't have anything to hide.

How could Carl talk to her like that? How could he go from *I love you* to *I think you might be bent* in the space of weeks?

She would prove him wrong. But she knew that the harder she tried to do that, the less likely he would be to drop his suspicions.

The door opened and she span round. "Sorry, folks, but can you give me a—"

Lesley stood in the doorway, hands on hips. "You sending me away?"

"Sorry, ma'am." Zoe rearranged her face. "What can I do for you?"

"You get on OK at Lloyd House?"

"I'm off the hook, if that's what you mean. For now."

Lesley raised an eyebrow.

"It's OK," said Zoe. "I'm being paranoid."

"So, we've charged Gatiss and Fulmer. The woman too, Sheena McDonald. She still insists the place belongs to her. I want you going through the legal documents to find any evidence that it doesn't."

"Happy to."

"Still can't find bloody Trevor Hamm though."

"The others won't tell you?"

Lesley barked out a laugh. "Even in prison they know he can get to them."

"Maybe Ian will know."

"Ian has told PS he has no idea where the man is. And for once, I believe the little runt."

Zoe nodded. "I sent Connie to the school the kids were supposed to be on exchange with. They're organising for them to go home, or for their parents to come for them."

"Poor buggers."

"Yeah." Zoe dropped her head. Five of the children had escaped without being abused, but the virginity of the two oldest girls had been sold for a high price. Fulmer, Gatiss and McDonald would pay dearly for that. Especially McDonald, she imagined. Juries didn't look kindly on women who did this kind of thing. Fulmer and Gatiss wouldn't get off easily, though, especially if they found themselves on the wrong end of a murder charge for their involvement in the two bombings. Which was, she knew, far from certain. For all the work they'd done, there were still a lot of unanswered questions, and from the sound of it, Fulmer and Gatiss weren't going to be helping answer them.

CHAPTER NINETY-SIX

"We need to find Hamm," Zoe said. "Or he'll be back in a few months starting the whole thing all over again."

"I want you liaising with Sheila Griffin. Share any intelligence you have with her. Someone will be hiding him. We have to find out who that someone is. We have to find out who blew up that plane and what the connection with Hamm was."

"You still don't think Hamm did it?"

"Get a bomb on a plane? In Karachi? No, Zoe, I don't. That sounds like the work of the kind of people who might have wanted Umar Abidi dead back home. Not that Hamm wasn't involved."

"Ma'am," replied Zoe. It did make sense. The Trevor Hamm she knew wouldn't be likely to pull off something like that, but he wouldn't hesitate to take advantage of it if he could.

Lesley pulled out a chair and sat down. She yawned. "Did Rogers tell you Ian's been charged with perverting the course of justice?"

"No surprise there." Zoe was relieved she wasn't being investigated along with him.

"Means you've got a vacancy in your team."

Zoe looked through the glass partition at the two constables. "You plan to promote one of them?"

Lesley followed her gaze. Connie and Rhodri sat at their desks, eyes on their computer screens but hands not moving on their keyboards or mice.

"Good God no," said Lesley. "I've got a much better idea." She pushed the door to the inner office door open and placed two fingers between her teeth. She whistled, making Connie almost fall out of her chair.

The door to the outer office opened and Mo walked in.

Lesley turned back towards Zoe. "Your new DS. Will he do?"

Zoe stood up, smiling at Mo. He spoke to each of the constables in turn then came into the office.

"He'll do just fine," Zoe said.

CHAPTER NINETY-SEVEN

Sofia closed her eyes as the plane took off. Three rows behind were two women she recognised. She'd seen them at the hotel, when she'd been looking for Andreea.

The plane shuddered as the landing gear was retracted. She gripped the armrests, forcing herself to breathe in and out. Images of the Wizz Air plane invaded her mind. The children who'd followed her. The one who'd run off to join her friends. The two she'd picked out at random. What they'd been through, because of her.

She still didn't know why she'd been told to find those particular children. There had been plenty of them on the plane, thirty maybe. But Trevor's men, and by extension Trevor, knew which ones they wanted.

She shivered and pulled her coat tighter around herself. She still wore the white cashmere coat, the one Trevor had given her. She'd been given the opportunity to go back to the house and collect her things. But none of it had been hers: it was all Trevor's. No matter how expensive it all was, she wanted none of it. She'd give this coat away as soon as she arrived in Bucharest.

She wiped away a tear, thinking of her parents. They wouldn't be waiting at the airport, they couldn't afford luxuries like travel to the city. She would have to take a bus. The UK authorities had arranged for Andreea's body to be transported separately. She would be arriving a week later.

Sofia leaned on the cold window and wiped her face. She had spoken to her mother, told her she was coming home. She hadn't told her about Andreea: she wanted to do that in person. The thought of it made her blood run cold.

The farm would be unchanged. Drab, dusty, and poor. The life she'd worked so hard to escape. But there were people there who loved her, and who needed her. She blinked back tears and thought of the dogs, her family's three Alsatians. They would be delighted to see her. They would search for Andreea for a while, sniff her on Sofia's clothes. But they would soon forget.

She, on the other hand, would never forget how stupid she had been.

CHAPTER NINETY-EIGHT

Zoe slammed the car door and went to open the boot. She pulled out three plastic bags containing her mum's belongings, most of which had been acquired in the last week.

Nicholas opened the passenger door and helped his gran out. Zoe eyed the pair of them. Nicholas was too soft on her.

Annette shook off his hand. "I'm not an old codger yet. Perfectly capable of walking on my own."

"Sorry, Gran."

Zoe grimaced. *Be nice to him*, she thought. He was only being kind.

She dragged the carrier bags to the front door and waited for Annette to follow with her key. Annette turned it in the lock and pushed the door open. Junk mail and red bills had piled up behind it in the week she'd been gone.

A curtain moved in the house next door: a young Asian woman. The city was still reeling from the attacks. Randle had held a press conference informing the public that organised criminals and not terrorists were responsible. But racially motivated attacks had increased.

"Come on in, girl." Annette fumbled in a chest of drawers in the hallway. Zoe froze: was she looking for booze? As far as Zoe knew, her mother hadn't touched a drop while she'd been at her house.

Annette caught her daughter watching her. She glared at her and brought a purse out of a drawer, waving it in Zoe's face.

"You don't trust me, do you?"

"Can you blame me?"

Annette harrumphed and went into the kitchen. Zoe resisted pinching her nose at the smell of dirty crockery and the overflowing bin. Nicholas stepped in front of his grandmother and started to tidy up.

Zoe watched him, torn between an urge to stop him and pride in her son. When no hot water came out of the tap, he boiled a kettle.

"Fancy a cuppa, Mum?" he said. "Gran, you must have coffee somewhere."

"No thanks," said Zoe. Annette curled her lip.

"You stay for a bit, eh Nicholas?" Annette said. "Help your old gran get this place into shape?"

Nicholas looked at Zoe. "I won't be too long. Stay and help."

"I've got a meeting."

"It's Sunday."

"People don't stop committing crimes cos it's the weekend, you know."

She leaned towards Nicholas and gave his arm a squeeze. "Watch her, OK?"

He nodded.

"Bye, love." Annette gave her a challenging look.

CHAPTER NINETY-EIGHT

"Bye, Mum." Zoe let her mum kiss her on the cheek, resisting an urge to wipe it.

She walked out of the house, kicking aside the unopened post. It went back for a month. She hurried to her car and opened the driver's door, grabbing her phone as she did so.

"Zo. Everything alright?"

"Yeah. Look, I know it's your day with your family and all that..."

"Catriona's taken the girls shopping for dresses. I made an excuse."

Zoe laughed. "That's alright then."

"You need me to come into work?"

"No, Mo. But I can't stop thinking about the New Street bomb. The woman in the green headscarf. I want to find out who she is, and I want to find Hamm. I thought we could make a start together."

"Cat bought some new coffee beans yesterday. Peruvian roast. She thought you'd like it."

"Perfect. Give me ten minutes."

I hope you enjoyed *Deadly Terror*. Would you like to try my bestselling Dorset Crime series? The prequel novella *The Ballard Down Murder* is available from my website and introduces the new characters DCI Lesley Clarke will be working with when she's transferred to Dorset. Get your copy at rachelmclean.com/ballard-book.

Thanks for reading!
Rachel McLean

READ THE DETECTIVE ZOE FINCH SERIES

Deadly Wishes

Deadly Choices

Deadly Desires

Deadly Terror

Deadly Reprisal

Deadly Fallout

Deadly Christmas

Deadly Origins, the FREE Zoe Finch prequel

Buy from book retailers or via the Rachel McLean website.

ALSO BY RACHEL MCLEAN

The Dorset Crime series – buy from book retailers or via the Rachel McLean website.

The Corfe Castle Murders

The Clifftop Murders

The Island Murders

The Monument Murders

The Millionaire Murders

The Fossil Beach Murders

The Blue Pool Murders

The Lighthouse Murders

The Ghost Village Murders

The Poole Harbour Murders

...and more to come

The McBride & Tanner series – buy from book retailers or via the Rachel McLean website.

Blood and Money

Death and Poetry

Power and Treachery

Secrets and History

The Cumbria Crime series by Rachel McLean and Joel Hames – buy from book retailers or via the Rachel McLean website.

The Harbour

The Mine

The Cairn

The Barn

The Lake

...and more to come

The London Cosy Mystery series by Rachel McLean and Millie Ravensworth – buy from book retailers or via the Rachel McLean website.

Death at Westminster

Death in the West End

Death at Tower Bridge

Death on the Thames

Death at St Paul's Cathedral

Death at Abbey Road